WHERE'S BOB?

Also by Ann Ireland

A Certain Mr. Takahashi (McClelland & Stewart, 1985)
The Instructor (Doubleday, 1996)
Exile (Dundurn Press, 2002)
The Blue Guitar (Dundurn Press, 2013)

WHERE'S BOB?
ANN IRELAND

A JOHN METCALF BOOK

BIBLIOASIS
WINDSOR, ON

FIRST EDITION

Library and Archives Canada Cataloguing in Publication

Ireland, Ann, author
    Where's Bob? / Ann Ireland.

Issued in print and electronic formats.

ISBN 978-1-77196-227-8 (softcover).--ISBN 978-1-77196-228-5 (ebook)
    I. Title. II. Title: Where's Bob?
PS8567.R43W44 2018   C813'.54   C2017-906993-4
                                              C2017-906994-2

Readied for the Press by John Metcalf
Copy Edited by Cat London
Cover Designed by Gordon Robertson
Typeset by Ellie Hastings

Published with the generous assistance of the Canada Council for the Arts, which last year invested $153 million to bring the arts to Canadians throughout the country, and the financial support of the Government of Canada. Biblioasis also acknowledges the support of the Ontario Arts Council (OAC), an agency of the Government of Ontario, which last year funded 1,709 individual artists and 1,078 organizations in 204 communities across Ontario, for a total of $52.1 million, and the contribution of the Government of Ontario through the Ontario Book Publishing Tax Credit and the Ontario Media Development Corporation.

PRINTED AND BOUND IN CANADA

MIX
Paper from
responsible sources
FSC
www.fsc.org   FSC® C004071

For E.J.I.
and in loving memory of B.B.I.

1

LYDIA FORCED herself to keep looking down at a world that shrank by the moment. La Pirámide's lavish architecture receded into a gleaming beach jewel, half-buried in the sand and surrounded by palm trees. Breathe, she reminded herself. Hands gripped the harness. Wind blasted her face, tasting of the sea and grilled fish. She'd told the boys not to send her up too high and they must be down there, cackling. They found her fear to be funny. What kind of idiot agrees to be a human kite?

'You could use a new perspective, given the rocky year you've had,' Iris noted in her persuasive way. Iris was Lydia's seventy-year-old mother, faintly visible now as she loped along the beach like a tiny gold beetle, waving both arms towards her daughter dangling in the sky.

The towing boat rode the waves parallel to the western edge of the bay. This side was where rich people lived in sprawling haciendas. Somewhere a dog was barking. Scooped still higher, she sucked in a breath and felt her skin flattened by wind, her nostrils sucked dry. For one dizzy instant she could read the sign advertising Corona beer, before the sudsy mug bled into an undifferentiated blur.

The motorboat shrank to the size of a pebble and it was the stream of its wake that she watched intently, a consolation that someone knew she was up here, the shadow of her parachute bobbing on the turquoise water below.

She was suddenly fiercely alone.

Bite of panic. Lydia lurched forward in the seat, caught by the flimsy bar that pressed into her waist. It was an old fear, that a mother's attention might suddenly falter and she would leave her child alone in a department store or even, once, famously, in the middle of Bloor Street at rush hour.

A pelican flew past with something wriggling in its beak; they were comrades of the sky. The boat at the end of the tether entered open water and right away, Lydia felt the extra snap in the line.

Faint thump of salsa beats rose from the resort's free-form pool. The motorboat, after making a quick tour of open sea, began to circle back towards the beach where Iris stood waiting. Lydia felt her mother's excitement more than her own, a familiar sensation of Iris taking over her most intimate self.

She could make out rows of striped loungers and the thatched roof of the bar. Hotel guests bobbed up and down in the modest surf as they clutched their drinks. The boat started to slow down so that she might drift gracefully onto the sand where Tico waited, ready to grab her legs.

So elated was she at feeling her feet hit sand that Lydia forgot she was attached to a harness and a collapsing parachute. Before Tico could get to her, she dashed forward, waving in triumph to her mother who was scrambling across the beach towards her. Yanked hard by the parachute, Lydia lost her balance and pitched forward, managing at the last second to break her fall with her left hand. A jolt of pain ripped from wrist to shoulder.

Sound poured in from all directions and for a moment she regretted returning to earth. So peaceful riding high in the sky, a weightless muted universe where the woes of life receded to pinholes. But now the world was packed with

8

voices and pumping music and the roar of jet skis. Someone wrestled to release the harness but Lydia did not rise. She was an astronaut returning to the field of gravity, heavy as the sea. She might stay prone awhile, hot sand digging into her temple. But it was not to be; a pair of strong arms reached from behind and lifted her to her feet in one swift motion.

'I'm a nurse,' a man's voice said in her ear.

Lydia felt the world spin and suddenly she was puking into the sand.

Iris was at her side, a whiff of coconut oil. 'You looked so glorious up there,' she said.

'We'll get you to a chair,' the nurse advised and Lydia managed, with his help, to hobble over to one of the plastic chairs. She heard him introduce himself as 'Joe,' and he worked in Emerg at St. Mike's in downtown Toronto: her city.

People crowded around, chattering advice. Someone brought a glass of ice water which she gulped down.

'That's quite a goose egg popping up on your forehead,' Iris said. She reached over to touch her daughter's brow.

'Keep your head down,' the nurse instructed.

Lydia was immediately hit by a fresh wave of nausea.

'Our first full day of holiday,' Iris told the assembled crowd. She sounded plaintive.

The nurse began to rattle off a series of questions: date of birth; do you know where you are now; anything other than your forehead hurt? Yes, my wrist.

Joe asked her to move her fingers. Lydia managed this and winced.

'Roll your forearm from side to side.'

Lydia obeyed and let out a whimper.

'Oh, really,' Iris said under her breath. Lydia recognized her mother's exasperated tone.

Joe squinted, managing to look professional despite the fact he wore only a pair of skimpy bathing trunks. He was bald, in the way of men who shaved their head, and even in her dizziness, Lydia noted where his hairline was, or would be, if he let it.

'You should have this looked at,' Joe said. 'Probably just a sprain, but we can't be certain without an x-ray.'

Lydia digested this information. 'Where should I go?'

'Must be a clinic in town.'

'Can't we just ice it and wait a few hours?' That was Iris.

Joe drew himself up to his full height, towering above Iris, who prided herself on being tall and fleshy in all the right places, the sort of person one didn't easily challenge. 'You could do that,' he said, 'but I'd be inclined to go for the film. Better to know what's going on in there.'

Iris looked put out. She didn't like being contradicted. A woman in an old-fashioned bathing suit, the kind with a skirt attached, came up and slipped her arm around Joe's back. She had long greying hair and a pale complexion. The pair of them stared at Iris, who waited a beat before responding, 'Right then, I'll take my daughter to the clinic.'

Gathering up sunscreen and beach bag, Iris looped her arm around Lydia's, seemingly unaware of the growing bruise on her daughter's wrist.

Lydia took a tentative step towards the path; the day had begun with such promise, the two women sloshing through breaking waves as they hiked along the beach just after dawn, wearing only their bathing suits. Gulls circled overhead while resort staff raked sand and hauled loungers out of the shed, setting them in neat rows facing the sea. Toronto's icy sidewalks felt far away.

Iris had peered at her daughter and said, 'You have a very nice figure,' though she spoiled the comment by adding—'Make sure you hold onto it, now that you are a single woman again.'

2

MARTINA MADE THE quick decision not to tell Alejandro about the phone call. How did these people get her cell number? She kept it private, only intimate friends and family, and this was the fifth call in as many weeks, a muffled voice: 'I am watching you.' How original. The crank calls began with Alejandro's declaration of candidacy for the post of governor of the state. He was getting calls too, but made light of them. Everyone in public life in this country got threatened. One could be brave, but one must also be attentive, and Martina had become more attentive in recent weeks, glancing into the back seat of her car before sliding behind the wheel and never walking solo after dark. She'd booked the installation of an alarm system in their apartment, though Alejandro snorted at the concept, claiming that the guys installing alarms were the same thugs who knew how to disable them, and would be sure to visit one night as they slept.

An enemy could be a *sicario* hired by other candidates to get rid of a pesky rival—or cartel members who didn't like the sound of Alejandro's vows to clean up the state, to ferret out corruption, extortion, to eliminate the kidnappings. Maybe they feared he meant it.

More important and much more heartening, Martina reminded herself, were the voices raised in passion, men and women taking to the streets, pumping election signs printed with photos of her husband. University students held weekly rallies for the cause. Change was in the air.

Alejandro paced the apartment with his phone tucked against one ear, gesticulating emphatically. All the men in his family were physically expressive, unlike her more self-contained relatives. He craved an audience. Odd—she was the one in show business but she never sought attention away from the camera.

'That is not what we discussed,' Alejandro said, pitching his voice low to prove that he was a man in command of his emotions.

He was sweating so hard that the back of his shirt had stuck to his skin. He'd have to get this under control if he was to keep appearing before crowds. On her television show, *Martina Viva!*, she was well aware of how her guests dealt with their nerves and she frequently barged in with thorny questions the moment fear crackled.

This morning she was hunkered down in her home office, a corner of the living room that she'd fitted out with a desk and laptop computer. Before they headed to the coast tomorrow she needed to finish laying out next week's show. First guest was an actress of Martina's vintage—pushing 50—a lively woman who'd been on the show several times and could be counted on to confess her indiscretions.

She watched the back of her husband's neck grow heated, his hairline closing into a V at his collar as he listened impatiently to Trina at campaign headquarters. Martina knew every inch of his skin, every blemish, every tender spot, the way he wouldn't allow her, or anyone, to touch the lower spine where a disc had herniated. No one but she knew he was in near-constant pain.

Alejandro's voice rose a notch. 'This is what I have decided. Check our Action Plan and you'll see I'm right.'

After the interview with the actress, practically a national institution, a lesser known guest would be given the chance to capture the attention of the nation. In this case—Martina scrolled down the screen—an earnest boy who sang socially conscious songs of his own composition.

Outside, the familiar chime rang out, followed by a murky recorded message: the tamale man was clipping down the street in his bicycle-and-cart combo, selling his wares. Pockets of old Mexico were still common, even here in the state capital.

Alejandro had dropped all pretense of being the quiet but effective leader and was now barking orders as he stood by the window that looked down into mid-morning traffic. He fumbled trying to roll up a sleeve with his free hand, then winced as pain pierced his lower back.

Martina closed the laptop, went over and leaned into his shoulder. Sometimes she thought of him as being a large, not-quite-tamed dog. She'd plucked him from the ranch and tidied him up, but there was still something of the *campo* in him, no matter how tailored his suit, how smooth his shave.

Startled at the interruption, he stared at her with those wide-set brown eyes. He heard himself and was appalled, and began apologizing to Trina as the flush receded from his cheeks.

In the rear bedroom, a commodious space with a window that looked onto the courtyard of the complex, she noted her husband's suitcase flopped open on the bed. Still empty, though he'd piled clothes and electronic gadgets next to it. At the last minute he'd toss as much as he could into the case and work the zipper around. Her own suitcase was neatly packed, zipped, and standing upright against the wall. They'd leave for the resort the next morning.

Alejandro was a commotion of nerves; the upcoming meeting at the La Pirámide was crucial. 'Make or break,' he kept insisting. Her husband was never content unless she fell into the vortex of his drama, a habit that she fended off whenever possible.

She rolled his socks into a ball and squished them into a corner of his suitcase. The beach would be lovely and she envisioned curling up on one of those loungers with a silly tropical drink while Alejandro met with his people.

3

THE TWO WOMEN stepped out of the taxi in front of a storefront clinic on the main drag of the beach town. Lydia, Iris noted, looked like hell, her pallor green. In the taxi, she'd laid her head against the back of the seat and said, 'So it continues.'

'What continues?' Iris made the mistake of asking.

The terrible year, of course.

Iris would have none of it; self-pity was not part of her vocabulary.

She hooked a hand under her daughter's good arm. The town was sweltering, cut off from the ocean breezes. A scattering of tourists cruised the sidewalk to paw over stalls containing souvenir t-shirts and hats. The shops held the usual trinkets, rough versions of the real handicrafts that one could still find in the mountain villages: carved wooden masks and silver jewellery, a great culture reduced to mounds of straw hats with the name of the town emblazoned on front.

Lydia eyed the Clínica sign dubiously. 'Is this legit?'

'It's what's available,' Iris said in a firm voice.

The front doors stood open and inside, two rows of folding chairs faced a wall covered in posters illustrating the warning signs of diabetes, stroke, and other maladies. The chairs were empty except one that held a young mother clad in blue jeans who sat clutching her baby. A fan in the corner blew warm air. Iris began to feel excited; this was the old Mexico. When she and husband number one, Lydia's father, Richard, got married back in 1969, they'd driven south from Toronto and holed up for a year in various Mexican towns, overstaying their visas, which led to difficulty at the border on the way home. This section of the coast was undeveloped in those days, and even nearby Cancun was little more than a mangrove swamp and deserted beaches.

As the two women settled into stiff-backed chairs there was a clatter at the doorway and Iris turned to see paramedics wheeling in a man humped under an orange blanket. A woman, likely his wife, accompanied him. While the medics parked the gurney in the front of the waiting room, the wife turned to the small audience and shrugged apologetically. The patient moaned and gathered his knees up under the blanket as the medics disappeared, driving off with a crunch of gravel.

'Where is the clinic's staff?' Lydia wondered aloud. 'He looks to be in bad shape.'

The wife was not making a fuss, as was the way with *campesinos* used to broken promises and the endless waiting for a better life. Iris had witnessed this fatalistic behaviour decades ago. Quite unlike Mexico City's upper classes, who would march in and demand attention ahead of anyone else.

The room got hotter and as the minutes slid by with no sign of a doctor or nurse, Iris felt her teeth grind; she, who was so sympathetic to this country, was finding her patience tried. The teenaged mother fed her baby from a bottle. The wife of the new patient occasionally whispered something to her suffering husband, though she did not touch him. Outside, car horns beeped, men called out in Spanish, vacationers swept by laden down with souvenir loot—while inside remained a dark and nearly silent cave.

Lydia held up her left hand; her pretty fingers had become sausage-like. 'Why did this have to happen to me?'

Could this tendency towards self-pity be why her husband paddled off in his canoe?

Lydia wasn't finished. 'I feel like I've stepped off a cliff, into nothing, into air,' she said. Stroking her throbbing forearm she added, 'It's been a rough ride since Charlie left.'

Iris, wary of the turn of conversation, nodded once.

Lydia pressed: 'When I phoned to let you know he'd done a bunk, I must say, Mum, you were not especially sympathetic.'

Iris understood she was meant to make up for some earlier lack, but what came out was wrong: 'You must reinvent yourself,' she said.

'Spare me the advice,' Lydia said.

Ever since she'd come out of the womb Lydia had worn that judgmental stare.

A woman in a white jacket emerged from behind a curtain and surveyed the room, her eyes immediately fixing on the pair of tourists. She came over with a clipboard and introduced herself.

'I am Doctor Alvarez.'

Iris nearly advised that the young mother and baby were here first, and that the man on the gurney looked to be in dire straits, but stopped: who was she to act as triage nurse?

Before Lydia could explain what had happened, Iris launched into the story of the mishap, speaking in Spanish, remembering to use the subjunctive form when required.

'You speak excellent Spanish,' the doctor said, but she was looking at Lydia. 'Your fingers are badly swollen,' she observed, speaking in English. 'Please try and wiggle them.'

She watched as Lydia performed this task, then touched the injured wrist, feeling the heated skin, and tapped Lydia's ring finger.

'This jewellery must be removed.'

Lydia's gold wedding band.

They should have noted this earlier, Iris realized. The band was pressing deeply into flesh and would soon cut off the finger's circulation.

The doctor motioned towards a door in the corner. 'Use soap and water and see if you can work it off.'

Iris followed her daughter but there was no space for her to squeeze into the tiny bathroom. Hovering outside the door, she watched anxiously as Lydia soaped her hand and began to yank and attempt to rotate the ring. It did not budge. Lydia gasped with pain and frustration.

'They'll have to saw off my finger.'

'I don't think it will come to that.' Though Iris wasn't sure.

Lydia emerged from the bathroom, hands dripping. Her face was white and the bump on her head had grown to the diameter of a silver dollar.

Iris tittered nervously. 'You look a sight.'

Lydia managed a laugh. 'We'll soon wake up,' she said. 'This will have been a tequila nightmare.'

Lydia was always very slim. Took after her father. Long-necked with a heart-shaped, pretty face and auburn hair. Shorter in height than her mother by at least four centimetres. The sort of woman who was called 'gamine'—or used to be when she was younger.

Doctor Alvarez disappeared behind the curtain, beckoning the teenaged mother and baby to follow.

Iris was thinking of how she might describe this episode to Steve when she phoned home to Berkeley, California, tonight. Or was it this evening that he was to address the Hillside Club with his photos of Bhutan?

The poor soul continued to writhe under the blanket. He might be a construction worker. She'd seen the ramshackle scaffolding outside buildings in town, where labourers, lacking boots and helmets, climbed nimbly in worn sneakers or flip-flops.

In a short while, Doctor Alvarez reappeared, mother and baby in her wake, the girl clutching a prescription and looking much happier as she strode back into the sunny street.

Gazing at the stuck ring, the doctor frowned. 'We must remove it quickly.'

'My finger?' Lydia yelped.

Doctor Alvarez smiled. 'One moment, please,' she said and she left the clinic, stethoscope shoved into the pocket of her white jacket.

Lydia said nothing, just looked straight ahead, resigned to whatever was being set in motion. The man on the gurney made an agonized groan and his wife shrugged again, embarrassed by the ruckus.

The doctor returned a moment later, accompanied by a burly man in a mechanic's overall carrying a pair of wire cutters.

'Holy shit,' Lydia whispered.

Dr. Alvarez stood aside while the mechanic lifted Lydia's swollen hand in his own grease-stained palm, jimmied the business end of the cutters between flesh and metal and made two quick snips.

The half-circles of gold spun to the floor and Lydia let out a surprised cry, then leaned to scoop them up, holding the sorry-looking crescents in her hand. A whoosh of blood raced to the end of her finger, pinkening it up. She seemed stunned as she toyed with the metal fragments. 'Now it's official,' she said. 'My marriage is kaput.'

Iris dipped into her purse and managed to locate a twenty-peso note which she offered to their rescuer.

'Follow me,' Doctor Alvarez said as she held back the curtain to the examination room. 'We will make an x-ray.'

'How old is the equipment?' Lydia whispered over her shoulder to her mother. 'Leaking how much radiation?'

Iris's heart went out to her daughter, the daughter whose life never seemed to go right. Years ago, Lydia had stood in the hallway of her house and explained to her mother in a tone of resolute acceptance, that she was 'a woman accustomed to disappointment.'

What a queer thing to say, to settle for. So much had happened in recent months: Charlie taking off; Annie messing up at university; Doug lasting just one semester at his institution of higher learning. Then the college where Lydia taught ESL went on strike.

Iris had brought her daughter here to let such trials melt away in a happy tequila mist.

It turned out that the x-ray indicated a wrist sprain, not a fracture. Iris accompanied Lydia and the doctor as they entered the examination room, a tiny cluttered space that was more like an office—very hot and stuffy, without so much as a fan to move the air. The doctor rustled about in her desk drawer and pulled out a roll of bandage. As she began to tape the injured wrist, Lydia let out a gasp of pain. The sound hit Iris's solar plexus and suddenly she struggled to breathe. Her head filled with angry bees and she lowered her head between her knees and almost toppled forward. Voices rose in alarm then a cool hand touched the side of her neck. 'You feel faint, *Señora?*'

The two women emerged into the blazing hot street after having paid Doctor Alvarez the equivalent of fifty dollars. Siesta hour was over. Hordes of tourists roamed the boardwalk, moving in and out of shops, fingering the pretty embroidered dresses and shirts.

'You managed to distract me from my pain by nearly keeling over,' Lydia said. She sounded amused by the episode.

'I feel too deeply; it's a flaw,' Iris said crossly. She spotted an empty cab with hand-painted lettering on its door that read: *Mamá, mi corazón.*

A fine sentiment: Mother, my heart.

4

WHY DID MEXICANS love noise so much? They cherished each sound, fondled it, applauded it, and ultimately paid no attention. Sometimes it enraged Martina, the infernal racket of her city. A group of men was installing a security gate next door, blocking the alleyway that ran alongside her building. They hammered and soldered as their truck blasted some gruesome *narcocorrido*. She knew better than to protest. She peered out the window to the cobbled *privada* leading to half a dozen modest houses and a bakery that was only open in the mornings. Suddenly her neighbours wanted privacy, after all these years? There would be honking at all hours from people who'd forgotten their gate keys. How would the gas truck get in? Imposing spikes poked up from the top of the structure. The workmen had attached their power cord to the city's overhead line to steal what they needed. It occurred to her that *they* were not yearning for a functioning government and judiciary system.

'Alejandro? Is that you?' Sound of key in lock, followed by a twisting of the doorknob and she waited, expectant, because of course it was him: who else could it be?

Her husband tossed his cap onto a chair and moved wearily into the living room.

'I toured a factory; I visited a school for the poor; I met with the fundraisers and donors; I worked out at the gym...' Here he paused and reached to clasp her hands. 'And now I seek only love.'

She laughed.

'Will you still cherish me if I become a professional politician?'

'Truth?'

'You are incapable of speaking anything less.'

She pulled away from his grip. 'I don't know.' Outside the workmen began to drill again.

'Yet it was you who encouraged me from the start.'

She looked down through the window as sparks shot from the wrought iron. 'I know.'

'Perhaps it will help if I tell you that Don Victor is coming to the resort to meet with us.'

She whipped around. Victor García Pacheco had ignored her requests for a television interview half a dozen times, had said 'no' even when she offered to drive to his studio in the remote mountain village.

'How...?'

Alejandro shrugged, a show of modesty that wasn't entirely convincing. 'He cares about what we are doing. He is, he says, 'intrigued.'' Alejandro unbuttoned the collar of his shirt and yanked his tie aside. An almost feral heat came off him. She'd taught him to dress like a man of consequence but the whiff of the fields would never entirely disappear. The shoes he tugged off his feet were sleek and shiny, and the moment she looked away, he'd pull on his battered cowboy boots.

'He's agreed to be your Minister of Culture?'

Alejandro made his way towards the kitchen, a galley space built in the days when everyone had a cook. Pulling open the refrigerator door, he crouched, as he was a tall man, and peered inside. She could almost hear his mind ticking as he surveyed the possibilities before deciding on a bottle of Dos Equis. Beer was a holdover from his early life, the life before Martina.

He popped it open, took a slug, then said, 'Not exactly. But we will soon convince him.'

When she returned to the bedroom she plucked her suitcase from where it stood against the wall and laid in the turquoise dress with the shimmering neckline, the dress that allowed her to float in and out of rooms.

5

LYDIA ATTRACTED instant attention from La Pirámide's staff and fellow guests who spotted her bandage, sling, and 3D goose egg. She responded to their questions by waving her good arm expansively. 'I was not meant to soar like an eagle.'

It took fifteen minutes to make it past the front desk. With the third or fourth query she launched into a detailed narrative, sounding brave and game, a much more attractive role than deserted wife.

'My mother nearly passed out,' Lydia offered to a couple from one of the Carolinas.

'An exaggeration,' Iris inserted.

By the time they made it to the patio bar, Lydia was sporting a broad smile. They managed to grab a table overlooking the sea. Everyone was pointing toward the water and they soon saw why: a manta ray leapt into the air, flashing its rubbery pectoral fin before dropping back into the sea. Settling into the pigskin and twig chairs, Iris laid a hand on Lydia's good wrist and said, 'I don't want you nattering on about how your poor old mother fell apart in a crisis. That part of the story could be deleted.'

'But it's my favourite bit,' Lydia said. 'You stole the show.' Her voice was pitched high and she tossed her hair in an exaggerated way. She had that lovely long neck; no wonder people still asked if she was a dancer.

No one ever asked if Iris was a dancer; she was proudly 'statuesque,' the sort of figure that men went for more than women.

Patricio, the waiter, arrived to wipe clean their table and take their order. He offered a bright smile of greeting, this time moderated by concern for Lydia. He set down a lava-rock bowl of guacamole and chips, its fragrance of cilantro and garlic a welcome intrusion. A breeze rippled across the sea, pocking its surface. Patricio left and returned with 'special margaritas' composed not from the usual syrupy mix, but straight-up tequila, Triple Sec, and fresh-squeezed lime juice.

The two women chimed glasses and drank eagerly. Then Lydia set her glass down and said with a frown, 'I won't be able to swim.'

Patricio snatched a bowl of ballpark peanuts from a neighbouring table and placed it between the women before heading off. Lydia stared at the mound of nuts in the shell with a dour expression, then reached with her good hand and struggled to crack one open.

'Let me do that for you,' Iris said.

'This is a taste of how it's going to be,' Lydia said. 'Getting older, the wheels starting to fall off.' She gave a wry smile. 'The bloom is off the rose.'

Iris peered at her. Forty-two was nothing—yet forty-two was also something.

'And how the hell am I supposed to cut my meat?'

'I will help.'

Lydia squinted as she eyed something near her mother's neck. 'What is that creature perched on your shoulder?'

Iris cocked her head just in time to see a thumb-sized insect lifting its stinger, a quivering prong pointed at the end like a hatpin. She screeched and leapt to her feet, drink airborne, and began to flap her blouse at the same instant as the beast shot venom into her shoulder. Everyone in the bar was watching but she didn't give a damn: where was it? Lost in the material of her top, readying itself for another go. A multicoloured creature helicoptered upwards and flew off lazily towards the sea, as Patricio, with a slightly malicious smile, came trotting over to clean up the mess.

'How many poisonous insects are there here?' Iris cried.

He dropped his cloth over the puddle and said in a cheerful voice, 'Everything in this place stings.'

By evening, Iris's upper arm and shoulder were flaming red and the sting had evolved into a constant itching. She gulped pills from the tuck shop, yet all they seemed to do was make her feel drowsy and slightly out of it. One activity could be counted on to distract: drinking.

Lydia frowned. 'Not so good with antihistamines, Mum.'

'I don't care.'

They'd booked dinner in the prettiest à la carte restaurant, perched on a terrace overlooking the sea. Palm trees loomed in the dark as fairy lights lit the cobbled pathway leading to the entrance. Music was supplied by a woman in a cocktail dress playing an electronic keyboard in one corner. *Que será será.* The day's warmth steamed off the stone path mixing with an offshore breeze. The two women grasped each other with their good arms and picked their way to where the maitre d' awaited, menus in hand.

His eyes cast over each of them in turn.

Would the *señoritas* like to sample a *copacita* of tequila first? Would they ever.

He offered tiny clay cups and instructed them to drink all in one go. Which they promptly did.

'Oh my,' Lydia said, pressing herself into her mother's side. 'That went straight to my brain stem.'

A line of candlelit tables snaked around the patio, following the shape of the shore. A few feet below surf slapped the shoreline, sending up starbursts of foam. The two women were seated at a table with a youngish couple.

'I'm Lydia,' Lydia said, introducing herself to the pair.

They were Neil and Lulu. The man, dressed in slacks and polo shirt, stood to greet them while his wife didn't shield her disappointment that they were being asked to share. She probably had in mind a more romantic outing. Iris sat herself down, letting her skirt float out to either side. Hot pink; a favourite colour when she had the nerve, and tonight she'd added a cape, keeping her throbbing arm well hidden. Lydia was wearing a batik blouse—did they still make those?—and some kind of peasant skirt.

'I am Iris, living since 2006 in Berkeley, California, home of the Free Speech Movement,' she said.

Lulu and Neil had no idea what she was talking about. Across the table, Lydia unrolled her napkin and placed her cutlery next to the plate engraved with the pattern of an Aztec calendar. Lulu stared at Lydia's bandaged arm.

'My daughter had a mishap while parasailing,' Iris said, and waited for Lydia to take up the tale.

But Lydia just sat there, not of a mind to tell the story yet again. So Iris took on the task of relating to their tablemates the tale of the crash landing, the trip to the clinic—omitting the fainting episode—which led to further anecdotes about the old days travelling around Mexico with Richard, her first husband. And later, with Jake, husband number two.

Lulu was a tiny woman, pressing forward on her chair so that her chest hit the rim of the table. She seemed content to let Neil, a fleshy, good-natured man, talk for both of them. He asked satisfactory questions: had Iris really eaten street food? Do tarantulas jump, as he'd heard they might?

Iris confided that as she and Richard perched on the back of a pickup truck, barrelling through mountains en route to Puerto Angel, she had thought—and here she paused, remembering the exact moment, Richard's long hair flying in the wind, his scruffy beard—'that we might never be like this again. And I was right; Richard ended up as a tax attorney.'

The soups arrived in pretty ceramic bowls.

'You've certainly led an interesting life,' Neil said. Facing her, he let his gaze settle. Narrow eyes, scarce lashes.

Iris understood that he was flirting, the way the young do with the elderly, as a sort of gift.

'I am still leading an interesting life,' she corrected him.

'Is that a cape?' Lulu flipped the corner of Iris's garment.

Lydia deigned to speak: 'My mother's a super hero.'

'I like costumes,' Iris admitted. 'My husband gave it to me.'

'Which one?' her daughter shot back.

A fair question. 'Steve,' said Iris. 'The current and, I expect, the last.' She turned her attention to Lulu; fragile-seeming women needed to be drawn out. 'Tell me, dear, where do you two live when you are not in paradise?'

Lulu named a town Iris had never heard of, up the Hudson River. She and Neil were pediatric dentists. This information was offered in a high-pitched voice, as if Lulu were talking to a young child. She then focused her gaze on her husband. 'Will you tell them what happened?'

Neil's good-natured face darkened.

'Go on, tell,' Lulu insisted.

Neil reached for his drink. 'I was working on a girl's upper left cuspid when—' He lifted the glass to his mouth and downed the wine. 'She leapt out of the chair, knocking over the lamp.'

'Oh my,' Lydia and Iris gasped in tandem.

'Neil's drill tore the inside of her cheek,' Lulu took up the story. Her small hands played with her soup spoon. 'She required twenty-six stitches, and there was a good deal of blood.'

'Enough detail,' Neil said.

'So now I'm it,' Lulu said, ignoring his plea. 'The bread-winner, while my traumatized husband figures out what he's going to do next in life.'

Fortunately at this moment the rest of their meal arrived. The waiter kicked open a side table, set the plates down, and served them with a flourish.

They began to eat under the starry sky. Plump shrimp swam around Iris's plate as she chased them with her fork. The singer had left the stage and was making the rounds, holding a cordless mike, singing *La Bamba*, that sturdy classic, though a rugged *marinero* she was not.

Iris shut her eyes and allowed herself to be transported to the mountain town where she and Richard had spent a month decades ago, staying in a room over the bar as mariachis sang on the street below.

The song ended with a drawn-out note and no one at the table seemed to notice Iris's coast into the previous century. Iris let a forkful of rice hover near her mouth. 'I was riding a burro in the hills of Michoacán when I felt it, the deep knowledge that I was carrying a baby in my womb.' She gazed at Lulu. 'Do you have children?'

Lulu carefully chewed her food and only replied after she'd swallowed. 'Not yet.'

Perhaps the word 'womb' had alarmed her.

'Don't wait too long,' Iris advised. 'The eggs get old—'

'Mum,' Lydia warned.

'What I recall most from being pregnant, is that I was always so damn thirsty. Would have drunk blood if it were offered. I had Raymond in the clinic in Pátzcuaro, an antique building with peeling walls and stone floors. Sharp contrast to Lydia's more conventional entry into the world in a Toronto hospital.' She tapped her daughter's hand. 'No fault of yours, dear.'

She knew by Lydia's expression that she'd gone too far, telling strangers things they didn't need to know. Iris sat back on her chair, leaving the translucent shrimp husks on her plate, and let her gaze slide over the other diners in their crisp summery outfits, voices rising and falling while the surf dissolved into sand below. Her skin felt alive, crackling with the day's sun. She spotted a thin man entering the restaurant, no wife or girlfriend attached to his elbow. He wore a shirt decorated with palm trees and tan-coloured slacks that could have used a pressing. His greying hair was tucked into a ponytail and he had a wispy beard and strong pointed features. She guessed him to be nearing fifty.

Noting her mother's stare, Lydia turned to look. 'I've seen him around,' she said in a low voice. 'He hangs about the pool bar and seems to know the staff by name.'

The man took a moment to scout the restaurant before making his way to a table near the chafing dishes. He grabbed a chair next to where a waiter was diligently folding napkins. Tapping a cigarette from his packet, the man lit up and helped himself to a shot of tequila. He drained this in one gulp and refilled, wiping his mouth with the back of his hand, then pushed the bottle away.

Iris recognized the moves of a drinker who knew his rhythm. She'd been married to such a man: Jake, the artist, back when she was running the avant-garde gallery on Scollard Street in Toronto. Just about lost her shirt during that enterprise.

'We were shut down by police,' she told her tablemates.

This statement was greeting by puzzled expressions and Lydia said, 'Topic change?'

Iris felt the usual flare of irritation when people didn't keep up with her thoughts. She told them about the Toronto gallery she'd run in the early 80s, about Jake and the ceramic vulvas he'd painted with bucolic landscape scenes.

Lulu laughed too loudly, demonstrating that this description had in no way shocked her.

Iris went on: 'One day as I was sitting at my desk, in marched a pair of Metro's finest to shut me down. They sealed the doors! ' Even now Iris sounded outraged.

'My mother has a scrapbook of newspaper clippings about the event,' Lydia said. 'Then she ran off with Jake, the sculptor whose work caused her gallery to be closed.'

'Oh my,' Lulu said, sawing at her steak.

Iris noted that Lydia seemed confounded by her lobster, probing with her good hand and recklessly tearing off a claw. Had she and Richard neglected to teach her how to deal with crustaceans?

'Who's for karaoke after dinner?' Lulu asked brightly.

6

WHAT ALEJANDRO didn't know, he didn't care to know. He'd been basking in her reflected glory for years, and everyone knew that because his wife was *Martina Viva!* he had been approached to run for the governorship. This was not vanity on her part, for Martina was neither vain nor deluded. Through her, he'd met everyone who counted in the state. Yet if he were to win, he'd be the one tossed into that high-stakes political world, invited to innumerable events and critical meetings, national and international—without her. He'd soon catch on that he didn't need her in the old way.

The phone rang, jittering against her pocket as she stepped out of Carlito's dry-cleaning establishment, her blue suit encased in plastic and draped over one arm.

She stepped onto the busy sidewalk, one hand clutching her clean garment, the other holding the phone to her ear.

'Yes?'

Pedestrians swept by, grazing her shoulders. Tacos al Pastor next door, a cylinder of meat glistening fat and juices, where men in suits lined up to grab a late-morning snack.

A familiar voice, Danielle, producer of the show, someone she spoke to several times a day.

'I have news,' Danielle said in the hushed voice she reserved for emergencies or when she was excited.

A convoy of buses roared by and Danielle paused again, waiting for a break in the noise. Martina leaned against the filthy wall of the restaurant.

'Yes?' she said again.

'Miss Brisbois has consented.'

Martina knew exactly what Danielle meant. She felt a whip of elation.

'But she's already refused; she's not doing any travel or press.'

'True,' Danielle went on, 'until she heard about our show on the refugees.'

It took Martina a few seconds to figure it out: a week ago she'd run a program-length interview with the head of an organization working to rescue the Central American refugees who were pushing through Mexico, headed to the glorious U.S.A.—and getting robbed, kidnapped, or murdered en route. It had been an extraordinarily moving session, as the man she spoke to had himself fled violence in Guatemala only to be left for dead in a burned-out bus in the northern Mexican state of Chihuahua.

'She wants to help,' Danielle said.

Martina let her clean suit collapse to the pavement. Miss Brisbois had recently won the Nobel Peace Prize for her tireless work with refugees, and everyone on earth wanted to talk to her. But she was reclusive, in ill health, hiding out with a daughter in a cabin on the west coast of Canada.

Danielle waited as another bus tore past, minus its muffler, belching diesel exhaust. Martina held her breath; her lungs, at this point, must be parchment.

'She'll appear on the show if it'll help the organization raise money,' Danielle went on.

'We'll run an on-air donation drive,' Martina broke in. 'And we'll make it a condition for other networks who pick up the show. I'll speak the mother tongue but there will be simultaneous translation as subtitles.' She closed her eyes, barely noticing as the crowds stepped on her clean suit.

This was what she'd been waiting for, to blow open the show from its conventional interviews with artists, intellectuals and celebrities. This event could launch a new decade of *Martina Viva!*

7

KARAOKE TOOK place in the party room at the far end of the resort, reached through a series of outdoor pathways. Insects battered the marker lights and the two women could hear laughter and the slap of cards being played on a nearby balcony. The loony pyramid rose ahead, a glowing centrepiece of the resort, an over-sized amber jewel lit from within. There were over two hundred guest rooms in the main building in addition to the pavilions where everyone else, including Lydia and Iris, slept.

'Watch it!' Lydia cried, grabbing Iris's elbow and pushing her to the side of the path as a miniature train tooted past, carrying passengers who couldn't be bothered to hike between pavilion and party room.

The auditorium featured a stage and several dozen chairs set in rows. At the back was the bar, and along the sides, tables held hot and cold food, just in case anyone could possibly be hungry again. The women grabbed seats at the front.

'There he is,' Iris whispered, nudging her daughter.

It was the man they'd been watching in the restaurant, the man whom they'd decided held intrigue because of his solo status. He hovered near the karaoke equipment, letting cigarette ash tumble onto the speaker as he talked to the young guy in charge of audio.

The backdrop on the stage was encrusted with silver stars, indicating, Iris understood, the concept of celebrity. Some of these stars looked worse for the wear, having been dragged out once a week for years. A silver disco ball dangled overhead, set in motion by high-powered ventilation ducts. Its light jittered over the mainly middle-aged audience. Dry ice shot from a pipe, stage left.

A man Iris recognized as being Patricio, their favourite waiter, bounced onto the stage and grabbed the microphone. Dressed in top hat and tails, he'd transformed into the master of ceremonies.

Iris twisted to get a better look at the audience: the men, scrubbed and wearing golf shirts and shorts, looked as if they had been dressed by their wives. These women wore sprightly patterned dresses and sandals. There was a sense of occasion, a determination to have fun. She wondered if they took her for being a widow, scooped up by her daughter in an attempt to bring cheer to her empty life. Iris stretched her smile wider, to reassure anyone who might be watching.

No sign of Neil and Lulu. Apparently they had better things to do back in their room. Iris felt her smile fade a notch.

The emcee performed a soft-shoe as he encouraged people to stand up and make fools of themselves. What happens in La Pirámide stays in La Pirámide. A vacation was a sort of dream, washed clean by the light of the following day.

The man with the wispy beard, whose name they had not yet discovered, settled into a chair to one side and was staring with frank interest at the two women. Well actually, Iris had to admit, he was staring at her daughter. He nodded a couple of times, as if imparting a code. Iris understood; he was daring her to get up on that stage. Her being Lydia. Yet it was Iris who rose from her chair, tugged by an insistent force. Someone let out a whistle of encouragement. The heat of the spotlight swept her towards the stage and she heard, very faintly, a squeak of surprise emit from her daughter.

The emcee stared at her with an expectant look that was beginning to tighten; she was taking too long to decide what to sing.

Then it came to her: of course. She would perform the ballad of a woman who weeps for her dead children by the river: *La Llorona*.

Iris filled her chest with air, glanced at the video screen as a ball bobbed over each word, but she needed no prompting. She'd heard the song wailed in nightclubs and cantinas from Veracruz to Acapulco, years before the invention of karaoke bars. Karaoke being a Japanese word meaning 'empty orchestra,' though she doubted anyone here knew this. The synthesized instrumental sound began as Iris placed a hand on her hip and began to sing softly, making them think this was all she had. The first few notes were wobbly, then she quickly recovered and her voice was strong and true as she built to the climax of the song. She let them have it in the final bars, breaking into a theatrical sob as her arms floated upwards. She sang of the mother who wandered the world searching for the children she'd drowned in a fit of madness.

When she was done, she bowed deeply, soaking up the applause, then Patricio seized her hand and walked her down the three steps to where her astonished daughter waited.

8

IT WAS COMING together, the frenzied work of organizing outside Press. The show would feature the interview with Ms. Brisbois, but the Nobel Prize winner was insistent that attention be focused on the Central American refugees and their wretched situation as they passed through Mexico to cross the Rio Bravo. So many never made it. Photographs of their plight would be displayed as a prod to 'shake the pockets of your viewers.' This was the phrase Ms. Brisbois used.

Martina related this plan to Alejandro as they did the last bit of packing for the trip down the coast.

'Sounds good,' he said in a distracted tone.

She slipped a pair of sandals into the side pocket of her suitcase. Tomás would drive them to La Pirámide and remain with them, ready to perform useful tasks. She didn't have a lot of faith in his competence, but he was Alejandro's nephew.

'She's agreed to attend a charity dinner, twenty thousand pesos a plate. All money goes to the cause.'

'She?' Alejandro said vaguely. His thumbs tapped the screen of his smartphone.

Martina realized he had no idea what she was talking about.

* * *

Lydia got her mother settled in their room, Iris talkative and giddy after her surprising performance. Then Lydia headed back along the path towards the lobby bar. Her wrist pounded despite the fact she'd just iced the wound. She'd been alarmed when Iris mounted the stage—afraid that she'd make a fool of herself—but the voice that filled the auditorium was not an old woman's quaverings. Far from it. Iris had been stupendous, a show stopper. Lydia shook her head, still marvelling at the nerve of it.

Guests had clustered around Iris wanting to know—had she been a professional singer? No no, nothing near, though Iris was flattered by the suggestion. She'd sung in community choirs but these days she stuck to showers, or the occasional hymn performed at a friend's funeral.

Lydia hastened down the path. She needed to score some pot if she had any hope of sleeping. The business with her wrist was sobering; she, who'd always been so easy in her body, was feeling vulnerable. Ever since Charlie had buggered off, she'd forgotten how to fall asleep in the usual way; marijuana was a reliable aid. She hadn't dared stash any in her suitcase for Mexico's drug laws were appallingly harsh.

The man with the ponytail was, as she'd anticipated, sitting in the lobby bar, which offered live music until midnight. Live music being the duo setting up a keyboard and laptop computer.

Iris had been so buzzed after her bout of karaoke that Lydia slipped her a Valium. Iris was weird about it, asking why would Lydia have Valium in the first place, especially on vacation, and only reluctantly would she accept the tiny pill. She asked how long Lydia had needed the drug, which wasn't the sort of thing anyone told the truth about. Iris was quick to blame herself for everything, including her daughter's insomnia, reaching back to oceans of guilt at having left the family all those years ago to hole up with Jake, the sculptor, in his converted garage.

There had never been enough of Iris, back then. As a child, Lydia craved more of her mother's attention, and the call to meet up at the resort came out of the blue. She couldn't help but feel flattered that Iris wanted to spend a week with her.

The man with the ponytail cradled what looked like a tumbler of soda water. His skin was crinkled by sun, his eyes small and bright.

'*Buenas noches*,' he said, lifting his glass in recognition of her approach.

A blender on the counter roared, its contents foaming lime green.

Lydia squeezed into a space next to him. The tourists were having a grand time, tipsy women in cropped tops, husbands in short-sleeved shirts, everyone shouting above the din. The two-person band started up, guitar and keyboard, the laptop programmed for rhythm and horns, a relentless chug-a-lug that allowed for no interpretive deviation.

'Bob,' the man said, extending a hand that felt cool and dry. 'What can I do for you?' Up close his blue eyes stared directly at her.

The bartender, a young man in a red vest who'd earlier been in charge of the pool bar, kept glancing over as he clapped a hand over the blender's lid. When Lydia met his gaze, he smiled, and not in the neutral way he'd displayed poolside, when she was with her mother. This smile lingered.

'You can order me a drink,' Lydia said.

Bob lifted a finger towards the bartender.

Other men were snatching looks at her from the length of the bar; men with wives. She shook her hair and pretended not to notice. But she knew how it felt to be touched and a heat raced through her body. It was a novel sensation, after all these months of feeling dry as dust. She slowed down her gestures, made them deliberate. In her twenties she'd been a member of a modern dance troupe; intentionality in movement was key.

'What will you have?' Bob asked.

'Beer.' She'd stay clear of the sweet concoctions. Within seconds she was holding a glass of watery ale in her uninjured hand.

'That was your mama singing in the club?' Bob wanted to know.

'Indeed it was.'

'She's something, man, she's wild.'

Lydia smiled at the beatnik lingo. 'I know it.'

'And you?' He leaned in, breathing nicotine.

At the other end of the bar, a woman let out a whoop. There was a time when Lydia would have been scornful about such antics, but now she felt a pang of jealousy. There was a knack to seizing joy.

'What happened here?' Bob pointed to her sling.

She gave him the capsule version of her misadventure. He appreciated the segment about the mechanic and his wire cutters.

'Such an elegant solution.'

'Hey Bob!' A yell from the midst of the clamour.

He didn't bother to look up, but Lydia understood that he was listening by the way his gaze shifted sideways.

'Come to our rescue,' the voice insisted.

Bob sighed. 'Be right back.' He slid off his stool and inched through the crowd to where three stocky men in their thirties stood, arms linked like footballers. As Bob approached, one of the men tugged him into the little group. Bob allowed this, without actually lifting his own arms from his sides, seeming to coast into place.

There was a hasty conference and within a few minutes Bob returned to her side, pushing back through the crowd without a ripple. She'd stolen his bar stool and he accommodated, pressing next to her, his bony hip nudging her waist. His wispy beard looked like an afterthought.

'You work here?' she asked.

'In a manner of speaking.'

'You don't seem like the all-inclusive resort type.'

'What type is that?'

She held up a hand. 'Sorry. None of my business.'

'And what do you think my business is?'

She held the glass of beer against her throbbing wrist. It felt good, numbing the persistent pain.

'Actually,' she said, 'I was hoping to score.'

Bob chortled. 'Were you now.' He slid his hands over his thighs. 'What makes you think I can help?'

'You look like a resourceful person.'

He liked this, nodding several times.

'Am I right?' she pushed.

Bob dug into his pocket and pulled out a handful of peso coins that he dropped onto the bar. She saw that he wore no bracelet, no all-inclusive stigmata. The bartender didn't reach for the coins right away, waiting until he was through pouring a trio of margaritas, a gesture performed without lifting the beaker or spilling a drop.

Bob touched Lydia's elbow. 'Let's grab a seat.' He motioned to the padded chairs that extended the bar area, each set gathered around a table. Most of these spots were taken by older tourists. He edged to a corner table laden with the band's equipment and pushed the gadgets and cords aside, making room for their drinks. The musicians didn't seem to mind and Lydia got the idea that they were used to it. She felt self-conscious: was this the dope dealer's table?

Bob said right away, 'Tell me what, and how much.'

For the first time since meeting him, Lydia was guarded. Maybe Bob was a narc, seeking to entrap witless tourists. Mexican jails were no picnic. Fine example she'd be to Doug and Annie back home, not to mention Iris in the Toucan wing, innocently snoozing while her daughter got shoved into the back of a paddy wagon.

'Think of me as being part of the service of La Pirámide,' Bob said, noting her hesitation.

She sucked in a breath, then said, 'Just five or six joints to see me through.'

He nodded, considering the request. 'That'll set you back sixty U.S.'

She whistled. 'Holy shit.'

He shrugged. 'Up to you, my girl.'

She cast a look to both sides—the usual cacophony of people enjoying themselves. Zip interest in this exchange, yet it had been years since she'd scored off a stranger. She began to sink into her chair and the throbbing of her wrist eased; relief was in sight. Since Charlie took off she'd needed weed to get to sleep and to relax when she came home from the college and its heartbreaking stories of human migration.

She waited to hear the drill. Would Bob slip the weed under her door, preceded by a discreet tap?

Not too late to axe the deal.

Bob checked something on his phone and while he was at it, texted a message, thumbs probing the keyboard. The gesture made her nervous: who was he summoning? The government cautioned travellers to stay clear of border towns and certain other areas of the country—and don't, above all, get involved in anything illegal, in particular, the drug trade.

Bob looked at her placidly. 'Are we on?'

Just before leaving Toronto there had been another grisly tale about decapitations, bodies drowned in acid then tossed in the river. There was the ad hoc graveyard in Veracruz, corpses piled one on top of the other next to a sign painted in the victims' blood. She examined the bar with its pastoral paintings of village scenes, and imagined tossing on the hard bed for another night as Iris got up yet again to go to the toilet.

'Yes,' she said.

'Got cash on your person?'

'Afraid not.' After twenty-four hours here she'd lost the habit of carrying a wallet.

He gave her a sidelong smile. 'You're good for it, I assume?'

'Certainly.'

'Bring me the money tomorrow.' He sank a hand into his shirt pocket and pulled out a cigarette package, and without making much effort to hide what he was doing, knocked out half a dozen neatly wrapped joints. He reached for a paper napkin, wrapped the weed into a rectangular wad and handed it to her.

'Lullaby and good night to the pretty lady from—'

'Toronto.'

'Canadian. Thought so.'

'You?'

He didn't answer right away, as if deciding whether he needed to respond. Then—'Detroit.'

'Really?' A pause. 'Why Detroit?'

'So many questions.' He reflected. 'I live in many places, one of which is here.'

Waves of bawdy laughter erupted from the bar area and the musicians laid down their instruments. Had anyone been listening to their romantic ballads? Yes, those two older women dancing with each other, reluctant to part as the last chord rang.

The musicians nodded at Bob as they passed the table and headed towards the hotel entrance for their break. The singer was dressed in an embroidered skirt meant to evoke a Mayan costume—she might very well be Maya—while her partner wore jeans and a white overshirt. The moment they left the impromptu stage, their smiles dropped.

Bob followed their departure with his eyes. Lydia watched his face circumspectly, the beat-up skin and high cheekbones. Hole in one earlobe. A bit pirate, but there was a refinement in his manner.

Sixty bucks for half a dozen joints.

He kept looking beyond her and started to chew his lower lip. She twisted to see what caught his interest, skating her gaze across the tiled floor to the cavernous lobby with its pre-Columbian bas-relief clinging to the stucco wall, and on to the reception desk, quiet this time of night. A woman swept the floor with a handmade broom. The tuck shop was shutting down and the same group of men Bob had spoken to earlier was hailing a taxi, heading to *Señor* Frog's. Bob wasn't looking at any of this. His stare fixed on three people approaching the reception desk.

They were Mexican: a woman in her forties with blond hair tugged back severely from her face was talking to the concierge. Demands were being made. Her lanky husband stood beside her with one hand resting on her waist, saying nothing. He wore a sweater knotted around his neck. Behind the couple, a younger man snapped his fingers and one of the bellboys came running to gather up their luggage.

Big city types visiting the coast on their holidays.

'Well well,' Bob said slowly. His fingers tapped his water glass.

The newcomers began to follow the bellboy, clipping across the tile floor in the direction of the Toucan wing.

Bob hunched over the table and spoke rapidly. 'That man hopes to be elected governor of the state in the Spring. Licenciado Alejandro Gutiérrez.' Bob looked excited. 'What might he be up to at La Pirámide?'

'Have you thought that they might simply be on vacation?'

'There is no such thing as a vacation in election year. His wife, Martina, is a prominent television interviewer. She talks to soap opera stars and pointy-headed intellectuals.'

'How do you know all this, Bob?'

'Something is afoot,' he went on skittishly. He rose from the chair and ambled toward the lobby like a man who wanted to smell the night air, and stood at the opening to the resort, stretching his arms over his head in an elaborate yawn. He squinted at the stone fountain, the palm trees, and the bandstand with iron benches that mimicked a traditional Mexican plaza's layout. After a few moments he sauntered back into the lobby and made his way to the desk. He muttered something to the concierge and patted his pocket, as if he'd forgotten his room key. As the concierge reached down to one of the cubbyholes under the desk, Bob muttered something again. The exchange ended with Bob slapping a hand over the other man's in a comradely way. Instead of returning to the bar, he disappeared down the hallway that led to the Toucan wing.

9

LYDIA PICKED UP her pace as she headed down the pathway that led to their pavilion. At night the resort transformed, a magical stage set with inky palm trees looming, their fronds whispering in the breeze. No garble of monkeys, no hearty imprecations to 'Dance!' in the activity pool. Invisible surf crashed as it hit shore and bled into the sand, an elemental rhythm. Deep nostril-filling fragrance of something sweet. She caught voices, sometimes entire sentences, as other guests passed, the men tripping along in their unaccustomed sandals. The lights that appeared at regular intervals attracted moths that beat against the glass bulbs, creating a strobe effect. The meandering pool gleamed a much darker blue than during the day, and though it was closed for swimming after dusk, Lydia could hear muted conversation and spotted clusters of people still wearing bathing suits, as if they hadn't noticed the sun's descent. A child let out a howl, allowed to stay up late but too tired to enjoy it.

Square lanterns indicated the Toucan side; round lanterns equalled Colonial. Urgency evaporated and she willed herself to slow her hurried pace. In a few moments she'd be sinking bare heels into the sand, gazing at the frilled waves as they rolled into shore—and she'd light up one of the overpriced joints.

A troupe of youngish people clung to each other as they made their way to El Disco Tropicano at the edge of the property. One of the men waved to Lydia: 'Twenty-seven below in Winnipeg.' He didn't seem like the sort of husband who'd paddle off in a canoe, but you never knew.

She'd check on Iris on the way to the beach, and maybe make a quick trip to the internet lounge to Skype Annie. Or was this the night before her Statistics midterm?

Lydia stopped short.

She couldn't remember.

And what about Doug? Her son was lousy at replying to her cheery emails, saying in a mystified tone when she finally got through to his phone: 'I saw your messages.'

He pointedly used the word 'saw' rather than 'read.'

He'd tried a year of college but it didn't take, so now he was doing makeup classes at the local secondary school, allegedly to pull up his marks for a future run at higher education. Images of home appeared: fresh stains on the Turkish rug, burner set to high and forgotten, all of this happening while Charlie hung out in his condo by the lake with friends he'd met in his Conversational Italian class.

Stop.

She reminded herself of how, just hours ago, she'd coasted high above the Bay, unfettered by domestic concerns.

Reaching the pavilion, she grabbed the railing and climbed upstairs one flight and hesitated outside the room. That's when she heard a familiar sound, Iris's throaty laughter.

Hadn't her mother said, 'Don't worry about me, not for one nanosecond. I'll be happily snoring when you return.'?

Lydia pushed the door open and peered inside. Three people sat on the balcony, crammed into plastic chairs around a low table. Iris spotted her daughter and announced 'Here she is!' as if her arrival were a much-anticipated event.

The room was dark, bathroom to the left, closet to the right. Lydia pressed past the beds and the TV monitor towards the little gathering outside.

Three smiling faces greeted her.

'Your rescuers,' Iris prompted.

It was Joe, the nurse who'd hauled her to her feet after her crash landing, and his girlfriend; what was her name? Gloria.

'Turns out they are staying in the room just above us,' Iris said, holding her glass aloft. 'I heard them talking about your unlucky episode, so I invited them for a nightcap.'

'Or two,' Gloria said. She was wearing a sundress with a shawl coverup. Long greying hair fell over her shoulders.

Joe eyed Lydia professionally. 'I understand that you got an all-clear with the x-ray, no fracture.'

'Thank goodness,' Lydia said, lifting the injured arm as she wedged past them to lean against the railing.

'We're visiting the ruins tomorrow,' Gloria said in a whispery voice that made Lydia tingle. 'I was asking Iris if you two ladies wanted to join us. We're hiring a guide with a van.'

These would be the famous Mayan ruins situated down the coast a couple of hours.

'I said I'd check if you were up to it,' Iris said.

'I'm not sure,' Lydia said and watched her mother's face darken.

Gloria and Joe explained that they were active travellers and liked to use the resort as a jumping off point for adventures. Another day they'd planned a bird-watching excursion. Then there was scuba diving off the nearby island, accessible only by watercraft.

'I'm like that too,' Iris agreed. 'Always on the go.'

Though she'd said a few hours earlier to Lydia—'Poke me if I get the urge to accomplish something while here.'

'I'm not sure what I'll want to do tomorrow,' Lydia said.

Iris's frown deepened. 'I thought you'd jump at the chance.'

'I don't want to plan.' It was never easy to stand up to her mother.

'I'd hardly call it a plan.'

'Why don't you go, Mum?'

'Well,' Iris straightened in her chair. 'I might just do that.' There was an awkward pause, then Iris said, 'You'll never guess what Joe does back home.'

Lydia was puzzled. 'He's a nurse at St. Mike's.'

The paddled leaves of the palm tree brushed the edge of the balcony. Monkeys leapt across the springy leaves onto the railing to make their deposits. They were known to bite.

'And so much more.' Iris tugged her cape around her chest while Joe sat upright in his chair, looking amused. 'Joe is …' Iris paused for effect. 'An ordained Zen priest.'

'Really?' said Lydia, genuinely impressed. Indeed, his head was shaved, though this was no longer odd among secular men.

'I'm afraid so,' Joe said.

'But you are also a nurse.'

'Of course.'

'Why 'of course'?' Gloria said. She seemed faintly annoyed.

Joe's expression barely changed. 'One needs to work in the world, and being a nurse is an extension of my practice.'

Iris bent forward, all ears. She was proud of her acquisition: a genuine Zen priest!

'And I'm a social worker,' Gloria said. 'I met him—' Here she pointed to her mate. 'In the nephrology unit where I was counselling outpatients. Trust me, I had no idea that he was an ordained priest.'

'It must be so interesting,' Iris said, cheering, as always, for the man. 'Do you meditate together?'

Gloria snorted. 'He didn't even tell me about this Zen business until we'd been dating for three weeks, and by then it was too late.'

'The die was cast,' Joe said.

Lydia examined the face of her rescuer. He had been so gentle and efficient, gathering his arms under her shoulders and heaving her to her feet. He sat now like an obedient schoolboy, hands resting on his knees. His skin pulled tightly over the bones of his face, in the way of marathon runners, or ascetics.

Gloria wasn't finished. She went on in the same tense voice. 'I don't believe in organized religions. They cause only suffering and trouble.' She tossed back the rest of her drink—rum from the minibar.

Joe didn't look disturbed. Maybe he was used to his girl-friend's anger.

'May I have another one of these?' Gloria thrust her glass towards Lydia.

If this were a year ago and it was Lydia holding out her glass for a refill, Charlie would say, 'Time to call it quits'—but Joe did not do this. He merely looked at Gloria with his wide open silvery eyes, feeding her compassion and forgive-ness, which could get creepy after a while.

'You can't separate Zen from who I am,' Joe said.

Gloria jiggled her empty glass until Lydia took it from her. She was attractive in a raw-boned way, with a long nose and full mouth. Too much pale foundation cream made her look older. Lydia guessed she made a modest stir around men because of her strong gaze and good figure, though the effect was less reliable now.

'I've been known to meditate,' Iris said. She turned to her daughter. 'Back in the 70s at a yoga studio, before yoga was in vogue.'

Lydia looked over the railing and spotted the three big-city Mexicans Bob had pointed out earlier. They were emerg-ing from the pavilion, talking quietly, and they turned left, heading towards the sea.

'I feel dizzy,' Gloria said, pressing a hand to her forehead.

'Then we will return to our room,' Joe said, rising from his chair.

10

AFTER DARK THE beach became a wild place again. The loungers had been dragged into the sheds and there was nothing but sand and wind and the sound of waves belting against the shore. The hurricane last fall had reconfigured the shoreline. Trucks had hauled in tonnes of sand and you could see where the resort's property ended and the beach shrank to a narrow strip in front of the budget hotel. No imported sand there. Lydia found her way past the children's wading pool and the washrooms, past the breakfast *palapa* that held ghostly shadows of wicker furniture and a faint smell of coffee. Tugging off her sandals, she felt cold sand ooze between her toes. The half-moon had risen and stars sprinkled the dome of sky.

There was no beach at the lake where she and Charlie took the kids each summer, renting the same cottage since Doug was in diapers. The children learned to jump off the dock and paddle about before they could speak in full sentences. Lydia's own mother and father had neglected this instruction, being immersed in their adult lives, and Lydia ended up taking swimming classes years later, making up for lost time. The sore wrist twitched at her side—how she'd love to peel off her clothes and jump into the dark, broody water.

She supposed cottage life was over too, along with the rest of it. The place was tainted with her husband's stealth disappearance. Charlie had planned his escape for maximum effect.

Lydia felt her chest expand as she drew in the cooled air, not a hint of the earlier sun-soaked torpor. She neared the shoreline where the sand grew damp and hard underfoot, then looked behind to see the trail of glistening footprints left in her wake, picked up by the scythe of moonlight. Scraps of debris had washed ashore, pebbles of styrofoam, a dead fish, a scapula of tiny shells—all of this would be gone by morning when guests arrived to claim loungers for the day. The sweepers and rakers would have been up since dawn, creating a stretch of pristine sand. La Pirámide lit up behind her like a Mayan temple, its sheath of glass and stucco meant to evoke an ancient place of worship. Further down the beach, a stolid high-rise building rose from the middle of a grove of palm trees; this was the budget hotel that catered to the March break crowd. Lydia walked parallel to the shoreline, letting water scoop sand out from between her toes. Calluses began to dissolve to pumice dust.

In the distance she could make out low rolling hills. This part of the country did not feature cliffs or interesting geography; it was noted for scruffy flatlands and swamps and dense jungle foliage—so unlike the Pacific coast with its dramatic cliffs.

She was aware of a wave rolling in on a deeper note, a longer reach, and when it hovered, lingering too long before crashing, Lydia scampered towards dry sand with a jolt of panic. She knew about rogue waves. They came out of nowhere and retreated to nowhere, and if you were in their way, too bad.

Heart pounding, she slipped one of Bob's perfectly rendered joints into the palm of her hand and lit up. Tough to keep it going, and the matches she'd picked up from the tuck shop were equipped with heads that snapped off. A breeze cantered across the open water towards shore, dousing whatever flame she managed to ignite.

Finally. The paper flared, then the weed inside. She inhaled once experimentally, then took a long draw. Her lungs expanded, trusty bellows.

Spasm of coughing. She drew in again, feeling the raw heat hit throat and chest. Something in her settled. It didn't seem nearly so dark now and she could make out the forlorn shape of a freighter, or perhaps a cruise ship, pressed against the horizon. A kiteshape leapt out of the water close to shore. Sting ray?

Charlie must have stood on the dock, dandling his foot in the moored canoe, thinking—now? Across the lake was the town and apparently that's where he'd paddled first, then caught the bus back to Toronto, leaving her and Annie and Doug to wonder what the hell.

This was what sent the fury node careering, that he could do this to them all, make them stand dockside under pelting rain wondering if he'd capsized, when he was, in reality, sitting at Don's Burger House tossing back an IPA, waiting for the Greyhound bus to roll up. Charlie was a man who left nothing to chance and he would know exactly what they were going through. He must have told himself—what? That freedom was worth it.

Goddamn his bones.

Lydia filled her lungs again.

Iris, when informed of his flight, let out a sigh over the phone and said, 'You recall how I left your father and you kids. It's not a pretty picture, but sometimes necessary.' It was a couple of months before Lydia could bring herself to phone again.

Charlie didn't miss a day in his job as vice-principal at the east end collegiate. It wasn't his whole life that he needed to quit, just the domestic part.

Three weeks ago, Iris had called from Berkeley, jazzed by her plan. She'd bought a lottery ticket from the cancer hospital and—'I've won a week at a luxury Caribbean resort. Join me.' Iris couldn't resist adding; 'Who knows, you might meet a handsome widower.'

The weed was a herbal blast of sensuality, wicking her mind clean. Lydia continued to stroll along the shore, crossing into the neighbouring hotel area with its modest patio and eroded beach. She couldn't help but feel a certain disdain: imagine staying in such a dull place, crummy plastic tables, no umbrellas, an uninventive rectangular pool with one end roped off for children. Slogging through sand, she hit the far edge of this property, marked by a rock with the painted warning: Entering Unsupervised Beach Area.

This was what one was warned against, walking solo along deserted beaches in Mexico at night. No one raked the sand here. Her bare feet hit driftwood and tangled in a fishing line. Ramshackle houses dotted the hillside, lit by flickering television screens. These dwellings were built of concrete and rebar, topped by slices of corrugated tin. It would be wise to put on footwear before venturing further. Biting down on the joint, she managed to balance on one foot and slip into sandals without using her wounded arm. Tinny pop music thumped from a car parked alongside one of the huts.

The air had changed subtly, infused now with a faint odour of drains.

A four-legged creature zigzagged across the beach towards her, a shape cut out of the night. The pot was making her mind slow, brain warning of danger while her feet sank into the sand. She'd pick up a stick. Except there weren't any. Should she make a dash for it, head back to the hotel zone?

The panting dog circled her, its tail arched and stiff. An unknown breed, narrow muzzle. She'd entered the forbidden land. That was the pot talking; occasionally, marijuana made her paranoid. She continued to stand still, willing herself to look imposing and unafraid, and hugged her sling as the dog continued to circle, feet kicking up clumps of sand.

Her stomach clenched; here came dinner.

The dog leaned back on its haunches and began to growl. Lydia stood frozen, alone in this godforsaken place.

A sharp whistle and someone barked an order in Spanish. The voice came from behind her. The dog cantered towards the hill, where it stood for a moment, posing in dramatic silhouette.

A man pulled out of the darkness, and it took her a moment to recognize the politician, the man who would be governor. She hid the joint behind her back.

'*Buenas noches,*' she said.

Could it be that he didn't hear her above the sound of surf? A breeze loosened sparks off the tip of her joint and he looked pointedly at this display.

In Mexico they lock you up in some filthy jail and you languish, awaiting charges. Iris would frantically call the Canadian consulate, if there was one in town. This was how nightmares began.

The politician drew closer, sweater roped over his shoulders. No expression on his face, no welcoming smile, nor glimmer of hostility. He looked her up and down in a lazy way. She was wearing a tank top and one of those gauzy Indian skirts that she'd bought for the trip.

'*Buenas noches, Señorita,*' he finally said, and his tone was not friendly. 'I must tell you that it's not a good idea to walk by yourself at night,' he said, switching to English.

Her finger clicked against her joint, let it fall to the sand, and she made herself stare back at his face with its symmetrical cheekbones. The lights from the budget resort sparkled, but between it and them there was nothing, just this stretch of unkempt beach.

Bob had warned, 'Be discreet where you smoke.' Hence this walk in the dark.

The man kept staring at her, expressionless.

'A beautiful evening,' she said.

No response. He was an elegant statue, hair lifting in the breeze. A sound of a motor alerted them to an airplane heading inland. The politician glanced up and frowned. They both watched the starboard light as the small aircraft disappeared behind the palm trees.

She would slide past the man in a casual way and amble back to the resort as if she had all the time in the world. Iris would be asleep in the room, her soft purr of breath barely audible over the hum of air conditioner.

Before Lydia had a chance to act, a woman stepped out of the darkness—his wife, the television journalist, hopping as she sought to fasten the strap of her sandal. Her husband swung around, acknowledging her arrival. A wave curled across the sand to eddy around their feet, brimming foam.

The woman peered at Lydia and said, 'You should stay in the tourist area.'

'So I've been told.' Lydia glanced at the joint that lay on the ground, leaking tendrils of smoke. Her heart jumped in a weird way; maybe the weed was laced with meth. Would Bob sell adulterated goods? She knew nothing about the man.

The politician dug one hand into the pocket of his slacks while the other moved to rest on the shoulder of his wife. 'In your country it is perhaps acceptable to smoke marijuana, but we Mexicans do not like this. We have rigorous laws.'

'It is you people—' the woman said, smoothing the front of her dress, 'that cause problems in our country. If you didn't buy drugs, we wouldn't sell them. And we would not be in such a mess.'

This small lecture had taken place in English. A further admonition; they knew her language but she didn't know theirs. The woman took a step forward and kicked sand over the smouldering joint.

'I will be more careful,' Lydia said, and loped past them in a studied gait, tongue lying like a slug in her mouth. She felt the pair watching her progress as she tramped along the scruffy beach towards the combed sand of La Pirámide.

11

THAT'S FOR ME,' Iris said, pointing to the activity menu. 'Archery is excellent for balance and concentration. I always thought I might be good at it. '

Squeals of laughter rose from the activity pool where a member of the Star Team was conducting an aerobics class.

Lydia looked stern. 'Not such a good idea, Mum, considering your fragile bits.'

'You should talk,' Iris said, noting her daughter's injured wrist. She gave her own thigh a hearty slap. The hip had been replaced two years ago, an arduous few months, but well worth it. 'There's metal and plastic in there.' She paused and added in a softer tone. 'We might as well have it out now; you are not to fuss about me.'

The two women marched past the beach volleyball court where girls in bikinis lunged for the ball aided by bare-chested men, not all of them so young. The girls neighed like thoroughbreds, tossing hair over their shoulders.

To one side, the shore sloped to the turquoise sea, which was sequined with bathers. The women stopped beside the meandering swimming pool with its tiered series of waterfalls.

'Have you ever imagined such a place?' Iris said.

'Not in my wildest dreams,' Lydia said.

In her tone Iris detected a certain contempt, an easy disregard for the sort of people who demanded artificial waterfalls and nonstop entertainment when they left home, not to mention six restaurants, five bars, and a snack bar that was open 24/7.

The pair threaded between loungers laden with oiled-up vacationers, past the beach bar where a trio of blenders scoured fruit into cocktails. Discreetly, Lydia tucked her good arm under her mother's elbow. Iris tossed her blonded hair, noting that people were watching her progress. She was used to a certain amount of attention, and not just from geezers. She did not cater to the commonly held belief that women of a certain age couldn't hope to attract notice. A person creates her own visibility, insists on it.

They reached two cots at the end of the row, webbed plastic with gaily striped cushions, decorated with several damp towels. Cots claimed by hotel guests who were nowhere in sight. Iris stared like an engineer at the low-slung recliner. Whoever designed these things didn't take into account that a segment of the population needed something to grab onto while lowering themselves. After a few seconds of hovering, followed by a thud and wheeze of vinyl, Iris was settled. Beside her, Lydia glided effortlessly onto the other lounger, brushing the damp towel aside. People must not claim turf that they didn't need; if the world paid attention to this basic principle, they'd all be in less trouble. A waiter came by with iced margaritas, which they gratefully seized. Soon, Iris shut her eyes against the sun and fell asleep.

When her eyes fluttered open half an hour later, the Mexican family who'd been parked nearby had disappeared. Her drink, what was left of it, was baking in the sun, the ice cubes long ago melted. Lydia sat cross-legged on her cot, reading with pen in hand, ready to underline pertinent passages.

Iris said in a lazy tone, 'Are we allowed to mention Charlie?'

'Of course,' her daughter replied.

'Because, no matter how this unfolds, he remains the father of your children.'

Lydia cast those huge brown eyes towards the sky, as if the obvious had been spoken, as indeed it had. Clichés popped out of Iris's mouth around Lydia. It was because she was trying too hard to act motherly, a role she'd never taken to in a natural way.

'When you share kids, you share for good,' Iris added.

The statement hung there in all its banality.

Lydia dropped her stare to the sea, a widow searching the horizon for her husband's vessel. Charlie had disappeared on water, heaving off from the dock in his carefully restored Chestnut canoe, showing a previously unrecognized romantic nature. Charlie was escaping. That's how Iris saw it, because she was a champion escaper herself.

'Have you heard from him recently?' Iris asked.

'We're on speaking terms, because of the kids.'

Well, that was something.

Iris tread carefully. 'How are Doug and Annie doing?'

'Not so well.'

'I suppose they are angry.'

'Of course they're angry. A parent disappears one summer afternoon; it's pretty traumatic.'

The arrow hit its mark for Iris had done a similar bunk when the children were young. 'I've made a point of always being the one who leaves, never the one left behind,' she said.

A child stood on the beach, crying, as he frantically searched left and right for a familiar face. Iris sat up straighter, ready to spring into action, and was half disappointed when the boy's mother shouted from her cot, 'Miguelito! *Ven acá!*'

'Recall that I made a point of assuring you and your brother,' Iris said, 'that I was not, in any way, leaving *you* two.'

Lydia gave a barking laugh. Iris understood that she was to take this as a expression of disbelief.

She'd turned up at Jake's door that evening, thirty years ago. His place of residence (a term he used ironically) was a patched-together affair, a combined garage/studio hidden in an alley near Kensington Market in downtown Toronto. What an adventure it had been to slip away from the brick house on Roxborough Avenue West and waltz into this shack with its wood stove and concrete floor. Jake stared at her with wide open eyes, then grabbed her in a bear hug. He couldn't believe she'd taken up his dare.

It was all wonderful and mad, until she got sick.

Should she let her daughter know about her relationship with Richard, how he was always holding her back, insisting on following the stifling routines of daily life? The adventurous young man she'd travelled with all over Mexico had gone back to school and become a tax attorney. He insisted they join the golf and country club! It would have killed her to stay with such a man.

Just beyond the group of loungers, a trio of men in safari suits began to lift three Roman columns off a dolly. With odd ease, for these props were made of styrofoam, they planted the columns upright in the sand. When this task was completed, they unrolled a strip of red carpet leading to a dais, then set up rows of folding chairs, clicking them open with one foot.

Destination weddings were all the rage. The sun cast a shadowless heat over the proceedings. Soon the wedding party arrived: women in breezy cocktail dresses and high heels picked their way over the stone path and onto the carpet, clinging to the elbows of their escorts wearing tropical shirts.

'*Señoritas,* you are finished?' Patricio arrived to grab the empty cups.

'*Otra margarita, por favor.*' Iris used the opportunity to practise her Spanish. And where was his hometown, she asked.

He named a village in the state of Michoacán.

She knew this charming village with a seventeenth-century church planted on the main square. Excitedly, she told Patricio how she'd spent time there *'hace muchos años,'* many years ago, had rented a house with—her memory failed for a moment—with Jake, her second husband. She managed to stumble through the sentences in Spanish. In Berkeley she made a point of speaking to her Salvadorian cleaning lady in her native tongue.

The wedding party began to blast that ballad from Titanic.

'There are *problemitas* in Michoacán,' Patricio confided as he dropped empty cups into a trash bag. *'Los narcotraficantes.'*

Iris had heard; marijuana was grown in the hills and there were meth labs hidden in the forests.

'But the Yucatan has largely escaped such difficulty,' she said.

He shrugged. *Pues...*

Iris didn't live in a cave. She'd read about dismembered bodies dropped into tubs of acid, students gone missing. Most such events were clotted around the border, right?

Sí, sí. Patricio didn't sound convinced. With his thick hair and wiry build he might still be a teenager.

The country had always been lawless. She and Richard were drinking mezcal in a cantina in Chiapas when *un borracho* staggered through the louvered doors waving an antique gun. Everyone hit the floor, terrified gringos included. Most visitors would have hightailed it back to the States after such an episode but Iris's opinion was, why travel if you wanted things to be the same as back home?

As Celine Dion's voice crested, the wedding party continued to assemble, observed by tourists humped on loungers, dazed by sun and piña coladas. The bride and groom hadn't anticipated onlookers when they'd pored over the brochures back home, photographs showing Romanesque columns, acres of empty sand and the glistening Caribbean sea. Brochures wouldn't show the squealing children tossing sand at each other or illustrate the chubby man with hairy shoulders emerging from the water, snorkel in hand, shorts dragging off his bum. A member of staff carrying a clipboard positioned herself to the side of the proceedings and fended off the curious in their drooping bathing suits, asking them to please not interfere with the photographer's sight lines. These tourists in flip-flops seemed to want to stride into the middle of the event. It reminded Iris of Shakespeare productions back in the 1970s, where the audience was obliged to take part in the action, shouting encouragement to Hamlet or handing Lady Macbeth her dagger.

The party made its way to the folding chairs. A trickle of applause, and at last the bride appeared, click-clacking down the stone pathway, wearing a fairy dress of white chiffon, a camilla in her hair. That must be her father, a youthful-looking man, sporting a handlebar mustache.

'What a remarkable garment,' Lydia said, referring to the dress. 'Do you think it's made of surgical gauze?'

A light breeze coasted across the beach, catching the hem of the bride's dress in a provocative way. At this photogenic moment, a child carrying an inflatable whale darted behind the couple, forever captured in the event. Cheers erupted from the volleyball court and a ball popped skyward, narrowly missing the bride's head.

Lydia rose from the lounger, heading back to the pyramid where she would Skype Annie, her eldest. Annie was currently enrolled at a small university in northern Ontario, majoring in something called Environmental Studies, a field of study that didn't exist when Iris went to school.

Iris realized that she had to pee. A few years ago she wouldn't have thought twice, no plotting required. Age was a series of growing awareness of body parts. Cautiously, she lowered one leg then the other onto the sand and scrabbled for her sandals. In case anyone was watching, she offered a tight smile. Her hip was acting up. She hadn't been as dutiful as she might have been during post-surgical rehab.

She gave herself a vigorous push, then plopped back down on the cushion. If she could just reach the umbrella pole and use it as a hoist. The buildup in her bladder pressed; that was another nuisance in getting older, one went from faint need to urgent in the blink of an eye.

Patricio swanned by with a tray of drinks but she couldn't bring herself to ask him to help, though Mexicans were notably kind to the elderly. She pushed again—hovering before toppling back with a squelch of flesh on vinyl.

'Mum!' Lydia raced across the sand.

Apparently Annie was not available.

Her cry alerted everyone within a kilometre and soon all were staring at the sight of Iris lurching to her feet to seize the umbrella pole.

Lydia scooped an arm under hers. 'Don't try that on your own again.'

They crossed the arched bridge together, over a pond filled with carp and dun-coloured turtles. Flamingos stood on their delicate stalks, self-aware in their kooky, florid beauty. The pyramid loomed, gold paint reflecting the blazing sun. Cortés and his men cut through the jungle with machetes, entered a clearing and were dumbfounded.

* * *

Alejandro crouched on the floor after tugging his trousers so they wouldn't bag at the knee. She'd taught him that trick. He picked up her freshly washed foot—the left one—and cradled it in his hands. He began to inspect each toe. Earlier, she'd wiped the leftover polish from her nails; the smell of remover made him sick.

He dabbed the tiny brush into the vial of cherry red; Martina was partial to bright colours. She had pretty feet, not a trace of bunions or callouses or corns, despite thirty years of wearing high heels. She lounged on the padded chair and closed her eyes as he worked, feeling the coolness of polish as he swiped each nail in turn. It took all his concentration, and for once he didn't talk. Toe by toe he worked, so tenderly. Not wanting to break the mood, she said nothing, even when she felt the brush lap over bare skin. He lowered her foot when he was done, placing it carefully on the ottoman, then lifted the other and began to paint, starting, as always, with her baby toe. She felt entirely calm, all thoughts and worries draining from her mind. She wondered, would a state governor continue to paint his wife's toenails?

12

THE TWO MEN stood behind the towel hut on the beach. It took Lydia a moment to recognize the politician, for he was wearing bathing trunks and nothing else. He looked, she decided, like the Spanish crooner, Julio Iglesias, same thin lips and wide forehead and too-white teeth. She would ask Iris if she'd noted the resemblance. Iris had bought her first computer so she could watch Julio perform on YouTube.

Standing a metre away from the politician was Bob, his hands plunged deep in the pockets of his cargo shorts. The men appeared to be having an argument, speaking in low urgent tones. Lydia recognized the body language of male anger, the way each was careful not to step over the invisible line that separated them. Alejandro gesticulated, his fingers strutting emphatically in the air. Suddenly, he tossed his towel over his shoulder and strode off, while uttering some dismissive comment. A comment that evidently enraged Bob, who began to follow the politician, albeit at a distance, letting loose a rush of Spanish in the same half-whispered tone. The politician, keeping his back to Bob, raised both hands in a shrug as he unhurriedly made his way to the pool area.

Bob halted and looked deflated by the abrupt desertion. Spotting Lydia, he let his eyes rest on hers for several seconds, but made no other sign of recognition.

Lydia wheeled about: she had to get out of here, this embalmed resort with its perfectly kept grounds and buffet tables laden with sculpted food. It clawed at her, the sudden need to enter real life, to smell car exhaust and to hear the clamour of traffic and adults at work.

It was Cleo from the front desk. Usually found staring at his computer screen, troubleshooting the small but persistent difficulties of guests, Cleo wore this uniform of pleated shirt and tan pants. He was crouching next to the entrance of the resort where it met the public sidewalk.

Three men in separate vehicles had tooted and waved at Lydia during her half-hour stroll by the roadway. She'd waved back, feeling free in a way she hadn't experienced in months. Annie and Doug were fending; she would have heard if they were dead or if the house had burned down. For the first time since Charlie disappeared, she saw that he had offered her a kind of liberation by running off. It occurred to her that she'd closed down her body for months, locked the doors and pulled down the blinds. Winter of the soul. But now, as the sun blazed, she felt almost naked, her limbs long and lean, flexible as a teenager's.

Cleo's shirt stretched across his muscled back. He rose to his feet and turned to face her, holding a brush in one hand, a small pot of paint in the other.

She peered down at what she recognized was a shrine, the sort seen planted on roadsides to commemorate where someone had crashed and died. This one was built like a miniature chapel, knee-high, featuring a Gothic arch. Inside, a plaster stature of the Virgin dangled garlands of flowers. Was that a baby pacifier strung on the Virgin's necklace? The exterior of the shrine gleamed with a fresh coat of blue paint.

'Who is this for?' Lydia asked.

'My son.'

'I'm so sorry!' She let out a gasp of sympathy. 'What happened?'

'Motorcycle accident. Last year.'

'I'm so sorry,' she repeated. She'd seen it on the roads and highways, a man whipping along on his motorcycle with a child or two tucked behind—no helmets of course. Had Cleo been the driver?

Apparently not.

'My son drives too fast.' He pointed with his brush to the area beyond where they stood, to where the road allowed a U-turn. 'He worked at the swimming pools and carried his equipment on his back.'

'What was his name?'

He pointed again, this time to the shrine. Embedded on the façade of the little chapel were pebbles spelling out: Cleo.

Cleo Senior had looked younger in the shade of the resort's lobby. His face, exposed in raw sunlight, showed a hatchwork of lines and a deep crease between his eyebrows.

'After the accident, my wife takes our daughters and returns to her family in Durango.' Cleo found the lid for the pot of paint and clamped it down. 'So I am alone, wife gone, daughters gone, my son disappeared to heaven.'

Lydia picked a stem of bougainvillea from the vine that spilled over the wall and leaned over to twist the magenta blossoms around the Virgin's necklace. When she rose, she saw that Cleo had begun to hike up the slope towards his workplace, phone pressed to his ear.

13

ANNIE'S IMAGE broke up on the monitor. Chunks of Lydia's daughter froze then snapped into focus, a bit of forehead, scraps of hair. Then abruptly Annie was fully present on the screen. She appeared to be in her dorm's communal area, a poster of Bob Marley stuck on the wall behind. Lydia had tacked up the same poster in her own dorm in the mid-nineties.

'You and Grandma having fun?' Annie said.

'You know Grandma, fun follows in her wake. Did you finish the project for Psych class?'

Annie's face looked guarded. 'It's not a project, it's an assignment. And I couldn't do the conclusion because'—she sighed dramatically—'he wanted this formal recapitulation that didn't suit the material. So he made me take it all back.'

'Oh no,' Lydia said, full of sympathy.

'Equals ten percent grade deduction because I'm going to be one freaking day late.'

Lydia didn't point out that this was a standard penalty. At the college where she taught ESL they invoked the same.

'I don't even know if I want to continue with Psych,' Annie went on.

'What do you mean?' Lydia said, keeping alarm from her voice. Annie had already changed her major twice. Last year it was Environmental Studies.

'It's boring. Maybe I'll switch again.'

'To what?'

'Carla's doing Fine Arts. It's pretty cool. She made a sculpture out of hay and dangled a plastic nose over it.'

Iris would think it was just great if Annie decided she wanted to become an installation artist.

'Don't rush into a decision,' Lydia counselled.

'I knew you'd say that. I wasn't even going to tell you.'

'Wait until end of semester before making up your mind. Remember how keen you were on becoming a shrink.'

'Yeah.' Annie sounded doubtful. She twisted in her chair and called out to someone in the room.

'Annie?'

Reluctantly, her daughter swung back to face the computer screen. 'What?'

'Promise me you'll wait until I get home before you drop any courses.'

'When do you get home?'

She'd only told the girl half a dozen times. 'In five days.'

'What?' Annie said this to someone Lydia couldn't see. 'Take it with you! How should I know?' Back to her mother. 'Listen; there's stuff going on here. I should go.' One palm fanned the air in farewell as the other pressed the mouse button.

I'm not going to worry, Lydia reminded herself as she left the stuffy room full of overheated computers and entered the lobby of the resort. She'd pledged to remain offline this week. So far it wasn't working. She peeled off her wrap and headed to the beach where soon she was pillowed by the sea, sculling with her good arm towards her mother. The wounded arm floated easily, water becoming a sort of sling. A decade earlier, she'd chased a slimmer, faster Iris on Lake Huron without a hope of catching up. Today, her mother bobbed just above the surface, hair encased in a bathing cap, eyes shut, barely moving.

14

WATCH ALEJANDRO—the way he keeps looking around while he's talking.' Bob was keyed up, chewing his lower lip. 'He's expecting people,' he went on in a conspiratorial tone. 'Putting together a posse for his run at the governorship.'

Sr. Gutiérrez was almost too good looking, and his casual clothes didn't fool Lydia. This was a man accustomed to wearing tailored suits, not these chinos and polo shirt. He lay on a cot, feet crossed at the ankles, arms folded behind his head. There was nothing relaxed in this pose; each limb was taut, ready to spring into action. He tilted his head to speak to his wife, Martina.

Martina's hair was untouched by pool or sea water, perfectly coiffed and camera ready. She lay in a cot beside her husband, wearing a metallic wrap over her bathing suit and dangling reading glasses in one hand. She seemed amused by what he'd said and reached over to touch his hair—such an intimate gesture that Lydia averted her gaze. The pair had positioned themselves next to the adult swimming pool, not the one containing a noisy swim-up bar, but the one reserved for serious swimmers, empty as usual. The third member of their party roamed the rim of the pool speaking into his cell phone.

Bob cocked his head, listening to the one-sided phone conversation. 'A meeting will be held here with a certain high-ranking official,' he translated.

Moments ago, Lydia had clambered out of the ocean, feeling her winter skin pucker from salt water. Iris was still languidly floating over the waves. When warned of the danger of sunburn, she'd crooned in a voice so relaxed it barely registered—'Who cares?' She disliked being cautioned about the world's perils; at best, Iris would pretend to listen, nodding amiably, then ignore everything that was suggested. This went for vitamin supplements, sun exposure, and the need to brush one's teeth in purified water.

Bob continued to translate, leaning forward on his bar stool next to Lydia's. 'Our friend is talking to a driver, giving directions; people are coming here from the capital.'

'Mexico City?' Lydia said.

Bob hesitated before correcting her, still trying to pick up the conversation. 'Capital of the state; that would be Chetumal,' he said. 'We are, in case you didn't realize, in the state of Quintana Roo.' He pronounced this 'Kintana Roe.'

Bob wore a pair of baggy shorts held up with a belt, buckle shaped like a cannabis leaf. Patricio slipped a cup in her hand filled with one of his specialties, orange liquid topped with foam. It tasted like an alcoholic milkshake, which was more or less what it was. During the minutes she'd been sitting next to Bob no fewer than three men had come up to him, punching his shoulder, saying, 'More of the same, my man,' or 'Double my pleasure,' as if Lydia weren't there.

She recalled the sensation of seawater pushing against her back, a seductive buoyancy. She'd closed her eyes and allowed herself to be cradled, embraced. It had been a while since she'd let anyone hold her this way. She glanced towards the sea again, searching through the crowd of bathers until she spotted Iris cutting sidestroke towards the yellow rope that marked out the safe swimming area. Iris would be attracted to just such a line.

The man speaking into his phone barked a few words before dropping the device back into his pocket. Sr. Gutiérrez called out to him and the two conferred.

'The group will be here within ten minutes,' Bob said, piecing together the exchange. He grabbed his cup of non-alcoholic juice and took a gulp. 'Martina wants to return to their suite for the meeting, but her husband—' Bob strained to hear. 'They seem to have a difference of opinion.'

Martina Gutiérrez sank back on her lounger after shrugging in apparent resignation. She slipped a massive pair of sunglasses over her eyes and lay staring skyward; let the men do what the men will do.

Bob straightened to his full height on the stool. His teeth were a hodgepodge, suggesting impoverished or distracted parents. Deep vertical creases framed his mouth and his chest was slightly concave. He'd taken her up as another single person at the resort, Lydia understood. At meals, he'd swan over with his tray and point out some item of food that she might try. When they ran into each other elsewhere, he'd skip small talk and impart grisly tales from the local news. This would include a litany of car crashes, home invasions, drive-by kidnappings and unsolved murders. He seemed to take pleasure in relating these details, as if he wanted her to know what was going on outside this artificial paradise. He stood closer than he needed to and frequently touched her as he spoke.

She found herself looking at his hands now, slender fingers and tanned skin. He perched next to her on a bar stool. The torpor of late afternoon heat made her drowsy and she let her knees fall open. Even the activity pool had taken a break from its relentless fun and music.

The path leading to the beach was filling as a small man strode towards them, flanked on either side by bulkier men with broad Indian faces.

'Hey ho,' Bob said and pulled out a toothpick and began digging at a molar.

The compact man in the centre of the group did not look like a hotel guest. He was a slim, dark-skinned Mexican, walking nimbly, though judging by his weathered face he was well over seventy. He wore a white costume identical to what the *folklórico* dancers displayed the night before: wraparound pants made of rough cotton, a breezy overshirt and a red kerchief tied at the neck. His sombrero was wide-brimmed, an old-school shape, not the turned-up cowboy style favoured by the younger generation.

'You recognize him?' Lydia asked.

'I certainly do,' said Bob. 'Ask any Mexican.'

As if to demonstrate this, the bartender switched off the blender and stood with his hand on the lid, gawking at the approaching group. A couple of chambermaids stood to the side of the walkway, giggling as the men passed.

'Who is he?' Lydia asked.

Patricio supplied the answer in a reverent voice: 'El Pintor.'

The painter.

Lydia wished Iris were at her side now. Her mother used to exhibit Mexican art in her gallery in Toronto, hectic surrealist conglomerations that landed like a thud in local art circles.

'Victor García Pacheco,' Bob said. 'Better known as Don Victor, painter of the people.'

'Never heard of him.'

'Which says more about you than him.'

Lydia pumped for more information. 'What kind of paintings?'

Bob lifted a hand and let it flutter. 'Images on ceramic, mosaic tile, frescos, canvas—updates on Mayan glyphs, animals, fantastical creatures …'

El Pintor continued his stride, even as he glanced in amusement at his surroundings. The faux pyramid reflected light off its jangled surface in a hundred directions. It hurt to look at it, certain times of day. The painter stood still and, making a visor with his hand, gazed for several seconds at the vast, improbable jewel, then gave a raspy laugh.

His group began to cross the arched bridge that traversed the miniature jungle. They stood in the middle of the structure, pointing into the foliage, having spotted the flamingos. The painter stopped again when he reached the beach area and leaned over to unsnap his sandals, which were clunky affairs with rubber tire soles. As he rose, he winced and pressed a hand to his knee before continuing.

The tourists paid no attention to the newcomers, despite the artist's eccentric dress. If they thought anything, it would be that the man was part of the evening's entertainment. As he neared the bar before turning towards the pool area, Lydia succeeded in catching his eye. He offered a curt nod, no hint of a smile. This was a man accustomed to respectful attention.

Don Victor was fewer than a dozen metres away when he shielded his eyes and gazed over the beach, scanning the rows of loungers filled with greased tourists—and squinted at the outdoor shower where a pair of children yelped under the rush of cold water. Their mother oversaw sand removal before letting them venture into the restaurant. El Pintor continued to take in the scene until he saw what he was looking for: the politician and his television star wife awaiting his approach on the elevated deck.

He briskly climbed the steps towards the little group.

'What does he want with the candidate?' Bob wondered aloud. He leaned hard into Lydia's shoulder as he strained to see better.

The artist and his men reached the pool area, a clatter of shoes on tile. Alejandro swept the newspaper off his stomach and rose from the lounger, his wife close behind. Martina's wrap was a sarong, knotted under the neck.

Bob started to hum tunelessly.

'I saw you arguing with him, with Alejandro,' Lydia said, in a tone that sought to appear offhand.

Bob lifted his weight from her shoulder and tilted his head so he was looking at her. Those unblinking blue eyes were unsettling. He flashed a smile that held no amusement and she felt a chill settle between them.

'Whatever you observed was not what you think,' he said.

'You don't know what I think.'

He turned away, in no mood to argue.

The group of Mexicans stood in the shade where Alejandro and Martina had camped out and immediately a waiter appeared to take their drinks order. A boy raced over with a stack of fresh towels while another staff member dragged deck chairs into a circle. This all happened in less than a minute, though no audible order had been given.

The meeting, for this was surely what was going on, began with El Pintor reaching into his voluminous pants and pulling out a cigar. Soon the stench of Cuban tobacco drifted over to the bar area where Lydia and Bob sat.

'Could be something to do with Don Victor's interest in the environment,' Bob mused, in his usual voice. 'They're hustling a deal—government will protect the ocellated turkey in exchange for Don Victor creating a public mural.'

'He could start his environmental concern by putting out that cigar.' Lydia made a face. She gazed back at the water; no sign of Iris. People were starting to drift in for lunch. She leaned forward on her stool, squinting hard; her distance vision wasn't what it used to be; the world lacked its old definition. She reminded herself that Iris had the right to go anywhere she pleased without checking in. Chances were she was ambling along the shoreline, drying off before lunch. Many people were doing this, oblivious to the perils of UV rays. Or she'd made new friends, joining them for a preprandial shot of tequila. She would be demonstrating the correct way to tap salt on the wrist, squeeze lime, and lap up the whole affair in sequence.

Her mother's absence had the old effect on Lydia: she felt herself tighten, never sure whether Iris was gone for days or weeks—or had merely stepped out on an errand. She would trot up the front steps of the house in her high heels, late and often breathless, having forgotten about her daughter's dental appointment or the parent-teacher interview; her own life was far more dramatic and complicated than a mere child's.

15

'I'LL BE FINE,' Iris insisted. 'Remember our agreement?'

Lydia remembered; she was not to fuss.

'And besides, who is the wounded party here?'

'Moi.'

'Correct. You two go to town and enjoy yourselves. I have no wish to leave this chair for the next several hours.' Iris was sitting on the balcony of their room, the fat biography of Catherine the Great open on her knees. 'I'm finding this woman's life fascinating.' She patted the page.

Page twelve, Lydia noted.

'I'll never be able to face Steve unless I get through at least half of it.'

Bob was waiting by the driveway where the buses drew up. He looked on edge, drumming his thighs. He'd dressed for town in a collared shirt and slacks.

Lydia wore a sleeveless dress that hit just above the knees, a dress that contained a fraught history and had once ended up on the floor of her car. It was Bob's idea that they should walk to town, an easy three kilometres. He bounced off the pillar and touched her shoulder in greeting. It felt a little like a date. She planned to buy souvenirs for Doug and Annie, maybe a serape, or silver jewellery.

They made their way downhill on the cobblestone path, passing the gazebo and the parrot snoozing on its perch in the ornate cage. The sun was high, unrelenting, mitigated by an ocean breeze that would not be with them for long. Heat pulsed off the stone walls while palm trees leaned away from the sea, buffeted by remembered winds.

Reaching the main road they inhaled pungent diesel fuel from the buses grinding by. Barefoot men tended the flower beds decorating the lush meridian of the busy boulevard. Lydia glanced down at the shrine to Cleo Junior and noticed a change: a tiny wooden cross was propped next to the figure of the Virgin. She could make out the patch where the grieving father had crouched, twin smudges for his knees.

They stepped onto the sidewalk and were immediately ambushed by the stink of drains emanating from the curb-side sewer. Bob pressed forward, undaunted by the heat and smell, and Lydia had to rush to catch up.

'There's a heavy dude I need to see in El Centro,' he told her. 'After that we can hit one of the local dives for a cold one.'

Where did he get this lingo, she wondered. And asked aloud: 'Do I go with you when you meet this man?'

'No you do not,' he said, and added, 'for your own good.'

He seemed euphoric, or maybe just tight with nerves.

They marched past a group of villas under development, cheerful stucco cabañas with balconies. A sign advertised time-shares featuring sea views and 'luxury details.' Bob shook his head: 'Two decades ago I strung a hammock between a pair of palm trees here. The *señora* made our meals and I spent all day body surfing. Me and some boys from Progresso, but that's another story.'

A forklift bucked over the sand, scooping up a load of boards. Workmen perched curbside, eating lunch out of insulated buckets. They looked no more than sixteen years old, hard-muscled, waving when they caught Lydia looking. She raised her sprained wrist to wave back, and winced with pain. The arm fell back into in its sling, a tender creature that must be protected. The swelling had eased; she could now use the hand for certain tasks, like pulling on underpants and cutting food.

Across the street a development looked stalled, rusted rebar sticking out of concrete, wheel tracks full of muddy water, and an advertising billboard had faded to a sepia blur.

'Developer got on the wrong side of the mayor,' Bob said, and he tossed an arm over Lydia's shoulder. Was this a comradely gesture, she wondered, or the prelude to romance? She'd lost the knack of reading the signs, it had been so long. She sneaked a look at him. Those grizzled cheeks evoked outlaw, a mug shot as different from Charlie's fleshy, clean-shaven face as she could imagine. His body, bony and nimble, overtook the memory, already fading, of Charlie's solidity. After a moment of hesitation, she wrapped her good arm around Bob's waist and felt the jazzed-up energy in him, the dampness of his shirt and pulsing of skin against skin.

He glanced sideways. 'Rare to see a woman at La Pirámide without a man.'

The statement wasn't exactly flattering.

'What's your story?' he asked.

'Which one?'

'The most current.'

'Well ...' she started. Then paused. 'I am no longer married.'

'Good,' he said in an encouraging way.

'It wasn't my choice.'

'Seldom is, kiddo.' He held her gaze and it startled her, the intensity in his expression, an intimacy that she hadn't invited or expected.

They passed the ornate entrance to La Mansion de las Brisas, a colonial-style hotel, and made room for a group of tourists approaching from town, laden with shopping bags. Their bracelets were yellow, not the blue ones that signalled

La Pirámide. Lydia and Bob offered brief nods, rather than the full greeting reserved for kin.

'I teach ESL,' she said.

'An honourable profession.'

'I have two kids.'

'Bet they've got their heads screwed on right.'

'Hard to know, at this point.'

'Give them time.'

'And you?' she asked.

'No kiddies, far as I know.' Then he added, 'When you come from a family of gangsters, you learn an unusual skill set.'

They stepped through a pocket of intense heat.

'Gangsters?' she said, trying not to sound too interested.

He looked at her. 'Did I say that?'

They were passing the hidden entrance to Posada Buenavista, the smallest and oldest hotel on the strip. Its roof peeped up from amongst trees that had been planted thirty years ago. A guard stood at the gate, walkie-talkie in hand, and he stared at Bob before giving him an abrupt nod. Lydia felt a little proud to be with Bob, the one guest at La Pirámide who wasn't entirely respectable.

'That's not what I heard back at the resort,' she said.

'What did you hear, doll?' He squeezed her waist so hard it hurt, then let his hand drop. 'You must tell me everything about myself.'

'Word is you work for the U.S. drug enforcement agency.'

'Administration,' he corrected, then gave a off-kilter smile. 'D.E.A.'

The edge of town was chaotic, with three roads converging and a policeman trying to make sense of it all.

'I would have thought you were working for the other side.' When he failed to respond, she added, 'Given the fact you sell drugs.' She paused when he offered no response. 'Of course I wouldn't know.'

'No, you wouldn't.'

He turned his attention to the converging traffic, and Lydia got the idea he might disappear into its midst and never be seen again. Her dress was soaked with sweat and she found herself longing for the resort's scrubbed serenity. Bob darted ahead, ignoring waves and whistles from the cop, and the cars miraculously flowed on either side of him. He landed on the far curb where he leaned against a concrete pole, ostentatiously waiting for her to gather up the courage to follow. Traffic swarmed, criss-crossing lanes, honking, belches of exhaust.

She stepped onto the asphalt then lost her nerve. Finally the officer gave a signal, blew on his whistle, and for a few seconds everything stopped. She raced across the open road-way, clutching her purse.

Town gave off its own heat, with its rows of low-slung buildings and a wooden boardwalk that lined the main drag. This was where tourists congregated, ambling between souvenir shops, bars, and restaurants. Garish billboards loomed, urging visitors to try this beer or that tequila, to experience the mystical experience of swimming with dolphins or to try diving into an ancient *cenote*.

A young woman approached Lydia, carrying a clipboard. '*Señorita*, come with me to the caves,' she said, offering a brilliant smile.

A bus excursion to the capital city?

Buffet dinner on a paddleboat?

Bob warned, 'Keep away from time-share touts. They'll lure you with free meals and ferry rides and you'll get trapped for hours.'

'Where are we going?'

'I'm going to meet *Jesus*.' Pronounced Hey-Seuss.

'Is he your connection?'

Bob squinted as the tourists thronged past. 'I'll park you at his sister's place next door.' He looked amused, perhaps at her use of the term 'connection.'

'I don't want to be parked anywhere, Bob. Tell me how long you'll be and we'll meet when you're done.' She pointed to a patio filled with merry tourists. 'How about the Lizard Lounge?'

'That clip joint,' Bob said. 'But first, I want you to see where I'm going.' He paused a beat. 'In case I never come out.'

So she was his insurance, his backup. She checked his face: was he kidding? Bob just raised his eyebrows then patted her cheek, a patronizing gesture, and she pulled away, cross.

They passed the Scotiabank building where sunburned tourists lined up to use the ATM. Just beyond was a mini mall where boutiques displayed designer resort clothing in air-conditioned splendour, a far cry from the jerry-built stands offering kooky sombreros and synthetic serapes. And—*hola*—wasn't that the clinic? As before, its door was propped open and when Lydia peered inside, she spotted Doctor Alvarez crossing the floor, fingering a stethoscope as she approached a tourist clasping his bloodied knee.

Down this side street, traffic thinned and there were no boutiques or patio bars. There was hardly anyone at all—local or visitors—to be seen. The dwellings were modest affairs, some boarded up and others thrown together with cinderblock and patchwork materials. The celebratory sounds of the main drag drizzled into background.

Bob pointed out a barbershop. 'Our police chief met an untimely demise here last summer,' he said.

Lydia stared inside at the row of men sitting on chairs, waiting their turn. The television in the corner was tuned to a soccer game, except here they called it *fútbal*.

'What happened?' she said, feeling a thud of fear. They'd ventured far from the familiar confines of La Pirámide.

'He was cozying up to one of the *capos*, thus alienating others.'

'*Capos?*'

'Cartel bosses. They're fighting for turf; they all want control of *la plaza*.' He waited until she'd caught up. 'The dealing territory. Stick your flag in and defend it to the death.'

'Did they catch the killer?'

'Please, Lydia, you are betraying your naïveté.'

'Just tell me, Bob.'

'They did not. Them and Us are tricky concepts in this part of the world. Don't let the uniforms fool you.'

'If it's so tricky, what are you doing in the business? You got a death wish?'

He shrugged off the comment. 'I'm small time. They see me as performing a public service; I keep the tourists out of trouble. Otherwise, the idiots would be roaming the streets in search of weed and worse.' Bob nodded. 'Not good, kiddo, not good at all. And no one wants the tourists to stop coming.'

His arm slid around her waist and this time his fingers slipped under the fabric of her skirt. Two days ago she'd been a kite skimming high in the sky, tethered to earth by the thinnest of lines. Her world was changing.

They passed a tiny convenience store, the Coca Cola sign nearly as big as the storefront. Inside was sepulchral with rows of chip bags snapped onto a rack, an ancient cooler pumping against midday heat.

'This is where our paths diverge,' Bob said, and abruptly let go. He indicated a narrow street that petered off into dirt. 'My man's down there, in the blue house.'

Lydia spotted it easily, one of the bigger concrete buildings on the residential strip, protected by a waist-high brick wall, its nubbly flank painted Caribbean blue. Unlike its neighbours, the house looked finished; no rebar poked out from an anticipated addition and pots of flowers decorated the front yard. On either side were more modest dwellings, tin roofs, chickens squawking as they pecked at dirt.

Bob glanced at his watch. 'Lizard Lounge in twenty minutes, *más o menos*. Don't get into trouble.' He leaned over and kissed her forehead. There was a tiny pause, then he reached with his hand, and this time, instead of patting her cheek in an avuncular way, he caressed her face, rough fingertips taking their time as they trailed down to her neck. She shivered and immediately the hand lifted and he was gone, headed down the side street. A dog loped after him, hoping for a handout.

Lydia looked around to see if anyone noticed her standing there, alone. If they did, they didn't care. She felt an unexpected whip of freedom; the cloistered life of the resort was left far behind. Her skin sparked with nerve endings, and to remind herself, she touched her cheek, tracing a circle.

Walking back towards the centre she mused that, if she chose, she could disappear into one of the budget hotels. She could teach ESL to locals, scrape by, leaving Annie and Doug to their own devices.

With a jolt she realized—this must be close to what Charlie felt as he lowered himself into the canoe, chucking an orange life vest under the bow. By disappearing, he'd reappeared to himself.

A woman emerged from Hotel El Loro—the Parrot Hotel—a tourist somewhat older than Lydia, wearing a long skirt and sleeveless top, woven purse slung over one shoulder.

A long mournful horn blew; a cruise ship preparing to leave port.

The woman hesitated, opened her purse and peered in, as if checking to see if she'd remembered her wallet, then marched in a determined way along the street, away from the centre.

Lydia followed. This was the sort of thing Iris would do. She would end up speaking to the woman, finding out who she was and why she was here. A friendship would blossom.

The woman walked briskly past an auto repair shop where several men congregated around a battered Volkswagen Beetle. Then she crossed the road, followed by Lydia, skirting a newspaper kiosk whose dailies sported lurid photos of a recent car crash.

The smell of cooking oil pointed to a *taquería*. Inside, metal card tables were crowded with men eating as they watched the soccer match unfold on TV.

The woman veered off to yet another street, this one holding few signs of commercial activity. Lydia felt a creep of unease. She jumped just in time to avoid a girl stepping out of a house to toss a basin of dirty water into the gutter. Seeing Lydia's alarm, the girl started to giggle and raced back inside.

Iris would cry: 'Finally, the real Mexico!'

Lydia made a hasty calculation; could she find her way back to the centre? The tourist had stopped in front of a shop with the name Elvira painted on its window under the sign: *Salón de Belleza*. A beauty salon. The woman stepped over a dog that was sleeping in the doorway and disappeared inside the shop. Lydia caught sight of a fan propped in one corner. The stylist stood behind a client, coiling strands of hair into foil sleeves.

Lydia reached up with one hand and let her hair spill between her fingers. She could use a cut. A boy sped past on a bicycle several sizes too big for him and called out in English: 'Hello pretty American girl. What is your name?'

The resort with its immaculate jungle path and gardens, its fairy lights and pink flamingos, seemed very far away.

16

Not for the world would Iris let her daughter know this, but it was frankly a relief to be on her own, not that one was ever alone in a place like this. The girl had whisked off to town with Bob, a consciously disreputable person, yet a gentleman still. She'd seen his exchanges with tourists, the not-so-secret handoffs. Iris wouldn't be surprised if Bob had done time. She found herself feeling a pang of something close to jealousy as her daughter took off for her adventure in town, dress floating in the breeze of departure.

Iris picked her way over the hot sand, past the rows of flaked-out tourists whose chests rose and fell in the languid hours of mid-afternoon. A few desultory drinkers remained at the swim-up bar, hunched over cocktails. Not a soul was swimming in the infinity pool. A staff member roamed its perimeter, emptying ash trays into a pail.

She was glad to escape the balcony chair and the tedious biography of Catherine the Great. A few years ago, she wouldn't have thought twice about striding off on her own for this modest trek down the beach, past a clump of rocks towards the pier. But since this business with her hip she'd lost some of her corporal confidence. Something unwelcome had crept in—a tick of fear, the temptation to anticipate the walk's challenges and predict how the boards of the pier might sway in the breaking water. The sole railing was at the end and she might freeze in fear halfway along. Such an absurd thing had happened while crossing a suspension bridge with Steve last year. She couldn't go a step further; it was as if she'd been hit by a sudden paralysis. He'd found it funny at first, then became annoyed, not being a man who held much sympathy for nervous Nellies. Too many of her peers had started to cut back their activities, deciding they'd quit driving after dark or not bother swimming in the Yuba River, with its steep banks and unruly currents.

It was because she recognized this leaning towards caution that Iris determined to make the short hike alone. She wriggled between loungers to the boundary of the resort property where she pulled her hat low on her brow and headed towards the hard sand where waves hit shore. Scattered fish heads lay about, remnants of the fishermen's work this morning. Pelicans swooped, beaks ready to clamp the silvery flank of any fish witless enough to skim the surface of water. She smiled at a pair of tow-headed children engrossed in sandcastle building. A windsurfer shot recklessly towards shore, its sailor, a girl clad in a bikini, gripping the mast as the craft seemed sure to crash onto rocks—but at the last moment she veered off. Steve would be out there, having gotten the hang of windsurfing in ten minutes flat, his grizzled face and muscular chest looking like an ad for active retirement.

She left the groomed beach and entered public land where local families spread blankets to picnic by the sea. Feeling self-conscious in her bathing suit, Iris forced her spine to straighten. She reached the tricky patch where boulders rose to form a makeshift breakwater, creating a series of pools and eddies.

It crept up on one, the temptation to gradually eliminate the things you used to do, without admitting that these pauses were for good. You came to realize that it had been years since you'd last donned skates or skinny-dipped in the lake at night. Friends from Toronto had taken to wintering in Florida and boasting of grandchildren.

Iris had to remind herself of her grandchildren's names and she spent very little time thinking about them. Her fridge door was devoid of school photos and crayoned artwork.

A flock of squealing gulls circled above the rocks. She paused, catching her breath, then dared lift her gaze to view the end of the pier. Someone was standing there: a man. He leaned against the rail staring into the sea, and he looked like he'd been there a while, hypnotized by curling waves and the distant horizon. It was his clothing that gave him away, and the long grey hair that streamed from under his hat.

Iris approached the pier. At high tide you wouldn't be able to make it this far, or at least she wouldn't. Pilings rose above the waterline, rotting wood encrusted with barnacles and seaweed. Next challenge was a high step onto the platform and it would be convenient if there was a railing at this point, but there wasn't. Iris attacked the task by taking a deep breath before launching herself.

El Pintor stood staring at the sea, lost in his National Treasure thoughts. He seemed a frail figure under his peasant garments. Where were his minders? No doubt lolling on the beach, letting the old man fend for himself. Or perhaps he'd escaped their clutches, craving solitude, a sensation that Iris understood.

17

ELVIRA LOOKED up from her work as Lydia entered the shop. The woman who Lydia had been following sat on a chair, leafing through a fan magazine.

'You want eggs?' Elvira asked, in English.

Lydia was confused.

'Elvira sells eggs,' the other tourist said, looking up from a picture of the pop singer, Enrique Iglesias. He didn't look anything like his father.

'Can't I get a haircut?'

A shrug. 'I don't see why not. Ask Elvira.'

Elvira began wrapping the last foil sheath of her client, a middle-aged Mexican woman wearing shorts and a striped shirt.

'You wait,' Elvira said. 'Five minutes.' Then she spoke in Spanish to her client, who braced her hands on the armrests of the padded chair then began to walk tenderly, as if her back hurt, towards one of the empty chairs lined up against the wall.

'Aren't you before me?' Lydia whispered to the tourist.

'I'm waiting for eggs. Her son will bring them,' the woman said. She had a crisp accent. Perhaps Dutch. No doubt she'd spotted Lydia's bracelet from La Pirámide and discounted her as being an all-inclusive lemming.

The salon was not air-conditioned, though the fan was blasting a current of warm air. A child, perhaps eight years old, sat on the floor doing her homework, painstakingly writing numbers in a workbook. A radio yammered local news.

'It is terrible,' Elvira said, shaking her head. She grabbed a duster and began to whisk hairs off the upholstered chair. 'This country is crazy.'

The woman Lydia had followed said something in Spanish then turned to Lydia: 'They've found another burned car just outside of town. A couple of boys trapped inside, their bodies charred.'

Lydia winced. 'Drugs?' she wondered aloud as she settled into the chair.

Elvira repeated the word: '*Drogas*. Who knows? It is one thing, it's another. These are bad people.' She fastened a bib under Lydia's chin. 'You hurt your arm in Mexico?'

Lydia related her parasailing misadventure.

Elvira gave a sympathetic cluck as she sprayed Lydia's hair to dampen it down. 'Life is dangerous, yes?' She fished a pair of scissors from the jar of antiseptic fluid and started cutting. 'Don't worry,' she told Lydia. 'I am going to give you a beautiful style.'

The Dutch woman tossed her magazine onto the pile and said, 'Where's Paco? I need two dozen eggs.'

'Yes yes,' Elvira said, snipping away. 'Paco will come. He is collecting the eggs. Very fresh.'

Eyes closed against the falling clumps of hair, Lydia spoke to the Dutch woman: 'Do you live here?'

'Since six years.'

'You must like it.'

'I love it, I hate it,' the woman said. 'I quit my job back in the Hague.'

She pronounced this *the Hahge*.

'I was an elementary school teacher. My name is Olga.'

'Olga,' Lydia repeated, then offered her own name. Her ears filled with the sound of snipping. Elvira seemed to cut without looking, being far more engaged in the conversation and radio news than the task at hand.

'I write a travel blog and articles for magazines,' Olga went on. 'In return, I am able to stay in this absurd town—'

Elvira interrupted: 'Olga has "gone native," yes?'

Olga's leathery face displayed not a trace of amusement.

The stylist barked at the little girl in the corner, presumably her daughter, who rose from the floor and disappeared through a rear exit. Lydia caught a glimpse of a dirt courtyard and pecking chickens.

Snip snip. Elvira swayed her hips in time to the radio that was now blasting polka music.

'Too much here,' she said, holding up a hank of hair from above Lydia's ear. 'We shape this, thin it, make it chic, yes? Look, Olga, what do you think? Does she not already look younger?'

Olga squinted. 'You always say that.'

Lydia examined herself in the tarnished mirror; she did look younger. She never flinched from her own appearance, unlike some women. She must have learned this from Iris, who had no patience with females who whined about inadequate skin tone or an incipient double chin.

'Paco!' Olga cried, rising from her chair. She seemed delighted by the appearance of a small boy with bare feet, wearing a t-shirt that said *Special Agent*. He held a cardboard egg tray, each pouch containing a spotted brown egg, some with tufts of feather clinging. Oblivious to his mother and her client, Paco padded over to Olga, who leaned forward to accept the eggs and to receive a kiss from the boy on her cheek. Paco stood on his tiptoes then started walking in a tight circle.

Olga said something in Spanish while digging in her purse for coins. All the heaviness had gone out of her.

'Paco is a good boy, sometimes,' Elvira confided as she tossed a fistful of hair onto the floor.

This was turning into a pixie cut.

'But there are so many bad boys here.'

'There are bad boys everywhere,' Lydia said, fishing hair out of her mouth. 'Where I come from in Toronto, there are gangs. They break into our cars at night. We had a murder in the coin laundry two months ago.'

'Of course,' Elvira said, then aimed the scissors at her son.

Reluctantly, Paco snatched the coins from Olga and dropped them on the counter next to the combs.

'You will visit me soon?' Olga said. 'We'll make cookies and you will study English.'

'No no,' the boy sang, still strutting about.

His mother sounded cross. 'Olga teaches him English so he can work at the hotels when he is big.'

'No no,' the boy chanted, liking the effect it made.

Olga heaved the eggs under one arm and, without bidding farewell, left the salon.

Immediately, Paco stopped his dance and stood with his arms at his sides. His mother issued some order that he pretended not to hear. She repeated it in a sharper voice and this time he moved to the doorway and looked out.

'Paquito!'

The boy stepped back inside, small face pouting. His sister returned from the courtyard and plunked herself back down in the corner and opened her workbook. Somehow, through all this, Elvira kept cutting and Lydia's ears were now wholly uncovered.

Another flurry of cross language aimed at the boy. The snipping grew more intense, metallic blades pricking the skin above Lydia's eyes. What was left of her bangs fell onto the plastic apron.

'He never listens to me,' Elvira said. 'He won't study. He does—' she aimed the end of scissors at her son '—exactly what he wants and will not obey his mamá.'

Paco allowed a thin smile.

The woman with foil in her hair talked above the conversation, about something else entirely. The radio announcer spoke of the upcoming election and Lydia heard the name of Alejandro Gutiérrez. The girl in the corner succeeded in focusing on her homework, drawing a neat pattern of apples next to the number 6. Pulling her good arm out from under the plastic shroud, Lydia checked the time. She was way overdue to meet Bob at Lizard Lounge.

'Beautiful!' Elvira announced and twirled the chair around. She reached for a spray canister and shot varnish into Lydia's hair; Lydia managed to shut her eyes just in time.

'*Perfecto!*' the other client declared, looking up from her magazine.

Cautiously, Lydia opened her eyes and realized that Paco had squeezed next to her chair and was mugging into the mirror.

She looked, well, fabulous.

Where was Bob? Lydia drummed the face of her watch. She'd settled into a curbside seat at Lizard Lounge, surrounded by tourists who all seemed to know each other. None wore bracelets, indicating that they were a more adventuresome bunch who stayed in modest hotels right in town. They weren't especially young. They could be early retirees who'd cashed in the family home and fled to this beach paradise and still couldn't believe their luck. Someone was singing Mr. Tambourine Man off-key. That fellow in the Oakland As cap gave her long, soulful looks as he lifted his drink in salute.

Lydia peered at the intersection where she expected Bob to turn up. The corner was occupied by the same pair of women shilling time-shares and trips to underground grottos. She raked her fingers through her newly cropped hair, feeling the crackle of varnish.

Beer arrived in a frosted tumbler and she drained it quickly. She hadn't bought so much as a necklace or a fake pre-Columbian figure, nor did she have any impulse to shop. The air was saturated with moisture and she felt herself wilt.

No vehicles were allowed on the boardwalk, nothing motorized except tourist police astride Vespas. They were a happy contrast to the armed soldiers who guarded banks and money-changing establishments.

How long did it take to weigh weed and peel off the bills?

Next door to Lizard Lounge a woman pushed open the glass door of the Benetton clothing shop and let a draught of frigid air escape. She stepped outside, loosening her sweater, and lit up a cigarette.

Lydia decided she'd wait another ten minutes, then to hell with Bob, she'd walk back to the resort on her own or hitch a ride on the local bus. She was beginning to miss the comfortable lounger parked at optimal angle for views of the sea. And she was not Bob's keeper.

A familiar couple appeared. Neil and Lulu, the pediatric dentists, swinging along the boardwalk, bare knees and stuffed shopping bags. His face was a florid red, his nose starting to peel, but when he spotted Lydia he managed a smile.

'Where is your lovely mother?' He set his bags down and wiped his forehead.

'I left her reading on the balcony. I came to town with Bob.'

'Bob?' Lulu's smile tightened.

Neil looked around. 'Where is he?'

'Question of the hour.'

Lulu hadn't taken her eyes off Lydia. 'I like your hair,' she said. 'Did you get it cut at the resort?'

'I found a salon here in town,' Lydia said. Then she couldn't help adding, 'Seven dollars, U.S.'

'Was the place clean?' Lulu said, frowning. 'You wouldn't want to pick up lice, or something worse.'

The pair moved closer to Lydia, kicking their packages along the ground.

Neil said, 'Lulu is very anti-bacteria.'

'I should hope so,' his wife said.

Lydia squinted again towards the intersection. No sign of Bob. Just a kid making figure eights on his bike and a man balancing a stack of hats on his head.

'Join me,' Lydia said, moving her chair to make room.

Neil brightened and reached to pick up his bags until his wife touched his forearm. 'We should rest before this evening's event,' she said.

He tipped his head back and stared at the sky.

'This evening's event?' Lydia repeated.

'Don't you check the activity board?' Lulu said in her squeaky voice.

'Lulu has filled our agenda,' Neil said. 'We know where we're going to be every hour until the end of the week.'

His wife looked annoyed. 'It's the fiesta event where staff transform the entrance of the hotel into a marketplace with food stands and all sorts of crafts for sale.'

'Feels like the real Mexico,' Neil said, 'without actually being it.'

'This is our sixth year at La Pirámide,' Lulu explained.

'We got here the month they opened,' Neil said. 'They were still drilling holes to hang the hammocks.'

'I really do like your haircut,' Lulu said. 'Very Audrey Hepburn.'

18

A DOZEN MORE steps would do the trick. Iris felt like she was slogging through wet clay, not crossing wooden planks. Who was going to applaud if she managed to perform the heroic deed of walking to the end of the lurching pier, and who, other than herself, would care? Lydia would say, quite sensibly, 'What are you trying to prove?' and examine her mother for further signs of dementia.

Iris made it to the end, each step an act of will. Fear had invaded her body, a septic march through the bloodstream and she was mad as hell that she'd allowed it to enter. The breeze became a stiff wind on the long finger of pier. The moment she reached its end, she seized the railing and gripped hard, a sailor strapped to the mast. Only then did she dare gaze out to the turquoise sea. El Pintor's face, when she cast a quick look, was set into a frown, and not, as she'd anticipated, hypnotized by the view.

He breathed audibly, then spoke in a low mutter.

She couldn't make out a word.

He cleared his throat and repeated, this time in English: 'The sea has told me nothing.'

Just the sort of thing she'd imagined he would say. She stood very still as he continued to stare into the water's reflecting surfaces.

After an appropriate pause, Iris said, 'And what have you asked the sea?'

A distant freighter slid across the horizon.

For a moment she feared that he hadn't heard her, or worse, had decided that the question was not worth tackling.

'I have asked her—should I accept this grave responsibility? Should I change my life to help my country?' He spoke in heavily accented English.

Iris hardly dared to breathe. All feelings of panic had fled, for she was standing side by side with the national treasure.

'Have you come to a decision?' she asked.

He turned to look at her, his face heavily creased, brilliant eyes, high cheekbones. There was something in his expression that she recognized, and the sensation startled her: did he feel it?

'I am selfish,' he said, lifting his palms, and she had to strain to hear as waves lapped against the pilings. He made no effort to raise his voice. 'I want only to make my work, yet they ask me to enter this crazy world of politics. It is their opinion that I can help, that the people will listen to me.'

Without having any idea what he was talking about, Iris said, 'Perhaps they are right.'

'I'm an old man; why can't they leave me alone?'

'Do you want them to?'

A quick laugh. 'What is your name?'

She told him.

'And I am Victor.' He stretched out his hand and Iris clasped it, after prying her grip from the railing. She felt a rough workman's palm scratch against hers. Giving a half-turn, he squinted towards the beach where the multitudes had begun to thin out, heading back to their rooms to change before entering the lobby bar, and later, to visit one of the six dinner restaurants. The sun began its slide to the west.

'The tide is rolling in,' he said.

Tide. The word came to her: '*La marea.*'

He was startled. 'You speak Spanish?'

'To a degree.'

'Then we will walk back together and we will speak in Spanish.'

He was a small, wiry man who moved quickly, with no hint of stiffness as he skipped over the rotting boards. Noting her hesitation, he gripped her elbow to offer support.

Something Steve wouldn't think to do.

* * *

Neil and Lulu disappeared into the throng of tourists crowding the boardwalk. The last image Lydia caught was of Neil's broad back, his t-shirt sporting a cartoon of a burro wearing a sombrero.

Where *was* Bob?

She must be the only tourist in town who kept checking her watch. It used to drive Charlie nuts, her insistence on being prompt; she'd make sure they turned up at dinner parties on the stroke of seven p.m., wine bottle and flowers in hand.

She was half enjoying working herself up into a state when she felt, to her alarm, tears flooding her eyes. The feeling of desolation broadsided her at unexpected moments. Reaching into her bag, she found a rumpled tissue and wiped her face, hoping no one noticed. She knocked out several peso coins and laid them on the table. The bracelet didn't work here; this was the real world of money and commerce. She would find the blue house into which Bob had vanished an hour ago. She would hammer on the door and if he didn't appear, she would head back to the resort. Bob was not her responsibility. Never again would she wait on a dock or press her face to a window, waiting for some man to turn up.

Reaching the dusty intersection, Lydia turned right, away from the centre. Her wrist throbbed, as it often did in late afternoon. Arriving at the blue house, she hesitated before knocking on its door. A woman in the neighbouring yard was doing something with a chicken. When she spotted Lydia, she grimaced, then made an abrupt motion, wringing the creature's neck.

The blue house pulsed with music, its concrete façade doing little to dampen the noise. A live band, judging by the off-key trombone. She pounded the door as the neighbour disappeared into her house, carrying the deceased chicken by its scrawny legs.

A girl opened the heavy wooden door, peered at Lydia then rattled off something in Spanish.

'*Señor* Bob?' Lydia asked.

The girl ushered her inside and Lydia found herself standing in a tiled vestibule, faux-colonial chairs lined up against the wall. Beyond this, an open courtyard was crowded with a dozen men lounging on plastic lawn chairs. A quintet of musicians decked out like rhinestone cowboys played on a makeshift stage, black Stetsons and studded suits, needle-nosed boots.

Many pairs of eyes turned her way and she felt her heartbeat ramp up to a canter. Get out of here, she advised herself. A trumpet bleated. She turned to go, but then she saw him.

Half-hidden in a corner of the courtyard, Bob perched on one of the chairs, his legs tightly crossed, and he leaned over from the waist, as if his gut hurt. His arms hugged his chest and he was rocking, either in pain, or in time to the beat.

The girl who'd let her in made a motion towards the door. Sun leaked under its heavy slats. The men stared. Bob's mouth opened in a silent moan. Lydia began to move towards him, stepping over empty bottles as the men watched her progress through heavy-lidded eyes. No one was talking; they were past it. The musicians played on, a barrel chested man attacking the fat *guitarron*, strumming a relentless rhythm.

She edged alongside a table littered with the remains of a meal, keeping her gaze pinned straight ahead. Bob was looking pretty marginal, the freshly laundered shirt wrinkled and unbuttoned, his face pale, his eyes, baked.

A man stepped in front of her, blocking the way, and she stopped short. He was youngish, wearing tight jeans, and unlike the others, there was the ghost of a smile on his face.

'We will dance, yes?' he said in English.

The music changed abruptly, gearing down to a mournful ballad. The deadly horns blasted off-key. The man held his arms out.

Lydia lifted her wounded arm resting in the sling, indicating her disability. This did not dissuade her suitor, who swayed from side to side, the half-smile fixed on his face. He plucked her good arm and placed it on his shoulder and ran his hands around her waist. She felt herself flinch. Soon they were shuffle dancing, angling between sodden partygoers who barely lifted their eyes. His body was muscular and damp and she didn't dare break away. Her own moves were awkward as she sought to keep a distance from the man, but he insisted on pulling her back against his chest.

'I am Antonio,' he said.

His single earring rippled as he moved, a tiny metal Kalashnikov. His face was wide and innocent-looking, long lashes, full lips. A whiff of something chemical emitted off his skin.

Men followed their dance with bored, aimless stares as Antonio edged towards the vestibule. 'This is not a place for you,' he said.

No kidding, she thought.

The singer let out a coyote howl.

Antonio let go and stood with his thumbs hooked in his belt loops. '*Adios, Señorita,*' he said. It was a command, rather than a sentiment.

'And Bob?' she said. She craned her neck and caught sight of him sloped in his chair, eyes at half-mast. His head snapped up and he stared at her, a bleak pleading gaze. The

111

music segued into something more rambunctious and the guests began stomping the floor. The ground shook seismically and someone tossed a bottle so it skidded across the tiles and landed near Lydia's feet.

'Go,' Antonio said.

Bob's mouth worked but he seemed to have trouble controlling it and even at this distance she could see saliva caked at the corners of his lips.

He'd taken some crap drug. Bob, who claimed never to sample the wares, had gotten himself too wasted to utter a coherent sentence, let alone walk out the door.

'You must leave right away,' Antonio said, his wide face tense.

She didn't need another warning. Except her bladder, tetchy since Doug was born, signalled she had to go—*pronto*.

'*Un baño?*' she asked apologetically.

Antonio looked at her as if she were out of her mind. Then he gestured towards the front door. Go out there, where the tourists are, people like you.

After mimed insistence, and cursing herself for drinking the beer, she found herself entering a dark corridor and lifting a sheet that served as a curtain, not sure what she would find behind it. To her relief, a conventional toilet sat on uneven ground. Upon further inspection, she noted that it was sitting on the dirt floor but not connected to any visible plumbing. She let the curtain fall behind her. The toilet was scrupulously clean as if it had just been lifted from its shipping box, which perhaps it had. She sat down cautiously, watching Antonio's boot tap on the other side of the sheet. Not daring to flush, she followed him back to the courtyard where Bob was obviously in trouble. Steering towards him was an older man in snakeskin boots who barked an order, and when Bob gave no response, the man sloshed beer over his face.

Bob tilted his head sideways then, very slowly, reached with one hand to swipe his cheek.

The man spat on the floor.

'It is the Saint's day of my Tio, not a time for doing business,' Antonio spoke in Lydia's ear as he pushed her towards the front door. 'Your friend makes a mistake coming today.'

'I can see that,' Lydia said.

'Go back to La Pirámide.'

Lydia looked at him; how did he know where she was staying?

The bracelet, of course.

'Have a safe vacation,' Antonio said, taking a step backwards, giving her room.

She cast a final look at the party. 'He looks ill.'

'*Señor* Bob is not well,' Antonio agreed.

She paused and took a deep breath. 'I should take him back with me.'

'This may not be possible.'

He stood between her and Bob, not exactly threatening, but firm. She couldn't figure out if he was trying to protect her, or scare her—perhaps both.

'What's wrong with you?' Lydia called across the room and received another pleading look in response. After another brief, considering pause, she pushed past Antonio and crouched next to Bob.

'What's wrong?" she repeated.

'That's complicated, kiddo,' Bob said in a thick voice. When he opened his mouth she saw a web of phlegm.

'Need help getting up?'

'I require assistance of the first order.'

'I'll hail a cab,' she said. And wondered if this were possible; it didn't seem like a street where taxis roamed in search of custom.

Bob waved a hand dismissively. 'It was not my intention to get high.' Pause as he drifted off then managed to pull himself back to consciousness.

'What did you take?' she asked.

'Inadvertently. *Agua.*'

'Water?'

'You may know it as crank.' A shaking hand reached out and touched hers. 'Crystal meth. Evil stuff.'

He was breathing too fast, scrawny chest squeezing in and out.

'One of my best sellers,' he added.

Lydia was appalled. 'I thought you just peddled weed.'

He nodded, as if that were an interesting notion.

'You're out of your league here, Bob.'

This roused him. 'These guys need me more than I need them.' He struggled for air. 'I know what I'm doing.'

She slung her good arm under his shoulder. 'Get up, my friend.'

'Everyone's gathered together,' Bob protested. 'All the *primos.*'

Cousins.

He had begun to wheeze asthmatically.

'Saint's day. Bigger than Christmas.'

She gave a heave. 'C'mon Bob, back to the mother ship.'

'He will not leave!' It was the stocky man in reptile boots.

'Jesus,' Bob said, making the introduction. Pronounced Hey-Seuss. 'Meet my friend from the resort…' he petered out.

'Lydia,' Lydia supplied.

Jesus glared at her. 'You dance with my nephew, Antonio; he's a *licenciado*, in law school. One day he will be attorney general of the state. He's not shit like these *pendejos.*' He nodded in the direction of the other guests.

Bob had begun slapping his knee to the beat. 'I love these *narcocorridos*, man,' he said. 'Stories of love, murder, mayhem and valour. They wrote this song for Jesus, story of his life.'

Jesus looked pleased.

'You are going down in history, *amigo*,' Bob said.

'In history, yes!' Jesus flagged down a girl who was carrying a platter of food. 'The lady must eat,' he said and grabbed a napkin and passed it to Lydia. His mood appeared to have changed abruptly. 'Everything is made *en casa*. You, Antonio,' he told his nephew. 'You too must eat.'

Antonio, obviously in awe of his outlaw uncle, took a napkin and jabbed a toothpick into a meatball. Lydia got the picture: Jesus, man of the hour, was not to be crossed, and so she too plucked a grey meatball off the tray and popped it in her mouth. Within seconds she felt the habanero chili smack the back of her throat.

'Can't do it, man,' Bob said, waving off the food. His face had turned the colour of wet cement.

Past the seated men, a door led to the kitchen. An older woman dressed in black stood there, watching with a disapproving expression.

'My sainted mother,' Jesus said. Then he added, without a shred of irony, 'Mexican men, we are close to our mothers.'

The old woman clutched a bottle of pop in one hand and a plate of food in the other.

'Time to split,' Bob said, and tottered sideways. 'I am not a young man,' he added, grabbing the back of his chair.

'You gonna die?' Jesus said.

'I certainly hope not.'

'You look like you O.D.'ing, man. I don't want something evil going down in my house.' Jesus snapped his fingers and a pair of teenagers roused themselves. He spoke a few words and the lads nodded, understanding perfectly.

They removed Bob from Lydia's grasp and began to drag him across the courtyard to the foyer while she hastened to keep pace. One boy kicked open the front door and suddenly Bob was tumbling into the street, arms windmilling for balance.

'This is most embarrassing,' he said, recovering. 'Don't let Jesus near *agua*; he gets mean as stink.'

'You're lucky to get out of there alive, Bob.'

He set a hand on Lydia's shoulder and began to hobble on the unpaved road. Something dribbled out the side of his mouth and he wiped it with his forearm. 'Remember that Jesus needs me more than I need him.'

'Does he know that?'

19

THE BAR SEEPED darkness under the palm fronds, a contrast to the sunny beach area beyond, and Iris felt the blur of cataracts veil both eyes. Last evening, Lydia had been alarmed when her mother pointed to a pink blob at the buffet and said, 'I'll have some of that ham.'

'It's beet salad,' Lydia said.

Sometimes it felt like the girl was totting up her disabilities, imagined or otherwise.

Iris, wearing sandals with heels, lost her footing as her eyes failed to adjust to the diminished light. Her drink landed with a splat in the sand, as did her book, and only by luck did she manage to remain upright. A sandal slid off her foot and she didn't dare reach down to replace it. She felt a gush of relief that Lydia wasn't there to witness the mishap.

A man crouched at her feet, picked up the book and silver sandal, then rose to hand both items to her with a bow. He smiled, showing perfect teeth.

'Cinderella,' he said in a delightful Spanish accent.

The politician was a dead ringer for Julio Iglesias, the singer she loved above all others.

Flustered, she launched into clumsy apologies, but he interrupted, 'May I help you with your shoe?'

Thank you, yes he could. Iris propped herself against the bar counter and stared as Sr. Alejandro Gutiérrez lifted her unsheathed foot in his hand. Did he notice the bunion? Perhaps not. He slipped the sandal onto her foot and checked that the strap was buckled before lowering her foot to the ground.

Patricio sent a fresh drink across the counter.

Iris watched the politician retreat, towel slung over one shoulder, hips swinging, fully aware that he was being watched.

* * *

Martina couldn't be nervous, not after all these years of interviewing men and women from many sectors of society. She'd interviewed the president of the Republic, for God's sake, and didn't feel as jittery as she felt now. She'd suffered tricky encounters with local politicos: that portly Attorney General in his shiny suit, cadre of bodyguards hovering, the old goat trying to flirt with her, make her see that he had no choice but to act as he did, to jail the protestors. Otherwise—'*todo va a ser caótico.*'

After that interview aired, she'd had to lie low for a month, heading off with her sister to a rustic lodge near Tepoztlán.

Martina Gutiérrez slid her iPad into its case, grabbed her purse and notebook, and headed towards the pavilion where Don Victor was waiting.

She'd been at this TV job for nearly twenty years. She'd interviewed every cultural figure that mattered, every politician and rebel, including Subcomandante Marcos (twice), and intellectuals of all stripes. If anything, these subjects were intimidated by her sharp questions and lack of toadying. Still, each guest thought he could outwit her, which is why few public figures turned down her request for an interview; they all figured they'd get the better of *Señora* Gutiérrez. They'd see her walk into the studio with her dyed hair, silk suits, and high-stepping shoes, and their balls would shrivel. As for the women she interviewed, they might laugh too shrilly or eagerly confide some personal detail to win favour. This was not a pretty business—and she loved it.

She held her chin up, chest out, body language reminding herself of who she was. One of the maids looked up from her mopping and smiled shyly. An arrow indicated room numbers and the special suite where Alejandro had parked his prize. She'd never managed to get her hands on El Pintor for an interview on camera, and lord knows, she'd tried. The man hid most of the year in his studio in the mountains and made a practice of batting away media. Fame was a distraction.

She followed the track of the infinity pool that curled its way towards the beach as it passed through a hot tub area and a goofy waterfall and swim-up bar. She wondered if her husband was fatally naïve, believing he could bring warring sides together. This weekend could be a mad idea, not just conceptually, but in terms of their safety. Mexico, since Calderón started his drug war, had upended its implicit rules of engagement, and it was now rule of the most violent and egregious—yet Alejandro was convinced that he could act as peacemaker and mediator; Martina wasn't convinced that anyone wanted mediating,

Past a sheltered area where tourists in bathing suits leaned earnestly over clay plates and pots, painting *folklórico* illustrations onto their surfaces. The outlines of these pre-Hispanic patterns had been pre-drawn, so their task was to fill in the shapes using a variety of bright colours.

Don Victor was on the upper floor facing the beach. They'd originally booked him on the ground floor suite, mindful of his age, but he'd made Tomás change it immediately, seeking a view of consequence. What was the use of sleeping by the sea if you couldn't prop open the door and watch the froth of waves catch moonlight?

For a simple man of the people, Don Victor was proving to be quite demanding; the kitchen had to make him unsweetened porridge for breakfast and the maid must not visit his room between the hours of nine a.m. and six p.m. because he might be working. He drank only old-world imported wine, not the local plonk served in the dining areas.

She knocked on his door.

It was four p.m., right on the button. An empty room service tray sat on the hallway floor, the remains of a sandwich and an empty yogurt container waiting to be cleared away.

She knocked again, more sharply, and hoped that she wasn't interrupting his siesta, or worse, his work. She felt this tentativeness with a kind of bemused surprise; she'd thought herself well beyond it. She reached with one hand to pat down her hair.

The door squeaked open.

And there he was, El Pintor ushering her in, a gentleman after all. He'd drawn the curtains so that the suite was dark, a contrast to the blazing sun outside. One bed was unmade and she assumed he'd been napping. A bottle of single-malt Scotch sat on the glass table next to a weathered tome by a scholar of Mayan glyphs. She could smell cigar smoke; any kind of smoking was strictly forbidden in the rooms.

He'd refused to let her bring camera and crew; this was to be an old-fashioned reportorial interview, notebook in hand.

Back in her room, Alejandro was in a state, waiting for this man to agree to sign on for the job as Minister of Culture. El Pintor was playing hard to get, not declining, yet not exactly jumping at the chance to serve his country. What a coup it would be for Alejandro's bid for the governorship if Don Victor planted his signature on the document. The populace would understand immediately the symbolic value: Alejandro Gutiérrez was not another corrupt politician seeking to fill his pockets with public money; Don Victor's signature was as close as they could get to a seal of authenticity.

This was the rallying cry that Martina inwardly spoke as she stepped into the room; it gave her the courage to proceed. Alejandro was fretting that she'd blow it by uttering one of her pointed, bordering on rude, questions—so exciting for the viewing public. But this was not television and her task was not to entertain.

They shook hands though it had only been a few hours since they'd been sitting together on the pool deck. The painter's skin was rough, an artisan's hands, so unlike the soft polished skin of politicians and professors.

Don Victor seemed drowsy, his eyes red-rimmed, his hair mussed. He looked around for chairs, but they were covered with his things, and, giving up, he gestured towards the unmade bed.

She felt the hard mattress squeeze as they sat down side by side in the gloom of the curtained room. Pulling out stenographic pad and pen, she quickly scanned her surroundings for clues to the man and his habits. A terrycloth dressing gown, provided by the hotel, hung on a hook on the back of the door. The closet was almost empty—two or three garments hanging from metal hangers. A sketch pad lay on top of the TV; perhaps he would show her some drawings if she played her cards right. A set of working drawings for a sculpture that hung in the *Palacio Nacional* had been bought in auction last year for a hundred thousand U.S. dollars.

'I am like a mole,' Don Victor said in his hoarse, whispery voice. 'I prefer to live in a tunnel or cave.'

His house in the mountains was dark, except for the studio. When he wasn't working, he needed to rest his eyes. She'd read that somewhere.

Martina lifted the cover of her pad and began: 'What made you leave the practice of abstract painting forty years ago, Don Victor?'

'I never left it,' he said and crossed one leg over the other. He'd rested his hands over his skinny knees, like a schoolboy.

'But there was a distinct change in style and materials beginning in—' she flipped back a page to her notes—'1976.'

'Was there?' He sounded surprised.

She'd had interviewees like this in the past; they made you work for every crumb.

'At the time you were still painting on canvas in a modernist mode.'

'Possibly.' A shrug. 'So long ago.'

'And before that, you were noted for your murals, often loaded with political and sociological iconography.' This wasn't good; she was telling him things about himself instead of asking questions. 'Would you say that you had a change of heart abut the modernist and postmodernist enterprise?'

He let out a sharp laugh. 'I didn't know such things existed.' He hesitated, and at first she thought she'd have to plow in again, but then he said in a ruminative voice, 'Would you trust a man who changes his heart as if it were old clothes or a spare tire?'

'One grows and finds new interests.'

'Or one stays a child.'

'Can you tell me more about that?'

'What is there to tell?'

'Are you talking about retained innocence or a sense of play?'

He stared at the wall, which held a pastel landscape in an Impressionist mode, typical hotel art.

'What do you think of this painting?' he said.

'Exactly what one would expect in a place like this.'

'Is it so bad?' He made a show of musing on her comment.

Under normal circumstances, she'd fire back, but she'd promised Alejandro that she would behave.

Don Victor spent a long time staring at the painting, a picture made in some factory in China that specialized in innocuous hotel decorations.

'Think of what it seeks to do,' he said. 'To cause serenity and a fleeting pleasure. Or perhaps to be invisible, an art seeking only its own oblivion.'

He smiled, Buddha-like.

She felt irritation rise; was he baiting her, or was this really how he talked?

'You are making this encounter difficult, Don Victor,' she said and pointed to the blank page of her notebook.

'It is not my intention.'

'Let's fill in some straightforward biographical information.'

'There is so much I don't remember.'

She'd heard that line before, usually from the mouths of politicians. 'I have not been able to uncover much about your early years as an artist. I know, of course, that you lived in San Miguel de Allende decades ago. Did you teach tourists at the Instituto?'

He wriggled beside her, perhaps in annoyance. Maybe this early life embarrassed him, because he hadn't come out of nowhere. Instead, he'd studied with eminent artists, had gained early recognition and was a popular teacher of foreigners. She'd seen photographs of him in those days, long hair and mustache, denim work clothes, a peaked cap.

'Perhaps I am simply what you see, an old man who puts his hands to work on whatever catches his eye. Why must I be something else to satisfy the salacious wishes of the public?'

The vague tone disappeared and his voice rose several decibels; she was onto something.

'The Mexican people are in love with scandal and the banal lives of soap opera celebrities,' El Pintor went on, now sitting upright on the bed, and she could hear his breath quicken. 'If I don't tell you some secret then you will make up your own.'

'You insult me, Don Victor; I am not that sort of journalist.'

'You want to know why I have permitted this interview and why I have consented to investigate the possibility—' the artist paused before going on—'the possibility that I might join your husband's campaign.'

Martina held her breath. Now. Finally.

'I ask myself these questions.' His gaze lifted so that he appeared to be staring at the ceiling. 'Your husband promises me much, art schools in every city, a sculpture museum... am I to believe him? Can he make this happen?'

'My husband is an honourable man.'

Don Victor lowered his eyes and gave a half-smile. 'Of course,' he said.

She seized on the pause. 'You've been heavily involved in the revival of the *folklórico* arts in our country—'

'Yes,' he interrupted. 'We must allow our nation's rich cultural history to rise above the wave of digital this, digital that. You must know that the Mayan figurines you see in the marketplace here are made in a factory in China.' His hands rose. 'I'm an anachronism. I risk becoming quaint.' His face sagged and suddenly he looked his age.

'You should interview a woodcutter,' he added, sounding almost sullen. He frowned. 'Why are you here?' he demanded. Before she could answer, he went on, a hint of aggression in his voice. 'Is it your husband's command?'

'Certainly not.'

A wry smile. 'Because you are not a woman to dance around the wishes of a mere man.'

'That is true.'

'I understand perfectly.' He reached with one bronzed finger, aiming towards her face. 'You people seek revolution, an upheaval of our sorry system of government—but it is hopeless.'

'Then why did you agree to meet with us, to discuss joining my husband's campaign?'

Victor considered this question and his tone changed again, became weary. 'Maybe I have been feeling lonely in my mountain hermitage. Maybe it's time that I engage with the public, with the idealistic politician—'

She pressed. 'Are you so lonely? What about the women in your life?'

She'd done her homework and knew about the first wife who'd left him, taking their son, now a middle-aged man whom Martina had tracked down in San Diego. Victor junior was running a restaurant and had no communication with his father.

When the painter said nothing, she prodded again; 'How important is family to you?'

'Family?' The guarded tone returned.

If they were sitting under the glare of television lights, she would plunge in now with one of her pointed comments about the sacrifices artists make if they work outside the sheltering umbrella of institutions, how they must contain a certain chilliness, even a ruthless aspect—but then she thought of Alejandro back in their room, waiting with clenched jaw.

'You haven't married since divorcing your wife,' she said in a careful tone. 'Yet you are not without female company.'

Silence.

What if he told her to leave, then left, himself, packing his few things into his satchel and taking off for the airport? Alejandro would never forgive her.

'So much less than people believe,' Don Victor finally said, then allowed a thin smile. 'Possibly I should not challenge these exaggerations. It makes me so much more interesting.' Palms raised. 'I can assure you, Madame Gutiérrez, that you are perfectly safe here with me, a man of my antiquity.'

At this moment, as if summoned by a predetermined signal, the door to the balcony slid open and a girl—one would hardly call her a woman—wearing a skimpy sundress, stood there, shimmering dark hair and perfect complexion, bare feet. 'Where's room service, Vic?' she said in a sleepy voice. 'I'm hungry.' She gave Martina little more than a glance, apparently seeing her as no threat.

Martina felt a nip of irritation; she'd been a girl like this once.

Don Victor rose to his feet. 'So much I forget these days; I almost forget myself.'

125

Martina had seen this girl before. It took her a moment, then she realized she was the sales clerk from the clothing shop in the lobby.

The girl disappeared back onto the balcony, letting the curtain fall across the glass door, and Don Victor said without a shred of embarrassment, 'A new friend,' as if this were an inevitable and even tiresome aspect of his life.

While he rose to pick up the telephone to summon room service, Martina slipped her iPad out of its case and pressed the power button. As the screen came to life, Don Victor let out a gasp of recognition, for glowing on the screen was a photograph of one of his own works, a clay tablet painted with pigments he'd made from the earth and plants in his village. Its surface was embedded with fossil-like objects fashioned from pieces of children's toys and ordinary domestic objects. At first, the viewer might guess it was something ancient, a Mayan or Aztec artifact pulled from the soil.

She tapped the screen and another tablet slid into view, backlit in a way that made it glow from within. This one was encrusted with fish scales and a bent spoon.

Don Victor hastily ordered soup and coffee, then leaned over the iPad. His messed-up hair, Martina realized, smelled like sex.

'What is this machine?'

She began to explain.

'Incredible!' He reached down and blotched the screen with his damp finger. 'Such light.' The next photograph slid into view. 'This is from my sequence of gravestones. Small monuments.'

He perched again on the bed beside her, cross-legged like a yogi. Apart from his spotted hands and weathered face, there were few signs of wear and tear.

'Let me see more,' Don Victor demanded.

For a man who resisted the digital age, the painter was captivated by the gadget.

As she moved through the images in the slideshow that she'd prepared, he appeared to love the technology more than the work it displayed, offering little clucks of pleasure. When she asked questions about his creative process, he ignored her, so captivated was he by the gleaming pictures. When the slideshow ended, he stretched his arms in the air and yawned.

'You must go now.'

Faint but distinct pong of armpits. The girl on the balcony was singing some pop song and the air conditioner had switched off, leaving the room soupy with humidity. When Martina left and closed the door behind her, she heard his growling laughter followed by what sounded like a playful smack.

As she stood in the hallway, she felt a certain humiliation, as if she'd been played by the man. He was crafty, a carefully constructed persona who knew exactly how he wanted to come across. The more she thought about it, the more she didn't buy his 'man of the people' act. He hadn't revealed a thing about himself, virtually nothing she could use.

A family of three generations was making its way from the beach to the rooms, children dragging pool noodles, parents draped in towels, a set of grandparents in floppy hats. The mother smiled at Martina, who instantly thought of her own children, one studying at college in Texas, the other running a language school in Cuernavaca.

Alejandro had no children of his own and he'd never developed a relationship with hers, a fact that rankled; he could make more of an effort. He liked to say that he preferred to focus his love and care on her, a sensation that sometimes felt claustrophobic. It was one of the chief functions of children: they distracted you from each other.

Alejandro was incorruptible. This was not necessarily a useful attribute. She suspected that her dear husband was viewed as a holy fool by some people.

An ear-scorching shriek came from above and Martina looked up to see a monkey with a baby clinging to its neck dropping from a palm tree onto the nearby balcony. A small crowd gathered below, snapping photographs.

In six months' time, she might become wife of the new governor of the state, a concept which began in the dining room of Sanborn's restaurant, where a group of Alejandro's party chums met to discuss strategy. Somehow that chatter grew into this looming possibility.

They'd agreed straight away that Martina would stick with her television show; she was not one of those political wives content to gaze starry-eyed at her husband while he loped from one stage to the next, adjusting his tie. She was a modern woman and so, by inference, he was a modern man.

20

THE AREA IN front of La Pirámide, normally a parking lot and driveway for buses and taxicabs, had been transformed into a traditional Mexican plaza. All day, hotel staff had been setting up kiosks and decorating them with brilliantly coloured serapes. The bandstand was crammed with musical instruments, including a wooden box that was to be used as a drum, or so Iris learned when she asked a young musician. He happily demonstrated, straddling the box, called a *cajón*, and leaned forward to thwack its front with his open palms. Half a dozen ukuleles—or near-ukuleles—lay on a cloth spread on the floor of the gazebo.

The instrumentation belonged to *son jarocho*, the young man told her. A type of music native to the state of Veracruz. Step dancers would perform on wooden planks, creating their own percussion.

Coals burned in giant grills in preparation for the barbecue. Vendors arrived by cab from town and set up handicraft stands, the usual bric-a-brac of cheap jewellery, woven goods, tin and copper plates—and pottery that was, no doubt, factory-made. Iris would buy something to help them along. Perhaps Steve would wear one of the plain hemp shirts.

A taxi drew up, nosing between the workers, and disgorged Lydia and a tottery-looking Bob. Iris felt a pang of something like jealousy; what had they been up to? She couldn't wait to tell them about her encounter on the pier with the artist. She made her way over, past a girl who was threading beads on a necklace, and managed to grab hold of Bob, who swung off balance. The poor man's face was a ghastly pallor.

'While you two were sweating it out in town,' she began.

Lydia cut her off. 'We're beat, Mum,' she said.

'I'll second that,' Bob muttered.

'I hope you'll be in shape for the fiesta,' Iris said, unable to keep disappointment from shading her tone. Perhaps they hadn't noticed the extensive preparations going on. 'This is the high point of the week. Staff have gone to a great deal of trouble.'

'I've had enough Mexico to last me a decade,' Bob said.

'I need a shower,' Lydia said and, with her arm tucked under Bob's, the pair made their way towards the cavernous lobby.

Iris stood alone, surrounded by activity. Men were hoisting a tower contraption made of wood and rope that she recognized as a fireworks display. A *castillo*. Studded with pinwheels and ladders, the massive apparatus rose to twenty metres. It had been ages since she'd seen one of these towers set off, hundreds of *bombas* shooting into the night. Jerry-built, and thoroughly unsafe, it was a delicious contrast to the resort with its impeccable gardens and gold façade. She felt a prick of excitement; the old Mexico was striding in.

Staring at the haphazard structure were the Zen priest and his lady friend: Joe and Gloria. They stood with their necks craned, arms draped around each other's waist. Gloria must have temporarily forgiven him for being a man of the cloth. His shaved head was pink from the sun and he'd tucked his t-shirt into his shorts. Gloria was far less tidy, wearing some sort of tunic, and Iris noted that her shoulders betrayed an incipient hump. Instinctively, she straightened her own spine.

Joe spotted Iris and looked at her with the frank open gaze she'd marked earlier; so appealing in a man.

'Is that thing going to stay up?' he said, meaning the fireworks tower.

'They usually do.' Iris's smile took in both of them. 'How do you suppose it balances?'

'Don't ask Joe about anything structural,' Gloria said. 'He lives in his head.'

'Not true,' Joe objected. 'I practise yoga.'

'Yoga,' Gloria repeated. 'I meant actual physical labour.'

* * *

Alejandro crouched over his laptop and didn't bother to look up when Martina pushed open the door to their room.

'How did it go?' he said in a perfunctory tone.

He'd been in a state before the interview, reminding her countless times that she must not probe in areas where Don Victor resisted, and that the matter of gaining a sensational interview was far less important than keeping the man onside. The future of the state rested in her hands. This, he underlined, was only a slight exaggeration.

'Not great,' she said, setting her things on the bureau. The walk back had heated her up. She waited for follow-up questions; they did not come.

'What are you doing?' she asked.

It took him a moment to respond. 'Arrangements. It's coming together.' A pause, then—'Ah!' He sounded pleased. 'Seems as if'—another pause as he squinted at the monitor—'we are to be graced this evening with the presence of El León.'

Martina stared at him. 'The Lion owns this joint. He owns half the resorts on the strip.'

'Precisely.'

'He's a drug lord. He's co-leader of—' She lowered her voice and whispered the name of one of the cartels fighting for control in the region.

'Why is this assassin joining us for dinner?' she added and felt a kick of fear mixed with excitement: El León was top of anyone's list for an interview.

Alejandro lowered his feet that had been resting on the glass-topped table and flipped the lid of his computer shut. When he looked at her, his face was sober. 'If I can prove my ability to negotiate a truce between the cartels—'

'I see.'

They looked at each other for several seconds; he needed her to believe. It was not folly to meet with criminals and if he could mediate between the *capos*… The citizens of the state wanted nothing more than peace and safety, to go about their business without running into another blood-soaked *manta* blanket strung over the highway, streaked with messages written in the bodily fluids of victims.

'No need for you to know the details,' her husband said. He had the tight face she'd seen when he spoke to underlings he wasn't sure about.

'I see,' she said again.

They had entered the stage where he was keeping things from her. For her own protection, he would insist, if she were to press.

His gaze shifted away.

She nestled beside him on the sofa and he patted her knee, obviously distracted. He was so full of his arrangements that he had forgotten what she'd been up to. She examined her husband's profile as if he were one of her interview subjects: what was he really saying under the glib words? She was an old hand at reading body language and subtext.

In those early years with Alejandro, she'd been the star, the one people jostled to meet at parties and conferences, but recently this had changed. She'd helped him move up the party ranks, starting by getting him out of those tweed jackets and into tailored suits and silk ties. You had to look like what you wanted to become.

'And what do we call El León when we dine with him?' she asked. 'Presumably he has a civilian name.'

His gaze swung back. 'Luis Bartolo. I have reserved a table. Tomás will join us, and I have no doubt that El León will not arrive alone.'

Drug lords rarely travelled solo, even when they entered one of their own properties. Martina envisioned a convoy of SUVs disgorging heavily armed bodyguards; a fine way to scare the shit out of the tourists.

'Surely he isn't in danger here,' she said.

Alejandro had just shaved and she could smell the splash of cologne on his cheeks. 'A man of this kind is always at risk of being cut down.'

He knew this would excite her.

Still eyeing Martina, he said, 'You're not sure I'm capable of pulling this off. I can see it in your face.'

'Not so!' she said, perhaps too brightly.

Ever since he'd launched his campaign, her husband alternated between arrogance and this transparent need for approval. Her family thought she was crazy, leaving Rafael all those years ago, a man of business with excellent family connections and father of her children. But she'd fallen for Alejandro's urgent way of talking, the way he'd seized the microphone at the roundtable discussion on Chiapas that she was chairing. And when it was her turn to speak, he watched intently, with not a hint of the bored demeanour she was used to enduring in men of her class. It was he who'd recalled they'd known each other as students at UNAM. He confessed that he used to watch her sitting in the broadcast booth of the student radio station, speaking in elegant sentences, smoking one cigarette after another.

21

WHAT DOES ONE *wear to dine with a thug?* Martina pondered, scrutinizing the array of frocks that dangled from the hangers. She, like most of her friends, had clothing custom-made by *Señora* Beatriz in the state capital.

Alejandro was arriving at his own decision: tan slacks or mouse grey? Sandals or leather shoes?

'He knows who your wife is?' she said.

'Of course.'

'Such characters tend to be shy of journalists.'

When they weren't hiring *sicarios* to kill them.

'El León,' Alejandro pronounced, 'is known to be a charming and cultivated man when he chooses.'

'Let's hope he chooses that mode tonight.' Martina settled on a sundress decorated with a cloud pattern. Slight decolletage, enough to provide mild provocation without sending an unwelcome message.

Alejandro checked his watch. 'We need to be settled at our table before he arrives. Tomás is making the necessary arrangements with the concierge.'

That would be Cleo at the front desk. Tomás was one of Alejandro's many nephews, in charge of logistics, including security. Martina had little faith in his organizational expertise.

'What about Don Victor?' she asked.

'He will, of course, join us.'

'Does he know about our esteemed guest?'

'He does.'

'And still?'

'Don Victor understands that one must be pragmatic in order to govern.'

Martina snorted; she'd heard this before. She flicked on the television to the news and as she lifted the dress over her head she could hear the familiar pop of gunshots, followed by wailing sirens.

When would it ever stop.

Alejandro angled himself while dressing so that he could watch the screen. The image showed a mountainous terrain, scrubby bush and unpaved roads. He froze as the camera changed locale.

This was the Art Deco-styled building on the main square of the city, and here was the Italian restaurant where they often gathered for Sunday *comida*. A lumpy body lay on its threshold, covered with a sheet. Blood seeped across the concrete sidewalk. Cruz Roja medics were hauling a second victim from Luigi's on a stretcher, and this poor creature was still alive and writhing in pain. The camera zoomed in closer, sure to examine every detail of the man's suffering, sparing the viewing audience noth-ing—and meanwhile, a few metres away on the street, an excited crowd circled and bobbed, cell phones tracking the action.

'Do you know him?' Martina whispered.

Alejandro said nothing for a moment, his face sick. Then he whispered, 'Pedro.'

The head waiter. A man in his mid-fifties, humourless, yet expert in his job. They'd held the same brief conversation with him for years: how is the family? Health of your mother? And the grandson across the border, is he studying hard?

Martina could see the horror in her husband's eyes, a deep, grave veil of hopelessness: this was what he was up against. This was what he hoped to prevent, the daily body count.

Even as the police began to tape off the crime scene, Alejandro and Martina knew it was just for show. The cops had no intention of gathering evidence, no illusion of future prosecution and trial; this was a pantomime of the judicial enterprise, acted out for the television cameras.

It wasn't just dealers hitting dealers any more; it had taken on a much broader swath of the public, even in this relatively quiet state. Anyone could get in the way of the cartels' business. Poor Pedro—what, if anything, had he done?

Or was he complicit, using his job as a cover as he organized meetings in that private room at the back of Luigi's? They'd never know the truth of it.

A pair of mug shots showed up on the screen and the plummy-voiced announcer (Ricardo: she knew him well) spoke soberly of the latest gangland slaying: five victims, including a child, a staff member, and patrons at the well-known restaurant where the bourgeoisie liked to gather for family meals. There was Luigi himself, leaning against the outside wall, apron gathered in his hands. How long before customers would return to his kitchen? A week? A month? Never?

A message had been left. Written in blood, of course: by what other method would one possibly communicate.

She could scream. She could toss a shoe at the relentless monitor. But she did neither, just stood next to her husband, the man who thought he might change a corner of his country.

'This must stop,' Alejandro said as he reached to clasp her hand.

The two of them, half dressed, continued to watch as the screen flashed another image, a slim man with a mustache lounging by a pool in one of the city's suburbs. He smiled directly into the camera. This was not a thug's face; he could be one of the station's announcers with his symmetrical features and light-coloured skin. One hand, long graceful fingers, clasped the paperback book that he'd left off reading to pose for this photograph. His eyes looked almost merry.

The cutline beneath: El León. The man they were to meet for dinner.

The picture disappeared and the camera swung back to the studio presenters, looking suitably grave. On to the next item of news, a fire in one of the pueblos in the state of Michoacán, probably caused by a meth lab explosion. Alejandro and Martina and thousands of others used to visit this town for its Day of the Dead celebrations, women in native costume, tiny sugar coffins for sale. The camera panned the pueblo's main square with its empty hotels and forsaken restaurants.

Martina slipped her feet into her sandals and crouched to fasten the narrow straps. She said, 'This is the man we are welcoming to our table?'

Alejandro grabbed the remote and snapped off the television.

He was beyond speech.

22

YOU'VE CUT your hair!'

'Indeed I have.' Lydia waited for a sign of approval which
Iris was a beat late in giving.

Not because she didn't think the new style attractive.
More that she felt the burden of Lydia's expectation.

'You look as you did as a child,' Iris finally said. Her
daughter's smile tightened. It came back, Lydia with a pixie
cut standing on the school's stage performing a recitation of
A.A. Milne's *The Dormouse and the Doctor*, while Iris hovered
at the back of the auditorium, mouthing the words.

Lulu and Neil, sitting across the table, hooted with
laughter at the ongoing performance taking place on the
fiesta stage. If you called a parade of guests coming up to
the microphone to cup their hands and enter the flatulence
contest a performance. Shades of Le Pétomane, the French
flatulist celebrated for his ability to blow out a candle with
an explosion of sphincter and to mimic the sound of a thun-
derstorm through the same orifice. Iris was not in a mood
to join their merriment. She'd been indiscreet. Worse than
indiscreet; she'd been a victim of her desire to impress these

new friends. She had sought to entertain this pair of dentists, people she barely knew or cared about, at the expense of her daughter. When Lulu had asked Lydia whether she had a family back home, it had been Iris who'd burst in to say, 'My darling daughter has been abandoned by her husband.'

That got everyone's attention.

She'd plowed on, turning to Lydia: 'Remember two summers ago at the cottage?'

Lydia's mouth froze into a stiff, unconvincing smile.

'When I pitched in to help Charlie make dinner?'

Beef stew and corn on the cob: Lydia had seemed happy at the time to leave them to it. Hadn't she swum across the lake that day, Iris paddling alongside in the canoe?

'You popped into the kitchen when we were working,' Iris went on. 'Charlie had been expressing boredom with his life, a sense that time was playing out in a predictable fashion, that it was time to make a change, though of course he didn't say what he had in mind. I sympathized.' She stopped, waiting for her daughter to speak.

Lydia did not.

'I may have encouraged him,' Iris continued, feeling the continued attention of her small audience. 'To follow his heart.'

'Oh, please,' Lydia said. She set her glass down hard on the table. The dentists exchanged a glance, sensing that Iris had gone too far.

As indeed, she had.

'I really do like your hair,' Iris said, but when she reached to touch her daughter's shorn head, Lydia rose to disappear into the crowd of revellers.

Lydia had lain next to Charlie that night at the cottage, in the whiffy bedroom that never got entirely dry. As usual, a mosquito found its way through the screen. The walls didn't reach the ceiling so you could hear everything in the other rooms. Charlie had just told her, in a tone of amusement, about his conversation with Iris. 'She's all for me taking off into the wild blue yonder,' he said.

As Charlie huddled next to her, Lydia, in her mind, fed him fantasies. He had no idea. He was, she decided, imagining his arms surrounding that plump, over-ripe body of the au pair girl two cottages over. He'd slither a hand between her legs while the girl texted some boy on her phone. He got off on her boredom as he lifted the edge of her skirt, waiting for her to object. But object she did not.

When Lydia turned to look at her husband lying next to her in bed, he had a tiny smile on his face.

***

'Are you in real trouble, Bob?'

'I wouldn't say that.' Bob added in a musing tone: 'There's a story going around that La Pirámide may soon have a new owner.'

Lydia waited for more.

'Change is in the air.' He pulled at his collar, as if he needed air. 'I'm a survivor, a cockroach when it comes to looking after Bob's interests.' Suddenly he looked fierce. 'I'll eat paint if I have to. Shit acrylic.'

Looking past his head, Lydia spotted her mother who'd risen from her table and seemed to be searching through the fiesta crowd for her, a look of cheerful expectation on her face. She'd lost her audience and Iris was not one who liked to be alone, even for a minute.

Bob nodded towards the faux plaza. 'The current owner is arriving.'

Lydia watched the shiny SUV roll up the hill and cruise to a stop under a palm tree. The rear passenger door swung open and a slender man in a linen jacket and slacks stepped out. He was followed by another man, blockier in shape, dressed in black. The driver emerged and stood beside his door, as if guarding the vehicle.

The man in the linen jacket trotted into the midst of the fiesta, hands in pockets, light on his feet.

'El León,' Bob said and pulled at his wispy beard.

The Lion.

'Should I be impressed?'

'You should be afraid.'

They watched as the newcomer and his colleague made their way towards a table that had been set apart from the others. Sitting there already was the group of Mexicans, including the city couple who'd sprung out of the darkness while Lydia was smoking weed on the beach—and the old artist everyone made a fuss over. Two men stood to greet this new arrival, while the woman who worked in television merely extended her hand. The newcomer clasped it for a few seconds and it looked like he might draw her fingers to his lips for a ceremonial kiss, but he did not.

'I'm not sure I want to be around for this,' Bob said, and abruptly he was gone, disappeared inside the cavernous lobby.

'*Señorita?*'

Cleo looked different in his street clothes, madras shirt and tight jeans. His hair was slicked back, comb marks sculpted by gel. The smile he reserved for guests who approached the front desk with their questions and small difficulties was not present; instead he looked at Lydia straight-on, not a hint of subservience. She understood that he was inviting her to dance.

Lifting her wounded arm out of its sling, she placed her good hand around Cleo's back while he cradled the other. The music revved up as a breeze spun the pinwheels of the fireworks tower. Lydia let her hips find the beat. His touch was barely there and it was almost like dancing solo, but then he would snap her against his chest. She wondered if it was part of his job to dance with single women at the resort— and wondered if she cared.

A musician strummed the harp while chanting a repetitive verse. Lydia tipped backwards, waiting until Cleo pulled her back to his chest, to his heart, his poor wounded heart. She felt his hand slide down her back, stroking bare skin. His breathing softened her ear, and she knew that if she wanted more to happen, it would.

'Come with me.' He nodded towards the slope of driveway.

That's what vacations were for, to soar over your usual life, to escape the tedium of gravity. An image arrived like a slap, a rogue wave—Charlie pushing off from the dock as she stood on shore watching the gathering clouds. Did he know he was leaving for good?

She managed to say, 'I'm sorry.'

'This is what you always say to me.'

She left Cleo there, arms hanging at his sides.

23

REALLY, IRIS TOLD herself, wasn't she getting past the stage of feeling an infatuation? Hard to mistake this heightened excitement attacking her body. The racing heart felt good— alive and in command, not headed for a ragged ending. The doctor told her last month that irregular heartbeats were a natural consequence of aging and that she need not worry unless she began to feel faint or breathless.

Circumspectly, she touched the inside of her wrist: since when did excitement become a prelude to disease? Such seizures kept one young.

The fashionable Mexican couple, he with sleek black hair, she, fresh out of the salon with blonded tresses done up in a perfect Hillary Clinton 'do,' sat at the table near a row of palm trees. The man she'd noted earlier stood nearby, scanning the crowd from left to right, very secret service. Could that bulge in his vest possibly be …?

These observations were a discipline to keep her from fastening her eyes on Don Victor. There was something both elegant and undomesticated about the man. His leathery skin looked pure Indian, especially the prominent cheekbones.

He fingered the rim of his hat as he lounged in his chair, legs stretched out, hardly at home at this faux-Mexican plaza and fiesta. Yet not ill at ease either. One got the sense that he could belong anywhere.

Martina Gutiérrez leaned forward at the table, caressing a cocktail glass with her manicured fingers as she spoke to the painter. Her politician husband watched the exchange with approval; wives were supposed to do this sort of thing, keep the guest of honour engaged.

Suddenly the little party ignited and began pushing chairs back and rising to their feet—all but Don Victor who remained resolutely sitting, as did Martina. A tall slim man, dressed in linen jacket and slacks, strode through the partying tourists, an easy smile lighting his face as he approached the table, arms reaching out.

Alejandro gripped one of the man's hands and touched the opposite elbow in a show of comradely welcome. The newcomer bowed as he clasped Martina's hand. She did not look as pleased as she might, Iris thought.

Staff snapped to attention as the group reassembled. No more leaning against kiosks waiting to be summoned; the whole square assumed a higher pitch of activity. Bartenders and waitresses scurried about removing plates and replenishing glasses while dodging the more boisterous tourists who'd taken to stamping their feet in crude approximation of the clog dancer. There was Joe, the Zen priest, dancing with hands on hips, his shiny scalp catching the last rays of sun.

The man in the linen jacket settled in the chair next to Don Victor. A trio of waitresses appeared carrying plates of tapas and other goodies that had come, Iris couldn't help noting, straight from the kitchen and not from the buffet table.

Iris positioned herself so that the painter might see her, and she raised a hand in breezy greeting.

He didn't notice.

She grabbed a shot of tequila, downed it in one gulp, and made her way across the plaza, using the backs of chairs as support. She reminded herself that the man had spoken to her first on the pier. Arriving at the table beneath the sheltering palms, Iris stood in front of the group, who looked up at her through narrowed eyes, as if her presence were unusual. The man called Alejandro Gutiérrez rose to his feet, as did the dapper fellow in linen.

Caballeros. Gentlemen.

In short supply these days.

'*Señora?*' Alejandro said, with a little bow.

Had the elderly *gringa* lost her way, his expression inferred.

She had decidedly not lost her way and to prove this, Iris spoke to them in Spanish, her tongue loosened by tequila, and even her body language changed, growing more animated. Wasn't it grand that the young people were resurrecting traditional music and playing with such *espírito*? She keenly hoped—drop in a subjunctive here—that it was more than a passing fad.

The Mexicans stared at her with puzzled fascination. She charged on, speaking of her gratitude at visiting their country again after all these years—*un país* so beautiful, such gracious people.

The language spilled out, uncorked.

The blond woman, who wasn't so young when one saw her close up—a heavy hand with foundation cream—slit her eyes as if looking into a sharp light. She would be used to that, the hard television spots bearing down.

Iris got hold of herself. She could almost hear Steve, and all the other men she'd known, whispering in her ear—'Iris, calm down'—and she halted the stream of talk mid-sentence.

Relief flooded the faces of her audience.

The music clanged on, the strumming *jaranas*, the thumping clog dancers, the boy smacking his palms against the flank of his wooden box. She looked pointedly at Don Victor and in response, he lifted his feet from the rung of the table and sat up straighter. Scarecrow fellow, no more

147

than five and a half feet tall, his old-fashioned sombrero now sitting on the table beside a platter of fish.

It was hardly an insult to ask a man to dance.

'*Te gustaría bailar conmigo?*'

The others leaned forward to see what the painter would do. Don Victor rose to his feet, muttering something to his tablemates that made them laugh.

If Iris cared about the opinions of strangers, she would have led a very conventional life. The papery hands met hers and soon the couple was swept by the crowd into the centre of the courtyard. The painter was shorter than Iris and he tilted his head to look into her face—such sharp hazel eyes. This man could see through skin and bone and Iris shivered, despite the heat. The concept of transparency was thrilling, if unnerving. He danced with none of the stiffness of most men his age, guiding her under his raised arm, using no more effort than necessary.

He was looking towards the table he'd recently vacated. She followed his gaze and saw the newcomer slinging an arm over the shoulder of Alejandro. A natural enough gesture.

Apparently not to Don Victor, who muttered the common insult: *cabrón*. His face became guarded and he began to sweep her to the edge of the plaza, zig-zagging through the crowd. Soon they were loping down the steep drive towards the road, that four-lane highway that lined the coast. Her new hip jarred as they trod downhill and she gripped the painter's hand for balance.

'Where are we going?' she asked.

He did not answer. It was unsettling to be so abruptly removed from the party. She could object, but she did not. Far more interesting to see what would happen next. In the old days she wouldn't need to remind herself of this sentiment.

They didn't stop until they reached the guards' booth at the foot of the drive. This modest hut usually held one of a rotation of attractive young men in safari-style uniform. It was empty now and Victor gestured, meaning they should duck into the cramped space. Evening traffic sped past a few feet beyond. A comic book had been tossed on the floor along with a crushed pop can.

'Sit,' Don Victor said and he wiped his sleeve across the bench.

Iris was happy to obey. Her entire body felt ambushed from the jog downhill. There was a strange expression on his face as he turned to her. She was panting; he was not.

'I think you understand me,' he said.

She nodded, though she wasn't sure what she was supposed to understand. They squeezed next to each other on the bench built for one. The sound of music and traffic was muted in the humid air. Something aromatic shrouded the tropical night— perhaps those purple flowers she'd admired earlier. Her heart continued to thump in her chest, a slightly alarming sensation. She felt Don Victor's thin shoulder press against hers, and then quite suddenly, his hand dropped onto her knee.

The old goat.

She had to smile. In a long life there had been many hands that had found their way there. Decades ago she would have been wearing a miniskirt and her skin would have been soft and smooth. She'd worn short skirts well into her fifties; why the hell not—she had long, coltish legs. Still did.

'Why did you follow me onto the pier?' he asked in Spanish.

'I did no such thing,' she insisted, perhaps too forcefully.

'It is difficult for me here,' he said. 'Everyone wants me to be something that I am not.'

'You aren't obliged to obey them,' she pointed out.

'Perhaps it is more important to help my people than it is to continue working in my studio, a solitary man, his small inconsequential efforts.'

'What is it that everyone here wants you to do?' The Spanish was tripping effortlessly out of her mouth.

'Ah,' Don Victor said and laid his head against hers. 'Do you believe I would make an effective Minister of Culture? Am I the sort of man who can inspire and lead?'

Was he being sincere or playful?

'Or am I just restless? Like most men,' he added.

'I have no idea what—or who—you are.' Iris peered out the doorway to the drive where clusters of tourists sauntered past on their way to town. The younger set hoped to experience the full range of nightlife rather than stay cloistered in the hotel to suffer amateur entertainment. Not so long ago, she would have been one of them.

'I bore you with my questions,' Don Victor said. 'I bore myself.'

The painter's hand, a disembodied creature, traced circles around her knee. She felt the familiar vibration of skin against skin, the promise of adventure. If someone were to walk by the hut and peer in, expecting to see Alfredo or Julio at his post, would he or she laugh at this elderly pair? The thought of this reaction diminished her pleasure for a moment, until she recalled her pledge to never let the opinions of others infect her activities.

'You are a beautiful woman,' the painter said in his husky voice. 'And you understand that I need to escape those people and that terrible man.'

The hand began its march, offering a squeeze, then a caress, now rising to brush the inner thigh. Her cotton skirt rose in tandem with the gesture.

'Tell me who you are,' he said.

'Have you got a week?'

'I have no time, and I have all the time in the world.'

Before Iris could begin to reply to his question, he launched into a description of his own life in his village, a quiet place where he was left alone. He'd chop wood for winter nights and work in his studio all day. Evenings, he might head out for supper at Lupe's restaurant and visit a local cantina. These places were used to him and made no fuss or demands. Don Victor sighed deeply and confessed that he'd been lured off his tranquil mountain retreat by a prod to his vanity and patriotism.

'Is it a sin to be vain?' he asked.

'I should hope not.'

He squinted at her in the mottled light.

'Are you vain?'

'Certainly.'

'Then we are the same.' His hand worked in slow, deliberate motions, sweeping up and down her thigh: red light/green light. She wasn't going to feign an attack of modesty. She closed her eyes, feeling the tingle of nerve endings shoot up her leg and waken her womb, the old familiar pulsing, only a little dulled by time. Blow off the dust and she was as good as new. Her breathing became long and deep as she felt herself being lulled into the dream, all of her attention focused on the flame that singed her inner thigh as the hand made its drowsy but meticulous way towards her—

He was nearly there, fingertips nicking the edge of her panties—thank God she'd selected black satin with a frill at the waist. Lydia had spotted the undies hanging over the shower rod and squeaked, 'Are those yours?'

A taxi rolled across the ramp and began to chug uphill, lights streaking the drive. Iris could see a pair of tourists in the back seat, rustling for pesos to pay the driver. She let out a startled laugh; it was Lulu and Neil, the pediatric dentists. They must have gone out and come back within the hour. Lulu, closest to the passenger door, stared out, her eyes catching Iris's and resting there for several seconds. Could she see through the dark?

It was so easy to shock the young.

Don Victor said, 'Do you want me to stop?'

'I will let you know.'

'Am I disturbing you?'

'I certainly hope so.'

The taxi disappeared and seconds later, there was a bleat of car horn, and the sound of tires grinding against gravel as a curb was barely missed. A set of high-beams poured down the drive outside their hut and Don Victor's wandering hand

151

froze. Iris peered into the blast of headlight; the vehicle was going far too quickly downhill. The SUV shot past, not hesitating to check if the sidewalk was clear before bumping over the ramp to the main roadway. A man's voice shouted in English and there was the sound of glass breaking. A bottle, perhaps tossed in anger.

'Pinche idiota!' Don Victor cried, and he leapt to his feet, hands pressed against the doorway.

***

Lydia paced the nearly deserted lobby. A celebratory racket emitted from Party Room A, the Mayan Lounge, where a cluster of foil balloons was tacked to the door. The wedding party had been at it since dusk, a tribute band pumping out classic rock.

What had Iris been thinking, inviting her to such a place where everyone was happily matched up, celebrating anniversaries and weddings? This was meant to heal her? She had not spotted another single woman in the place. Iris's gifts always seemed to contain an edge of judgment. There were certificates to spas and women's wear shops that Lydia never set foot in. CDs of German lieder back when Lydia was listening to New Wave music.

Iris was not in their room, nor on the balcony, nor standing under the shower trilling 'Ring of Fire.' Lydia had pulled up a chair next to the bed and tried to get hold of Doug via telephone. It was nine p.m. and according to their agreement, he should be home. No one answered. She tried again, deciding that he wasn't answering because he was hypnotized by World of Warcraft, trying to outwit some Taiwanese genius. He'd gotten a twenty-seven-inch monitor for his birthday: a death screen, splashes of electronic fire and pixilated blood. Charlie, conveniently, had walked out on all of this.

'Hey Mum, whattup?'

She found herself talking too quickly, relating the day's activities, feeling her son's attention waver. 'And you?'

Doug hesitated. 'I saw Dad.'

'Oh?'

'Tamara was with him.'

The recently divorced music teacher who liked to pop by Charlie's office for advice and consolation.

'Was she,' Lydia said in a steady voice.

'No big deal,' he said. 'We had pizza in the condo.'

'That must have been fun.'

'Yeah, I guess.' Then—'I love you Mum.'

He sounded plaintive, as if he were afraid for her.

Maybe Iris had gotten lost on the way to their room. The resort changed at night, its labyrinthine pathways lit by hooded lights, and she might have taken a wrong turn and found herself roaming the paths of the Colonial wing. Orientation was never Iris's strong suit.

Surely she wouldn't enter the inky sea, lifeguards long ago packed up and gone home. Yet it seemed plausible, Iris peeling off her clothes under the shaft of moonlight, tossing her sandals onto the sand then stepping majestically into the waves.

Lydia paused outside the party room door, and pressed her good hand against the wall. She felt a surge of nausea; must be something she'd eaten: buffets were notoriously unreliable.

The recent encounter on the dance floor had been unsettling. The man in the linen jacket had crossed the plaza and stopped in front of her, causing Cleo to melt into the crowd. She recognized El León, owner of the resort, and, if Bob was to be believed, owner of most of the resorts on the strip. He'd held out his arms and she didn't think twice; of course she accepted his invitation. She was not immune to flattery. He was careful to keep a correct space between them as they danced to a ballad. His hands, Lydia noted, were cool and dry and he peered down at her with an oddly guileless look.

'You are from the U.S.?'

'Canada.'

'Canada,' he repeated. 'A peaceful country.'

'Yes,' she agreed.

'But cold.'

She nodded in further agreement. The man moved in a casual, almost offhand way.

'This is the music of Veracruz,' he told her. 'We have different music and dances for every region of the country.' He guided her past the table where the journalist and the politician sat watching. Neither gave so much as a nod of recognition, no sign that they recalled her from the episode on the deserted beach.

Bob had claimed that El León was dangerous, but what could happen here, surrounded by music and tourists in the open air?

She felt herself relax and those cool hands pulled her an inch or two closer to his taut belly.

'You are an attractive woman,' he said then added, ' Of course men tell you this all the time.'

'Not often enough.'

This made him laugh. He moved from the hips, at ease in his body, unlike Charlie who was the sort of man who when dragged onto a dance floor, stared at the ground and counted out the beats.

'Bob is your friend,' El León said.

The statement caught her off guard. 'We just met a few days ago.'

'You rescued him from the Blue House.'

Lydia felt a flash of fear. 'How did you know?'

Crack of a smile. 'Not much goes on around here I don't know.'

He gripped her harder as tourists clanged into each other in an approximation of dancing.

'Bob is not who you think he is. He is not a good man.'

'And you are?' she said.

Tiny pause. Then the Lion abruptly stopped dancing and reached into his jacket pocket. He pulled out a business card and slipped it between her fingers. 'I will be honoured to invite you and your mother as guests at my residence on Thursday.'

She stared at the card again as she stood alone in the hallway outside the Mayan party room: under his printed name, Luis Bartolo, was a cell phone number. No address, no email, no webpage, and no profession or title.

'I will send a car to La Pirámide at seven p.m.,' he'd told her, then added, 'Stay away from Bob. The man has worn out his welcome.' In a gesture that felt weirdly intrusive, Luis Bartolo placed his hand over her wounded wrist and squeezed lightly through the bandage.

24

'YOU SHOULD KNOW,' Iris informed Victor, 'that this is not my first encounter with a Mexican artist.'

Was he a bit deaf? Most men were, after a certain age. Even Steve needed to be bellowed at if you got on his left side. He refused to acknowledge this minor disability.

Her voice rose: 'It was in San Miguel de Allende back in the early 70s. I'd come with my first husband, Richard. We took note of the young artist who taught at the Instituto. He knew of all the important American and European artists and spoke passable English. Wildly ambitious. Well, why not? I don't see that as a flaw. He'd dart between the Instituto, his studio, and the café where a bunch of us would congregate. He was working on a mural in one of the civic buildings. Some historical epic, copious blood and gore.' Iris paused at the crest of the hill, panting. It was hard to climb and talk at the same time.

Hotel staff were starting to douse the coals and drag the grills back to the shed. A boy had begun to climb the rickety fireworks tower with lighter in hand. The grand finale was about to begin, deafening bursts of gunpowder and twirling pinwheels and flashing lights. Iris felt the painter's hand slip away from hers and understood that he didn't want them to be seen together. Men could be such cowards.

'Turned out that our friend had a wife and children stashed in a nearby town,' Iris said. 'All the while, carrying on with the female students under his tutelage.' She offered a knowing laugh. 'Including yours truly, in one memorable afternoon.'

She waited to be asked for more, but Don Victor was staring at the fireworks assemblage, watching the boy reach to light one of the pinwheels that flared and began spinning and shooting off sparks. Hotel guests shrieked and pressed into the darkness. Staff seemed to find this chaotic retreat funny.

'He was desperate to escape to the north,' Iris continued after the first round of explosions plumed the air with magnesium dust. 'He saw himself as being far too talented for a provincial town.' Don Victor was paying attention to her now. Encouraged, she went on: 'When he invited me to go to the movie theatre, I was flattered. *Bonnie and Clyde*, dubbed into Spanish.' She paused, remembering the odd celebratory mood inside that flea-ridden movie house where locals laughed at the grisly scenes.

'When he put his arm around my shoulders, I didn't exactly push him away. When he slipped a hand onto my thigh—' She shrugged, as if to say, 'What was I to do?'

A piece of the fireworks structure sailed into the crowd, popping electric blue. A mass scream of delight. They'd never seen such a ramshackle thing, so lacking in security buffers. No yellow tape to keep spectators back. Iris remembered why she loved this country.

The painter was looking at her as if fascinated by every feature of her face. He drew closer and reached with his fingers, those dry broken nails, and began to stroke her cheek. Even in this light she was struck by the contours of his face. He was old, and somehow she'd forgotten that. What she'd really forgotten was her own age. Perhaps he was thinking the same thing, with this almost forensic examination.

'It wasn't *Bonnie and Clyde*,' he said, switching to serviceable English. 'It was *Dirty Harry* with Clint Eastwood.'

She bucked backwards and nearly lost her balance.

They peered at each other, twin expressions of disbelief. This was just the sort of thing that happened to her, an outlandish coincidence; there was a pattern in her life, no episode was random. The past nipped at her heels and this was far from the first time that past and present had collided.

'You are nothing like Javier,' she told this man in his peasant clothing. 'He was—' she waved a dismissive hand. 'Very Americanized.' Her tone was measured, but her heart was racing. She felt tipsy, not as secure on her feet as she'd like.

It came easily, the image of young Javier in his sneakers darting across the square of the provincial town, sketch pad tucked under one arm as he headed to the municipal building to add another element to the mural.

She folded this picture on top of the current one and felt another sting of vertigo.

He was telling her something. She tried to listen.

'Do not speak of this to anyone,' he warned.

'I don't understand.'

'It was many years ago in San Miguel de Allende.'

'Yes,' she said, in a kind of trance.

He leaned in further until she felt a hand squeeze her waist. This touch was not erotic; it was a sort of underlining.

'Don Victor is not a man who cares to pass time with *Norteamericanos*. And he is not interested in their commercial enterprises.' The painter went on, the English spilling out of him: 'He is a man of his country and people, a man who uses the old techniques in his work.' He allowed a quick smile. 'And he is venerated.'

A pause. Fireworks shot skyward then bloomed into a multicoloured waterfall.

'You old fraud,' she said.

'This is who I am now.'

'I thought for sure you'd be living in Brooklyn, working in a massive studio, selling splashy abstract paintings to oil companies.'

'So you still think of me, after all these years.'

'Occasionally.'

'Of course there were many girls—' He took a step back. 'But you were ready for anything.'

'I still am.' She nodded towards the table where Alejandro Gutiérrez slumped, now alone in his chair. Where had the others gone? 'You think I'm going to tell everyone that you were an epic skirt-chaser desperate to escape to El Norte?'

He squinted towards the politician. 'I do not want to become Minister of Culture. I am a happy man in my mountain retreat.'

His hand found her again, sliding across her lower back and settling on the slim waist that she was so proud of. 'Stay with me,' he said and scrutinized her with those startling, clear eyes. 'Visit me at my village. We can sleep together in my rustic house.'

'Don't you have a wife?'

'She visits her daughter and son.'

'They aren't your children too?'

He looked pained. 'Why do you talk like this?'

'You're asking me to sleep with you in the marital bed?'

He just stared back at her. A dare.

She'd always liked dares.

25

MARTINA WAS beside herself, pacing the hotel room, sliding the balcony door open to enlarge the field. Fireworks like gunshots. She'd left him behind in the fake *zócalo*, morose creature. Alejandro was a proud man, so certain he'd pull this off, create a magical pasture of peace where there had been so much violence. Something had gone terribly wrong and she clawed at her hair, going over every element of the evening. She'd been perfectly behaved, not allowing a shred of disapproval to leak from her lips. There was a higher goal here than letting El León know what she felt about his activities. He was such a composed man; you'd never guess that he was a thug. Unlike El Chapo Guzmán, the Lion was well educated and had beautiful manners. He was, in a word, attractive, giving off the whiff of a careless sexuality. She'd felt it in herself, the weird and ghastly attraction, even when his attention was directed elsewhere, towards the painter or towards her husband. He seemed to always have her at the corner of his vision, ready to supply what was needed, from passing the basket of tortillas to help in rising from the chair. He knew she was aching to ask questions, to shoot a photograph, to lay down El León's first ever interview with a member of mainstream media. She'd held his gaze, being a woman who never shied away from men who bristled with their own power and sense of menace.

She stood outside on the balcony now, drenched in the evening fragrance of salt water and frangipani, looking down as satiated tourists wended their way back to their rooms to play cards or watch television. Perhaps to make love.

Luis Bartolo had leaned in to speak with her husband, dismissing polite chitchat: 'What do you want from me?'

Alejandro's shoulders tensed. The plan was to feel out the cartel leader in a subtle way: would he agree to share the *plaza* in return for peace? Alejandro might point out, in a tone of utmost discretion, that if El León were realistic, he'd realize that the other side, with its unhinged leader, could create a great deal of difficulty. The balance of power seesawed. Bodies lay in creeks and open fields. An agreement was of benefit to everyone, yes? Tourists would stop coming if the body count mounted.

She should have warned her husband more vigorously, made him see it was a daft idea. El León was a man of immense pride and he did not like being offered advice about his mode of doing business. Alejandro, when he got excited, could be blunt in his speech, forget the subtle tone necessary to broach such a subject.

Sitting beside them, she'd watched their body language change, how Bartolo's hint of a smile turned rigid as Alejandro's gestures became wider and more emphatic. She'd seen her husband's noble plan fall apart; the more he talked and persuaded, the more El León's bemusement turned to sour boredom. Then, more critically, to anger.

She'd observed her husband sling an arm over Luis Bartolo's shoulder in a comradely gesture, and noted how the man stiffened under such an impudent touch. His bodyguard approached, hand twitching in his pocket.

'Why Pedro?' Alejandro had asked.

'Pedro? Who is this Pedro?' Bartolo said.

'Come on, my friend, why Luigi's? Why blow up the restaurant of a good man, guilty only of composing an excellent spaghetti bolognese?'

She could see distaste grow on Luis Bartolo's face as he shrugged off Alejandro's arm, but her husband kept leaning in, insisting on an answer.

Drink wasn't to blame for the catastrophe; Alejandro hadn't touched alcohol for three years. He'd spent this time scrupulously attending A.A. meetings. He'd answer phone calls in the middle of the night, whispering to Martina that a fellow member was in peril and that he must help.

He'd always had an eye for the heroic role.

The end happened quickly. The Lion pushed back his chair, barked an order to his bodyguard, and within seconds, he'd roared downhill in his SUV, enraged that Alejandro would suggest he share his *plaza* with the detested gang—a splinter group of his own crew of thugs and assassins.

And before he left, didn't the Lion consider Martina's husband with scarily alert green eyes, as if measuring him for a coffin?

'Leave me alone,' Alejandro said to her after Luis Bartolo fled the fiesta. Perhaps she should have stayed with him—but she'd been angry.

Martina pushed the balcony door shut, muting the sounds of vacationers, then flicked on the television. First she heard the voice, then the image spat into view. The familiar music, cheerful guitars and horns in jazzy mode, signalled that the program was beginning. As always, it took a few seconds to recognize herself, to understand that she could be in two places at once.

Their old friend, the great Octavio, now regrettably deceased, used to talk of the split self, the public and private, the difficulty of inhabiting both simultaneously. He was a master of managing the dual worlds himself.

She perched on the bed, remote control in hand. She rarely watched herself; it felt like a disembodiment, yet there she was, cashmere sweater and silk scarf, sitting in the studio interviewing Elena, one of the country's eminent playwrights and actors. She recalled the exchange well, though this was a rerun from four years earlier, broadcast today because Elena had won yet another award.

After the interview the two women had gone to El Hospital, the ironically named restaurant in the hills just west of the city. With Elena you could talk about anything. Such fervent intelligence. Such curiosity.

Martina watched and listened, as always searingly critical of her own performance, the slightly too-avid face as the guest spoke, a tendency to fawn over people she admired and to condescend when the network forced a pop culture icon on her. She'd even interviewed, for pity's sake, that sweet, troubled boy from Canada: Justin Bieber. He'd sat opposite her with the restless mien of a boy who'd been told he must do this, his pretty face incongruously matched with his gold chains, tattoos, and hoodie. They could hear the hordes of young girls massed outside the studio, screaming loudly enough to raise the dead. The boy scarcely noticed; it was the aural wallpaper of his daily life.

She looked noticeably older on screen, Martina decided, and touched her neck. Time to get more work done. The camera's eye was relentless.

She switched the sound to mute and watched the interview gain momentum. Hands and arms waved and there was an expression of surprise on Elena's face. She'd said something she hadn't meant to; this was Martina's gift, to encourage such moments of revelation.

Her phone made the discreet chime that signalled an incoming text. Half-looking at the television as she glanced at the tiny screen, she saw that it was Danielle, the show's producer.

'Ms. Brisbois confirmed for Monday session.'

Glory be.

'Good,' Martina tapped and waited for the the reply.

'Twenty-two stations signed on for simulcast.'

Her head whipped up to see Elena flicking a tear from her eye; she'd been recalling the suicide of her son.

'Good,' she tapped again. Both she and Danielle were deliberately understating their excitement. Perhaps she could get the Nobel Prize winner to confess to some trial of her own, as she, Martina, leaned forward in that attentive way, hands clasped over her knees, listening, always listening. She would nod as her guest spoke and never push through the delicate beat of silence; an interview contained its own rhythm and to hasten was to kill it. A counter running top of screen would track the mounting donations for refugees.

Alejandro had clamped a hand over hers in front of their sinister dinner guest, the man who owned most of the coastal resorts, as he announced: 'My wife would be delighted to interview you on her program so that you may offer your side of the story, tell the country about your heavy responsibilities, how you crave peace and order, like anyone.'

She'd stared at her husband with horror. Even now it lit out of her, anger mixed with something ranker—disgust.

The television screen showed her swinging her body to face the viewers in that guileless way she had mastered. She watched the little speech without hearing a word of it, and, more disconcerting, didn't recall what she had said. It was a performance of intimacy, for she operated as surrogate for the intelligent viewer who imagined that he might move in such exalted circles. While they remained at home, digesting their *comida*, she was tangling with everyone who counted, asking the questions the viewer might ask, if he ever got a chance.

Rarely did anyone turn down an invitation to appear on the show. On the contrary, they had their secretaries send press releases boasting of each new achievement.

The mouth moved; she had full lips, thanks to Dr. Lopez and his magical injections. A smallish head with a sharp chin. Cartoonists made much of these features, though perhaps less so in recent years. She noted that she was getting round-shouldered, perhaps from leaning towards each guest, indicating that he—or she—was the most fascinating person on earth. She straightened her spine as she sat on the edge of the hotel bed.

Once a week she lured viewers into the mock salon with its couch and club chair, its fireplace and the shelf with carefully chosen books. Works by contemporary Mexican artists decorated the walls of the set. She selected many of these pieces herself, visiting the studios of young men and women who were thrilled by the prospect of their work hanging on her false walls. Often they gave her a drawing or small painting for her own collection. The rooms of the penthouse apartment were full of these pieces.

Elena reappeared on the screen. An attractive woman in her early 80s, she wore a flowered dress and tan jacket. She was telling a story, using illustrative gestures, relating that well-known anecdote about the man in the black sedan who'd reached out the window to pass her an umbrella because it was raining. She was thirteen years old, holding her school notebook over her head in an attempt to keep dry. It turned out that her rescuer was an eminent writer on his way to the Opera House where his libretto was being performed that evening. He offered her a ride. Would she like to hear a modern opera from a box seat? She would. The excited girl was guided into the Green Room after the performance, and thus, legend goes, her theatrical career began. One did wonder about the relationship between middle-aged intellectual and ingenue. There were certain questions that could not be asked, even by Martina.

Heavy breathing.

Her husband was messing with the key card, sliding it in and out of the lock the wrong way. She could hear his laboured breathing. He was in a state; this was not going

166

to be an easy night. She would have to calm him down; it would not do for a future governor to be caught on someone's smartphone dropping his room key, crying out in frustration. It was the sort of thing that could be spread over the internet—candidate for governor fumbles and curses, a man so inept he can't open the door to his hotel room. Was he to be trusted running the affairs of state?

She opened the door and for a moment he stood still, arms hanging at his sides. He'd unbuttoned his shirt collar and he seemed to have left his jacket behind at the fiesta.

Worse, far worse, he smelled of tequila. It was emitting from his pores, perfuming his sweat.

The nightmare was beginning, she told herself in an almost clinical voice. He hadn't touched a drop in years, insisted he was done with it, but now he grabbed onto the doorway and pulled himself inside the room.

Get him onto the bed before he fell.

'I need to take a whiz.'

He managed to make his way to the toilet and since he didn't bother shutting the door, she heard every detail of his endless piss. She waited, sitting on the edge of bed, staring at the television screen.

When he returned, he'd left his fly unzipped. Fumbling in the dark, he worked at removing his clothes, making more of the action than he needed to, then collapsed beside her on the bed, half dressed. She reached out and touched his bare chest, half expecting him to shatter.

'Everyone left,' he said. 'I was completely alone. Where is Don Victor?' He laid his head on her lap. 'Why have you all deserted me?'

His hair was tousled and at age fifty-two he was still caught between adolescence and middle age. She understood that he was waiting for forgiveness. He lay staring up at her, watery eyes pleading. It terrified her, to see him so helpless. Was this how it would go each time his campaign went off the rails? He'd hit the bottle?

'You've betrayed a good number of people, including me. And yourself.' She sounded like a schoolteacher, a role that dismayed her.

'I don't understand.' A pout; of course he understood.

'You insulted the man.'

'You are one hundred percent wrong.'

She began to peel off her blouse, turning her back so he wouldn't get the wrong idea.

He propped himself up on an elbow. 'Do you think I am intimidated by this gangster? He needs me more than I need him.' He spoke with exaggerated clarity.

She didn't bother responding to the absurdity. Instead, she felt fury tingle through her body like slow-moving electricity.

And what about her career? With a single phone call, she could be pulled off air. Journalists were always in the cross-hairs of the cartel leaders.

'You're not afraid,' he told her. 'Not you, Martina.' It sounded less like a statement than a plea.

Grey pouches under his eyes. He could go from looking vital and healthy to ravaged in a matter of seconds.

'I am most certainly afraid.'

'Don't say that. I won't allow it.'

She tossed her blouse onto a chair. Cold air blew over her shoulders.

'Don't ever be frightened,' he purred and tried to reach for her, but missed. The effort put him off balance and he capsized onto the bed again.

She pulled up her legs and slipped out of her skirt.

Such a beseeching look; he needed her to be on his side.

'The man is not as powerful as he thinks,' Alejandro said. 'He pretends that he is king of the coast, that all his minions cower when he enters a room, but it is pure theatre.' He amplified this insight: 'Theatre of the Absurd.'

It would be a long night, and then there would be the morning to contend with, its ritual of apology followed by anxious sex, to prove that nothing was broken. She saw the future unfolding, how he'd hide bottles in the toilet tank and behind the Japanese screen, start chewing on mints, snore loudly at night. She'd be sick with worry every time he set foot on the campaign stage.

Martina began to weep, but she made no sound. This so alarmed him that he struggled to a sitting position and took her into his arms. She let him hold her, feeling the heat of his body and the erratic thump of his heart.

'Just this once,' he said. Breath like a cantina. 'I swear, never again.'

He stroked her head and looked over at the television, at the mute image of his wife as she made some crucial point.

'Who is this woman?' he said. 'I don't know her; take her away.'

She reached for the remote, snapped the power button and the monitor died. On the other side of the walls, the tourists were getting ready for bed. Sound of a shower. A glass door slid open and laughter bubbled. A nightcap was being enjoyed on a neighbouring balcony. Normal people doing normal things.

Martina lifted the spread, toppling the towel swan so that its bougainvillea petals dusted the sheets. Even as she executed this move, she felt something in her fade. Alejandro loved drama, but he should know that drunkenness was highly unoriginal. They were the couple written about in gossip columns, countless photos showing them entering charity galas or highbrow lectures. Dig a little deeper and you'd find her extramarital affairs, and his. One could feel deranged with the pedestrian arc of one's life.

He yanked off the rest of his clothes, tossed them on the floor, and fell beside her on the bed.

'What happened out there?' he whispered.

An existential question.

They could hear the little train tooting its horn as it trundled past, gathering up tourists who were too drunk or tired to navigate the pathways of the resort.

'Tell me,' he said.

All the bravado had leached out of him.

He squeezed her shoulder as she lay beside him. 'Tell me it's not so bad. Tell me, Martina.'

She smelled his fear, burned rubber, as his hand caressed her neck, so sure she would come back to him. Genial vacationers brushed their teeth and made love, these ordinary people from ordinary countries. Nations where criminals were caught, charged, and went to jail—and even stayed there. Rarely were there beheadings or bodies dropped in acid or mass shootings. Rarely did murderers escape from incarceration in laundry trucks or ventilated tunnels.

'You detest me,' he said.

'I don't detest you, Alejandro. But I'm afraid of you.'

That got his attention. 'Afraid of me?'

'You are not behaving like a man who seeks public office. Your carelessness scares me.'

The blue light on the alarm clock read just past midnight. In a few hours they would eat breakfast and be on their way back to the capital. She reached out a hand and touched her husband's cheek. A child's smooth, untroubled skin.

26

BOB FOUND THE two women at the breakfast buffet. He carried his usual plate of buttered toast and a boiled egg. Iris and Lydia were lined up at the omelette station as morning sun poured onto the terra cotta floor. Guests trickled in later than usual, recovering from the previous night's festivities.

'Ladies,' Bob said. But he was looking at Lydia.

'Rough night, Bob?' She noted his eyes were bloodshot.

'Sleeping is for the dead.'

'I shouldn't even be talking to you,' she said, half-serious. El León owned this place, which meant he owned the staff, including that young woman replenishing the fruit salad.

'What are you two talking about?' Iris said. She seemed confused as to where they might sit, holding her tray and casting her gaze in all directions. Last night there'd been an incident in the hotel room when Iris had been fishing around in her daughter's toilet bag for a Valium, and accidentally dropped the bag and vial onto the floor. When a groggy Lydia appeared at the bathroom door to investigate the noise, her mother was on her hands and knees plucking tiny pills off the tile floor.

Following the women as they carried their trays to a table next to the pond, Bob said, 'He's going to send a car for you tomorrow?'

'How did you know?' Lydia set her plate down with a clank. 'Why is everyone so interested in who I see and talk to?' She flexed her hand. The wrist was far less swollen now, though the skin had turned a mottled pink and blue, like an exotic salami.

'What are you planning to do?' Bob sat opposite.

'What man? What car?' Iris said as she attacked her eggs.

Lydia answered Bob: 'I haven't decided.'

'What else did El León say?'

'He warned me against you.' She waited for Bob to chortle with amusement but he did not. Instead he poked at his egg, then set his fork down.

'How often does the chance come up to visit a cartel leader?' Lydia said.

'Will someone please tell me what this is about?' Iris said.

Bob fixed his gaze on her. 'Your daughter has made a conquest.'

'Actually,' Lydia said, smearing jam on her toast, 'Luis Bartolo, owner of this resort, has invited you and me, Mum, to his home tomorrow.'

Iris stopped eating, crumbs lodged on the front of her t-shirt. 'Why on earth would he do that?'

'This needs to be stopped,' Bob said.

'Oh come on,' Lydia said, wearying of the topic. 'The man's not going to chop us into pieces; he's in the tourism business.'

Iris looked pale. 'Chop us into pieces?'

Bob shook his head. 'You still don't get it.'

The waitress stopped by with refills of coffee and seemed to linger longer than necessary. Only when she'd slipped away did Bob say, 'El León considers you gals as bait.'

This was ridiculous. 'Bait? To catch who?'

'Whom,' her mother corrected.

'I'm trying to tell you,' Bob said and laid his forearms on the table. 'Me, of course.'

'Stop all of this talk,' Lydia said. 'My mother and I have no intention of dining with a narco. We will spend our final days luxuriating in the amenities of La Pirámide.'

'That may not be possible,' Bob said.

'Meaning?' Now Lydia was cross.

'Meaning,' Bob said, 'Certain invitations are difficult to refuse.'

Iris was looking over his head; she'd spotted the Zen priest and Gloria arriving in the restaurant and returned their waves.

'Meaning we have to think of how we're going to get you two out of here tomorrow.' Bob tugged on his beard. 'Leave it to me, dolls.'

His solution, it turned out, was that the three of them would leave the confines of the resort and embark on a field trip.

'What sort of field trip?' Lydia asked, thinking of the sweltering beach town with its blur of car exhaust and stalls of trinkets.

Bob smiled. '*Las Ruinas.*'

'Oh, spare us,' Iris said, fanning the air. 'I've seen enough decaying pyramids to last me several lifetimes.'

'These ruins are different.'

'Luis Bartolo's driver will come and I won't be here,' Lydia protested.

Bob reached across the table and seized her hand. 'Exactly so.'

For the first time since their arrival in Mexico, a heavy grey cloud pulled across the sun. 'We might be in for a bit of weather,' Bob said as he left the women at the entrance to their pavilion.

27

MARTINA POPPED A handful of pepitas into her mouth, too many, too fast. Gulp of water. Even after all these years, she still got nervous in the minutes leading up to showtime. Especially today.

Nervous and furious.

So mad she hardly trusted herself to speak.

Ms. Brisbois was cancelled, as was the entire fundraising enterprise for the refugees, as were a dozen international broadcasters live-streaming the show. And no, Ms. Brisbois was unable to postpose her visit and it was indicated to Martina that even to ask for such an accommodation was ridiculous. Did Martina not understand that Ms. Brisbois had gone to considerable effort, not being in good health, to fly to Dallas from which destination she was prepared to fly to Mexico City and then be driven—

All too awful, too humiliating.

Ms. Brisbois let it be known that she was 'distressed' by the abrupt change in plans.

Martina had one person to blame: her husband sitting at home, wondering how his wife would manage this critical interview. 'You are the only one,' he'd pleaded, 'who can get us out of this mess.'

Us. A not so subtle reminder that they were, inevitably, locked in this together.

She slammed the counter of her dressing table with her fist; the jars of makeup jumped. Her floor manager, Dara, cast an arm through the open doorway and made the 'five minutes' sign. Martina nodded acknowledgement and examined herself with a professional eye in the mirror. Another dab of mascara, a dusting of powder on neck and sternum. She had a delicate heart-shaped face which, if she chose her expression carefully, would appear unthreatening to guests. She favoured the feminine approach today, wearing this beaded blouse and short black skirt. It made male guests feel she was playing a game that they understood. Today was different from other weeks, for she hadn't visited the dressing room to greet her guest and run over the direction the interview might take. She'd heard the racket of his arrival, that armoured SUV pulling up to the studio building, then the squish of Italian loafers striding down the corridor. The bodyguards' boots made a more percussive thud. Paco showed them all where to go and dashed off to the galley to fetch coffee and snacks. She glanced out the porthole window that looked onto the station's parking lot: it had begun to rain, unusual for this time of year.

Picking up her notes which were scrawled on index cards, Martina stood and smoothed the front of her clothing then took her customary trio of deep breaths to calm the parasympathetic system. She leaned over to shake her head, giving her hair a less disciplined look.

The corridor was institutional beige, undecorated and not even very clean. She liked the way one passed through this unpretentious sleeve, through the open doorway, and onto the fantasy set which exuded the atmosphere of a salon belonging to a prosperous intellectual with its faux fireplace, bookcases, modern paintings, club chairs, and sofa. Behind the sitting area was the stage where guest musicians performed before their interview. She'd seen and heard most of those who counted: classical, *folklórico,* and popular. Her audience, though far from touching the *telenovelas* in quantity, was a sophisticated crew much sought after by upmarket advertisers.

A glass coffee table held half a dozen books illustrated by well-known artists, many of whom were friends or colleagues, and all the volumes were personally inscribed to her. She felt more at home here than in her own living room. Certainly more in control.

Reminding herself of this fact, she positioned herself in the chair at stage right and tugged at her blouse and skirt while keeping an eye on the image in the monitor overhead. Her cameraman gave the thumbs-up, as did Dara, who would note if there was a problem with her makeup or clothing ensemble. The viewers of the program were an eagle-eyed bunch who felt proprietorial about her appearance and would spot anything amiss and let her know. Any time she changed her hairstyle, she invoked a chorus of applause, suggestions, and complaints. She often played games with them, adding a piece of oddball jewellery to see if they'd notice. Like that time on the Day of the Dead when she'd worn a small jade skeleton around her neck.

'Here comes our boy,' whispered Dana. She was not easily impressed by riches or notoriety. Today they had both.

Martina put on her game face: attentive, chin tilted, eyes wide open.

El León sauntered through the doorway in a beautifully cut dark suit with emerald-hued tie, shiny shoes. He surreptitiously checked his fly before hopping the single step to the dais and extending his hand. Whiff of aftershave. She rose to greet him; anything less would be an insult and she could not afford to provoke more displeasure from this well-groomed gangster. She felt the strain of her smile and realized that ninety percent of her fury was directed towards the man who sat at home, watching the moment unfold on television. Her own Alejandro, whose reckless actions had forced this parody of an interview. It was up to her to make amends, to sweep that evening at La Pirámide from the Lion's memory.

Sitting down after this cordial greeting, the Lion unbuttoned his jacket to reveal a pin-striped shirt. He was a slim man, well toned. No doubt his mansion sported a fully equipped gym, a personal trainer, and a masseuse who would apply her cool experienced hands to the man's sore places. Martina crossed her legs, showing off neat rounded knees and slender calves. She watched his gaze dart down in appreciation. So far so good—entirely predictable.

Amongst her viewers were cultural figures known all over the country. They made space in their schedule to watch *Martina Viva!* She had a certain vogue amongst university students, not just at UNAM but also in the smaller state universities, such as the one in this very region, whose students were eager to keep up with current events and the arts. She felt them waiting: how was Martina going to nail this thug? If anyone had the *cojones*, she did. Why else would she have invited the assassin to appear on her program?

The familiar jazz-inflected theme music faded and Martina looked closely at her guest. They say you can tell by the eyes, but his were perfectly conventional, even affable in their gaze. He could be someone's uncle, someone's brother—a live wire at fiestas, a benefactor to elders of his tribe. All of which might be true. El León lived, as was well known, in a goofy-looking, postmodernist castle in the suburbs of the capital, a creation designed by the same architect who built his fantasy resort project: La Pirámide. It was said that the windows of his castle facing outwards were slits, appropriate for archers to stick their bows through, and she wouldn't be surprised if he'd fashioned a protective moat around the edifice.

The Lion had his share of enemies.

And what was she? He eyed her with a kind of curious serenity; he knew why he was here. Out of the goodness of his heart, he was offering this chance to remedy a wrong.

She began the interview with an innocuous question, checking her index card to recall his real name: 'Luis Bartolo, you are considered to be one of the most ambitious developers of our coastline for touristic considerations, but what our viewers may not know is that you are also a great philanthropist.'

Her guest shrugged modestly.

Now the punch is coming, her viewers would think. Put him off guard, then jump in with the killer question, the one that undoes all that repellent, fake-aristocratic bearing.

Bartolo swung an arm over the back of his chair—the picture of composure. It would be with such a gesture that he would order his killings.

She sat forward on her chair, as if fascinated by the prospect of his answer.

'Yes,' he admitted. 'It is crucial that men of business who have achieved success ensure that the less fortunate of our country are given hope.'

It was all Martina could do not to snort. Dara did it for her, from a safe vantage point.

'Perhaps you could tell our viewers about some of these ventures.' She retained her attentive expression.

'Certainly.' He cleared his throat in a chairman of the board manner. 'I have founded an orphanage in the town of—'

Of course, an orphanage. What other institution would create an instant surge of sympathy. Bring on the photographs of hollow-eyed children playing baseball, eating bowls of nutritious *pozole*. He rattled off statistics, babies lost and found, and foster parents (vetted by the nuns) signed up, and the vast educational and vocational opportunities provided by this important charity. Of course it was a mere drop in the bucket, given the country's challenges...

She nodded vigorously, encouraging the recitation.

Back home, Alejandro was watching with trepidation: would she continue to behave herself?

'What do you see as the greatest problem that faces our country?' she asked. Quiz anyone beyond the studio and they would answer: security. Violence. Lack of a functioning justice system. Impunity. Corruption from top to bottom. Rule of the cartels.

Her viewers were getting edgy: how long would she allow El León to embellish his reputation?

Her guest touched his tie. 'We are creating legions of lost children, due to their parents' drunkenness, the desertion of fathers, drugs, broken families, intractable poverty, lack of education and literacy. If we can help these street kids thrive then we are helping the entire country.'

A rousing plea to the nation.

'These children that your organization helps are fortunate,' Martina said. 'They have been rescued from the streets and slums where they were threatened with starvation and heartbreaking abuse.' Now she looked directly into the camera, brow furrowed.

Our poor sainted children.

The website link for the Lion's organization ran along the bottom of the screen.

El León added his sympathetic expression to Martina's: they were a duet of the sensitive.

How many murders have you ordered, my friend? How many kidnappings and how many extortions have you supervised each day?

'Pardon?' he said, looking puzzled.

She must have muttered something aloud.

It had happened several times in the past year that she'd lost track of the interview while in its midst. She always managed to keep the same focused expression on her face —by now that was automatic—yet she would have no idea what question she'd just asked or what her guest had said in response. Luckily, only Dana seemed to have noticed these slips. Today was interview number 620 over a period of twenty-one years. She'd had the unsettling experience of interviewing someone whom she'd interviewed a dozen years earlier—and forgetting for several seconds which era they were in. The guest had suddenly aged, his cheeks grown haggard, and he'd lost his hair.

Back to the present moment.

'What do you view as your responsibility for any actions of your employees?'

A soft toss. Employees was one hell of a euphemism and they both knew it.

Flicker of tension at his mouth. 'Of course I am responsible for the actions of any employee who works on behalf of Bartolo Enterprises. I have no patience with CEOs who pretend that they are above the matters of daily organization, the small difficulties and crises that enter an office of consequence.' He nodded his head then said in heavily accented English: '*The buck stops here.*'

She chuckled. They were a cosmopolitan pair, weren't they? She pretended to consult her notes. 'There have been questions as to the nature of some aspects of your business.'

'Yes?' he said, unfazed. 'What sorts of questions? If your viewers think I will give away the secrets of my success—' Here he looked directly into the camera. 'Then all I have to say is that you must work very hard and not allow distractions and negativity to derail your project.'

For this banal advice she'd chucked the Nobel Peace Prize winner, the fundraiser for refugees, and a record number of foreign broadcasters signing on. In the living rooms of the nation, someone was tossing a shoe at his television set.

'Distractions such as what?' she pressed. 'Ethical considerations?'

His smile tightened, yet his eyes gazed at her with an expression of playfulness. She understood that he was enjoying the game, getting a kick out of her discomfort and her nerve—or lack thereof.

Perhaps, after all this time, he yearned to encounter an equal. Only weak men feared a challenge.

'Ethical considerations must enter the discussion,' he said. 'But perhaps you and I have different perspectives. What are

the stakes for you, *Señora* Gutiérrez, in making a decision?'
He paused to brood on this question. 'Perhaps not so great.
You decide what you are going to have for dinner, or what
questions you will ask your next guest—' He slid his arm
off the back of the chair so that he could press his palms
together. 'It is a matter of degree, of levels of complexity.'

'And what are the consequences of asking my guest the
wrong question?'

Now his smile verged on genuine. 'We will find out, yes?'

Martina felt a tingle of excitement and didn't bother looking at her index cards. Dana was waving, code for—'Get this
interview on track!'

The program was live; that was the source of its loyal following. What you saw was what was happening in real time,
minus the three-second pause in case a profanity was uttered.

'Then answer this: describe your personal involvement in
the illegal drug trade.'

The studio was silent, except for Dana's muffled gasp.

El León's smile didn't slip a notch, not a centimetre.

The opposite—his eyes looked her up and down; he was
sending that familiar message, the vanity of a man who
knows that he is attractive and is waiting for this knowledge
to be mirrored in her.

She leaned over, giving him a glimpse of decolletage.

'Your question betrays a great deal of ignorance, my friend.
You may be a beautiful woman, but you are not well informed.'

No tic of the eye, no signal issued to his bodyguard.

'So you deny that you are directly involved in illegal and
violent activities? That many people are terrified of El León,
and for good reason?' Her heart was ricocheting in her chest;
rarely had she felt so alive, and so near death. The television
lights burned and she reached for a glass of water.

'I have no control over how people perceive me. As you
know, the citizens of Mexico lack a certain sophistication—
they embrace the *macabre*.' This word was pronounced in
the French way, to indicate his degree of refinement. 'You

see the front pages of our newspapers—' He waved a hand in dismissal. 'A pornography of violence. This is not interesting or healthy. People should look at attractive images over their breakfast coffee. Great art or beautiful women. I don't understand this attachment to the ugly elements of life.'

'So you take no responsibility for the assassinations that plague Mexico?'

'I take responsibility for everything—and nothing. I am a citizen, as are you and even you—' He waved an imperious hand at the camera. 'We must all play our roles.'

'And how would you describe your role?'

Those manicured fingers laced together in a presidential pose. 'A leader, I would hope. But always, at heart, a businessman.'

'Do businessmen hire murderers to do away with competitors?'

Not even this question raised an eyebrow.

'You ask me to speak for other men? I wouldn't presume.'

'Do you hire murderers, Don Bartolo?'

Dana was making 'Cut' motions towards the cameraman, but Hernando was not about to go to music and the tranquil photograph of Palenque that appeared when technical troubles broadsided an interview.

'You are so interested in violence,' Bartolo said with a sigh. 'Why is everyone in this country obsessed with death? I am interested in life, as you should be.' Again, peering directly at the viewer: 'We must become modern people, not always looking towards the grave.'

Martina sat back in her leather chair and repositioned herself so that her legs were crossed the opposite way. She made a show of dropping her index cards on the on top of the catalogue of Gabriel Orozco's latest installation. She'd had the artist on her show soon after he graduated from art school; now, he was known all over the world.

'Let us be candid, *Señor* Bartolo,' she said in a new 'cut the bullshit' voice that her guest recognized for what it was:

another form of bullshit. 'You and I both know that you are one of the most dangerous men in Mexico. What I, and our viewers, want to understand is—why do you do this? How are you able to sleep at night?'

'I sleep very well. And I am the least dangerous man that you know. For any woman, the most dangerous man is her husband, or her lover.'

Tiny pause.

'Or a former lover.'

'I am afraid of you,' she said.

Only now did he offer a laugh that was merry. Then he reached over and patted her hand. 'You flatter me.'

Dana was waving. Time for the viewers' emails and texted questions. This part of the show was usually a breeze—Dana would hand over the printed questions and Martina would race through a few with her guest. It was a recent addition to the show; these days everyone expected to interact with a celebrated person.

Martina spoke to the camera: 'As always, we are interested in your comments and suggestions.'

Cut to the flower arrangement while Dana passed her the sheaf of printouts. It was almost comical how big the pile was, how messy in her lap.

She lifted the first sheet and read aloud:

How can you sit there and speak of orphanages? You, who have murdered the parents of those children who are now alone?

She forced herself to look at her guest. Never, in all these years, had she directly accused a guest of murder.

The man's smile froze, but there wasn't a hint of sweat on his brow, despite the television lights and his knotted tie.

'I'm afraid that your viewer lacks awareness of the situation.'

Period.

She was relieved to flip to the next email:

I sit here in my apartment, listening to you lie and lie and lie, and feel only disgust and shame—

Her voice quivered, but she soldiered on:

When will someone in this godforsaken country dare to tell the truth?

El León interrupted: 'Your viewer wishes that we would *"Speak truth to Power."'* He recited this phrase in English, not bothering to translate. 'Those in power must be held to account. Do you not agree, *Señora* Gutiérrez?' He leaned forward and clasped his crossed knees.

She met his gaze and stopped herself from lifting the water glass to her lips. It made a person appear nervous, to sip constantly. His face was open and transparent as if he were willing her to look within. She allowed the remaining sheets of paper to slip onto the coffee table.

Dana made a slashing motion with her hand and pointed to the clock.

A trio of female mariachis was bunching at the door, ready to step onto the stage and perform.

Martina pulled her gaze away from her guest and spoke to the camera, saying her customary wrap phrases, as if she'd just interviewed a scientist who'd made a important discovery, or an up-and-coming writer talking about his debut novel.

El León buttoned his jacket and rose to his feet. As he approached, camera still running, she felt a shudder of animal terror, but he merely reached for her hand and drew her fingers to his lips. Just for a second, she wondered if he was going to bite down, but this did not occur; instead, she felt moist lips brush her skin.

And then El León left.

His bodyguards flanked his tidy form as he disappeared down the gloomy hallway towards the bulletproof SUV parked at the rear of the station.

The mariachis climbed onto the set with their instruments, their studded costumes picking up the light. They'd performed for the president at his inauguration and since then had been on a roll, the novelty of attractive females playing traditional mariachi being irresistible. Martina shook their hands and settled back on her chair. Her knees wobbled, a sort of aftershock.

28

TOURISTS CLAD IN puffy winter coats over their shorts and
tank tops crowded onto the covered terrace, drinks in hand,
though it was barely ten a.m. A hard rain thudded on the
roof and streamed over its lip, creating a sheet of water.
Wind gusted across the sand, picking up trash from other
resorts. Staff dashed out to rescue the gaily striped lounger
cushions and dragged furniture into the shed. The glistening
Caribbean Sea had turned into a churlish grey mass hammering a coastline that threatened to become erased.

Iris hugged her cape around her shoulders and watched
her fellow guests stare gloomily into the distance. 'It's a
low-level tropical storm,' a man with a beard informed her.
'Expected to pass in a matter of hours.'

The temperature must have dropped twenty degrees. Iris
threaded between tables set up with playing cards and board
games. Few people were engaged in these pastimes; it felt too
grim, too desperate, too redolent of being trapped inside cottages in foul weather. A frazzled-looking woman was trying
to organize a quartet for bridge.

'I'd rather be back home,' someone grumbled.

Lydia had taken herself to the internet chamber. She was communicating with her ESL students back at the college. Iris viewed her daughter's employment with a mixture of admiration and alarm; classes were cancelled when enrollment was low and there were no benefits or pension. She wondered if Charlie was chipping in expenses. He'd always seemed like a dutiful man, but dutiful men did not flee their families.

Iris greeted her fellow guests on the terrace with a cheery hello and received rueful smiles in return and plastic cups lifted in salute. They were like children waiting to be given instructions. A staff member planted a handwritten sign announcing 'Casino in the Party Room, eleven a.m.'

Rain pelted down on a corner of the terrace that wasn't covered and a gust of wind caused everyone to shriek and drag the tables further in. Many guests were already well lubricated and had begun to sing rounds of what Iris recognized to be classic rock songs. Sweetly comical to watch portly middle-aged tourists bleating the rebellious songs of their youth. 'Rock the Casbah' indeed. She had her copy of *Catherine the Great* tucked under one arm, but it was far too noisy to concentrate on reading. The row of palm trees leaned sideways, leaves vibrating.

She spotted Gloria, girlfriend of the Zen priest, perched on a stool drinking beer alongside Lulu and Neil. No sign of Joe. Iris trotted over, rehearsing her opening line: Whatever that is you are drinking, I'll have two.

Gloria dragged in an empty stool with her bare foot.

'Where is Himself?' Iris asked as she settled in.

Gloria pointed to the sea.

'You lose the bet, my friends,' Neil shouted above the din. His cheeks were flaming red and he seemed huge next to his wife who sat on the rim of her stool, legs dangling, alert and excited.

Gloria, her grey hair caught in a ponytail, said, 'He's a damn fool,' but Iris could tell that she was pleased. They all stared through the rain at a speck that bobbed in the surf, arms wheeling.

Everyone was pressing the edge of the protected zone watching Joe as he thrashed in the sea, visible one moment, gone the next. Collective gasp as the tiny human disappeared into collapsing water. The surf made a constant undifferentiated roar and Iris could taste salty water as it spun into mist. Was there a lifeguard on duty? The raised stand was empty, dinghy chained beneath. A red 'danger' flag whipped wildly on its pole.

'I didn't think Joe would do it,' Gloria said. She was wearing a parka with yoga pants and Birkenstocks.

Joe hopped in the trough between waves, one arm raised in a hearty fist pump. There must be a hundred guests on the terrace at this point, Iris calculated, and most were two sheets to the wind—an appropriate metaphor. Gloria, who held disdain for Zen calm, was being entertained by Zen fortitude.

Neil draped an arm over Gloria's shoulder and said in a reassuring voice, 'He's not in over his head.'

'We're still a bit bombed from last night,' Lulu told Iris in her little-girl voice. 'We were the last ones standing at the bar. Staff had to boot us out.'

'We four ended up back in our suite,' Neil added. He was staring intently at the water.

'Joe taught us to meditate,' Lulu said. 'It was a riot.'

'I don't think Joe considers meditation to be a riot,' her husband said.

'I can never manage to sit still long enough to meditate,' Iris confessed, but no one was listening. She felt another pang: they'd found each other, these couples of a similar age.

Joe bobbed up and down, then disappeared again. Was anyone taking into account the possibility of a riptide? There he was, shooting out of a wave, only to be crushed by the next.

The man might require rescuing. This idea quietly took hold. Iris imagined herself pushing through the rain towards the foaming sea, life-saving pole clutched under her arm like a lance. Someone would capture the moment on his iPhone and send it hurtling through the blogosphere—she'd go viral. Wasn't that the term? She went so far as to stretch one leg out, testing her hip, which had been stiff this morning owing to the abrupt drop in barometric pressure.

Joe disappeared for several seconds under the water then popped up like a piece of driftwood. Gloria sat forward on her stool and Iris saw something vivid and alive in her face.

A ferocious gust sent the rain blowing sideways like so many tiny knives—and Joe was gone.

Gloria straightened. 'There!' she cried. 'His hand!'

If none of these hearty men and women was prepared to make a move, then it was up to Iris. They probably thought they were watching a movie. That's what people said these days, interviewed after some catastrophe: 'It happened in slow motion, just like in a movie.' No one knew what was real anymore, and now a man was going to drown because everyone believed they were watching a screen.

Iris gathered her cape over her head and stepped onto the pocked sand. She'd already kicked off her sandals—no sense in ruining perfectly good leather. The lifeguard's stall was a good thirty metres away. She'd have to tramp across the dinted sand, reach the pole and hook arrangement, and grab one of the life preservers. It wouldn't be easy, not in this wind that worked to push her backwards like a big insistent hand. Already she was soaked, cape plastered to her shoulders and chest. She strode forward, eyes squinting. It was all she could manage to keep a steady course. And what a racket! A moaning from the entire hemisphere; every tree and building had become an instrument through which wind shrieked. Was she crying? Certainly not: this was rain streaming down her cheeks. Hunched forward, she trod on like a woman in a Greek tragedy, crossing the island in search of her ship or lover.

Setting her hands on the rescue pole, Iris began to lift it from the pair of hooks. She could hardly see the water now—everything had turned into a grey gauze. She could just make out the frill of foam gleaming as it rose and fell then dissolved. No sign of Joe. She stepped on the hard packed sand that sloped towards water's edge, using the pole as a walking stick and realized, too late, that she'd neglected to grab the life preserver. Waves crashed and eddied around her ankles. Even in the shallows she could feel the suck of undertow. Her ankles cleaved into the sand; she was sinking, more shipwreck than Helen of Troy.

She felt a pair of strong arms grip her shoulders, followed by a male voice bellowing in her ear: 'What are you doing hiking in a typhoon?'

It was the domed head of Joe. He peered through the hammering rain into her eyes. 'Where is your daughter? Why isn't she taking care of you?'

'I don't require looking after,' Iris gasped as rain socked her mouth. She sounded like a stroke victim.

'We'll see about that,' Joe said, slipping an arm around her waist and aiming her towards the hotel patio.

Countless tourists were watching, gathered in a clump under the jutting roof.

The instant they arrived on terra firma, she shook her head and released herself from his grasp. She was breathing hard and shivering. This was exactly the sort of thing that could lead to pneumonia. There was a sudden, hectic burst of applause as the guests cheered the reappearance of the mariners.

Gloria swung off her stool to embrace her heroic monk, while Lulu, the pediatric dentist, raced to tend to the old lady who seemed to have ventured into the storm for no good reason.

Iris rallied: 'My room key blew out of my hand and I thought I could retrieve it.'

'I'm taking you back to your room,' said Lulu. 'Will your daughter be there to open the door?'

'I can manage, thank you,' she told the earnest Lulu. Grabbing her beach bag, Iris pulled her sodden cape over her shoulders and, head high, strode past the card players, teeth chattering inside her gritty smile.

The patio gave on to a corridor with several branches, one of which led to the main lobby. From there she could catch the little train to her room.

She stood in the corridor, disoriented. Was the lobby that way? She was shivering uncontrollably. Must douse herself under a hot shower—but which direction was the Toucan wing?

Iris felt it rise in her, the urge to weep. It didn't come often, only when she felt overwhelmed, all efforts thwarted. It was a challenge to find a place to be alone in this massive resort, yet this was exactly what she was now: alone. Surely a staff person would erupt from behind a door and Iris would laugh lightly and say, 'I seem to have lost my bearings.' They were all so sweet and considerate and would lead her to her room without making a fuss about it.

But no one appeared and she stumbled down the hallway, one hand brushing the wall for balance. Let this be a lesson, Iris told herself severely. If she were to end up in a local hospital suffering from severe pneumonia, as she had years ago, a result of wintering in Jake's frigid studio, it would serve her right for attempting an attention-getting rescue.

She paused in the hallway, not at all sure this was the right direction.

Finally, a door did open.

An old man and a girl stepped out, he holding her hand in a grandfatherly way. Iris nodded politely, then let out a choke of recognition: it was Don Victor, the painter. Or Javier, as she'd once known him. He seemed as surprised to see her as she was him. Her eyes scanned the artist's face then the girl's—this was no granddaughter.

Victor dropped the girl's hand. 'What has happened to you?'

Iris wondered if the expression 'drowned rat' existed in Spanish. She repeated the fiction about her room key spinning in the wind and how she'd attempted to chase it down. During this speech the girl lazily scratched her bare belly, fingernails trailing over a tattoo of a rose. Her hair was mussed; the room from which they'd emerged had a sign reading 'Games/Juegos.'

Victor spoke a few words to the girl and she shrugged then waltzed down the hall.

'I will accompany you back to your room,' he said and offered Iris his arm.

She took it. Truth was, she was feeling wobbly.

'We are not so young, you and I,' he said.

'Who was the *chica*?' She heard the sting of irritation in her voice.

For a moment he did not answer and it seemed that he meant not to.

'I forget her name,' he finally said.

'I've seen her before,' Iris pressed.

'Possibly.'

Then Iris got it. 'She's the gal who works in the boutique.' She stopped in the hallway. 'Don't tell me...'

'When women say "Don't tell me," they mean the opposite.'

Her lips were numb from cold and she shivered so violently that he grasped her whole body, rubbing her up and down as one does to a small child who has stepped out of the tub.

'You must get out of these clothes.'

She nodded and felt pathetically grateful for his care. She wasn't up to flagging down the train and heaving herself onto its seat. The very idea of stepping back outside brought on another attack of shivering. Victor steered her in an unexpected direction; it turned out there was a tunnel between the main kitchen and the Toucan wing. They stepped cautiously down the service stairs then made their way through a huge work area where dozens of cooks in aprons and checked trousers were busy at their stations. Iris perked up; she always liked being backstage. No one seemed alarmed by their presence and she was pleased to note that everything looked spic and span. They marched along until they arrived at another set of stairs at the far end of the tunnel. Here, they paused briefly while Iris gathered her soaked cape so that she would not trip while climbing. From there it was a short hike outside to reach the pavilion.

Iris knocked several times on her door, because, of course, it was locked. No answer. After all that business of the errant key that she'd invented to save her pride, she reached into her bag and plucked the key card from a zippered pouch. She held it in the air as if it were a great discovery, though it was clear that Victor was not the least surprised by its appearance. He understood the need to create diversion from one's weaknesses.

Upon entering the room, Iris switched off the air conditioning and swung open the balcony door. The rain had stopped and sun cracked between heavy clouds. The air was so humid she could drink it in a pinch. A pair of monkeys squawked in the nearby palm tree, hoping for a forbidden snack.

'Bible rays,' she noted, pointing to the horizon. Between billowing clouds, the hazy rays of sun streaked down.

He was at her side, reaching to unbutton her blouse.

'What are you doing?' she stuttered.

'You are cold and wet.'

They were speaking in English. Just as well; she was incapable of recalling anything but the mother tongue. Iris stood near the open balcony door and allowed him to unfasten her blouse and peel it from her drenched flesh. He'd already hung her cape over the back of a chair; it would take days to dry.

He worked her sodden pants down to her ankles and stood back, letting her step out of them. She was down to bra and panties. There was a time, not so long ago, when she would have stood proudly naked in the light of day, aware of a man's approving gaze.

She half-hoped her daughter would return now as the

National Treasure reached behind her back, chin grazing hers as his practised fingers unhooked her strap. The bra dropped to the floor and her breasts swayed, unfettered. They were still full and unlined, more than presentable. His thumbs slipped under the elastic of her panties and slid them over her ample bottom and hips, down to her ankles, until she was able to step out of them. He had to crouch on the floor to do this. Creakily, and pressing a hand to his knee as leverage, Victor rose to his feet. He examined her body, taking his time. 'Beautiful,' he said in his raspy voice. Then—'Come to bed.'

'What are you going to do?'

'Make you comfortable.'

Searching in the cupboard for an extra blanket, he tucked her into the queen-sized bed and pulled the curtain across the balcony door.

Her eyelids were heavy as she watched Victor tug off his shirt and wiggle out of his cotton trousers. Underneath he wore exactly nothing. When he snuggled in next to her, Iris sighed in gratitude. His presence was medicinal. Warmth flowed from his papery skin to hers.

Immediately she fell asleep.

When she awoke half an hour later, she felt a weight on her thigh and realized that Victor had flung a leg over hers. His creased face was so close that she could count his eyelashes. She superimposed that other face she'd known decades earlier and wondered if he was doing the same with her.

'Were you watching me sleep?' she asked, unnerved.

'Of course.'

She was warm but not hot, nothing feverish. She felt his genitals slump against her thigh, then stiffen with a modest jerk of attention. He gave a little hum then reached to push a lock of wet hair away from her forehead.

'You are the only one who knows who I am,' he said. 'People believe that I am this peasant who works in clay and grinds his own pigments and lives in his shack on the mountain. What they don't understand is that I am hiding. Hiding all these years. From you.'

Oh please. Still, Iris couldn't help but feel flattered. The old boy knew all the lines.

'Don't be ridiculous,' she said.

'Not just from you, of course,' he conceded. 'I must stay away from everyone who knew me in those days.' Her hair had fallen back over her face and he fastened it behind her ear. 'Any of those guys could—blow my cover.' He was proud at nailing the idiomatic expression in English.

'Would that be so terrible?' She felt his other hand roam down her back then settle between her legs.

'Maybe not,' he mused.

Iris could tell that he enjoyed talking about himself, weighing various possibilities. She wondered if his current wife was an uneducated girl from the hills. He wouldn't want someone who was too curious, with ambitions of her own and a knack for surfing the web. She would wear traditional embroidered dresses, suitable for the wife of El Pintor. Perhaps at this moment she was squatted on a stool slapping masa into tortillas.

'I'll take you home with me,' Victor went on. 'You will be safe; I will be safe. You'll learn to cook like a Mexican.'

'I don't think so, Victor.' She stifled a yawn, placing a hand over her mouth in case her breath was foul. The image was briefly tantalizing: she bet his house was perched high on the mountain with a view of the valley. There would be a limitless sky, unobstructed by buildings or dimmed by city lights. She could learn about constellations and astral navigation. After a time, she might write a memoir of her experience, the sort of thing that would catch on: elderly woman reinvents herself in a foreign land.

He made a show of pouting. 'Only you can tell me who I am.'

'And who will tell me who I am?'

He giggled, an odd sound coming from the National

Treasure.

'In a short while you'd want someone different,' she said, recalling the girl from the boutique.

The hand burrowed between her legs, but she was too numb to feel anything.

'You don't believe me,' he said.

'Do you not have political obligations?'

He snorted. 'They invited a killer to dine with us last night. Can you imagine? I'm an artist—they thought I wouldn't know. I must return to my village: what else can I do?'

She recognized the tone; he was waiting for her to rescue him from the life he'd fashioned. She reminded him of his earlier self, that young man who'd made out with the pretty foreigners and craved a studio in New York's SoHo district. He'd imagined himself dashing uptown for openings in his denim jacket and long black hair, girls everywhere. His young eyes peered at her from his crinkled face.

Oh, hello hand. He gripped the skin of her thigh. Perhaps they could delude each other for a few weeks or months.

The maid pushed her cart down the hallway, a grinding sound followed by a knock on the door. Don Victor raised his head. '*Quién es?*' he called.

Short pause while the maid sorted out this voice. She replied in English: 'Enedina,' and began to slip her key card through the slot.

Iris pulled the sheet up so that her breasts were covered. Let Enedina make of the scene what she would.

29

THE WOMAN WHOSE name tag read *Rosa* flipped Lydia over like a fish on a platter and started pummeling her back. The air was heavy with the fragrance of lemons and a soundtrack played rhythmic surf noise. In the resort's Paradise Spa, recorded sound mimicked the real noises that existed outside its walls. Lydia dangled her injured wrist alongside the massage bed. Beside her, on an identical platform, Iris moaned as a masseuse dug into her fleshy back.

There had been an unsettling event that Lydia still couldn't get her mind around. Iris had ventured into the heart of the storm in search of her room card. Just like her mother to chase after it, instead of sensibly asking Cleo at front desk for a replacement. Was she one hundred percent all right in the head?

Gloria lay at the other end of the spa, getting the hot stone treatment. Moments earlier, she'd said in her throaty voice, 'Joe has me do this Tantric sex thing.'

Synthesized parrots squawked. Lydia pressed her face into the stirrup, a pouch covered with a hygienic cloth. 'Ouch!' Rosa had dug her thumb into a hard nub at the back of her head.

'We sit cross-legged and face each other without moving,' Gloria went on. 'You ever been in an erotic trance?'

'Can't say I have,' Iris reported dreamily.

'The universe slows down. Sex takes forever, a lifetime.' Gloria gave a muffled laugh.

'I don't know if I'd like that,' Iris said. 'Seems to me it takes long enough as it is.'

Steam rose from the mud bath. Lydia and Iris had splashed around there first, preparatory to this energetic massage. The idea was to keep Iris warm, the blood circulating.

'What mischief have you ladies been up to?' Gloria asked.

'Since you ask,' Iris said, 'it turns out I've been offered the chance to upend my life again.'

'If someone is upending her life,' Gloria said, 'then we want to know about it.'

Iris let her chin rest on her hands. 'You may recall this man with a distinctive appearance who recently arrived at La Pirámide.'

'The fellow you were dancing with at the fiesta?' Gloria asked.

'The very one. He is an eminent artist.'

Rosa lifted one of Lydia's legs and began to slap the flesh briskly, then lowered it and resumed digging into flesh with her thumbs, stalking the meridian from ankle to knee.

'He has proposed that I join him in his house in some mountain town,' Iris said.

This caused a rare moment of silence from the women.

Lydia raised her head. 'You can't be serious.'

Rosa lifted Lydia's good arm, pulled on it once, then crooked it at the elbow and began to work on the palm, pushing her thumbs into the doughy mounds. Lydia gasped; the probe seemed to attack her ovaries, a flash of white heat.

Iris didn't answer the question directly. 'What would it be like to embark on a radically new life at this stage of the game? Mistress of a sainted artist, living in some dusty town, chasing chickens off the patio? Would I start grinding cochineal, to help El Pintor create his pigments?'

200

'What's cochineal?' Gloria wanted to know.

'A parasitical insect that lives off cacti,' Iris supplied. 'Used to create crimson dyes.'

Rosa tugged on each finger in turn, finishing the gesture by tweaking the tips hard. 'Are you tired of Steve already?' Lydia asked, when she'd recovered.

'By no means, though I do wonder if this marriage is destined to be my final chapter.' Iris wriggled on her bed. She sounded strained, even a bit desperate. It was alarming, this new tone, and Lydia wondered if her mother was feeling trapped by the relentless march of age, the sensation of doors closing.

Rosa muttered an instruction and Lydia obliged by turning over to her other side. A towel was adjusted. Squirt of lavender oil basted her skin.

'And what did you decide?' Gloria asked.

Lydia half expected Iris to say, 'How can I say no to such an intriguing offer?' but instead her mother replied in a subdued voice: 'I don't want to live in a godforsaken hill town with some old man I barely know. It sounds too queer, too hard, too far away.'

Never had she heard her mother speak this way, with grave acceptance of her fate.

30

MARTINA BATTED away the idea, but here it was, creeping at the edge of consciousness: she found the assassin attractive.

Perhaps 'attractive' was the wrong word. Yet it was a heady business to feel that a man was so unthreatened by her. As she'd ramped up her questions he had not sprung to defend himself or dismiss her observations. He didn't care a damn what the viewing audience thought of him, for the Lion would continue doing exactly as he wished.

The taxi dropped her off in front of the apartment. When the kids left home to enter their various enterprises, it had been she who insisted that they scale down, sell the centuries-old money pit that leaked, and move to this apartment in a mid-century modernist building that their now-deceased friend had designed. Not a flashy piece of architecture, but solid, featuring clean lines and plenty of light.

Hector, the concierge, looked up from his newspaper. 'Flowers for you, *Señora*.'

She warily plucked the bouquet from Hector's hands. Gifts from assassins should be treated with caution. She flipped open the tiny card while stepping into the elevator.

You are a formidable woman.

This brief message was followed by his initials. The bouquet itself was a conventional, albeit expensive, mix of cultivated roses, obviously chosen by his secretary.

Martina smiled as the elevator doors popped open on the fifth floor.

Alejandro was pacing the living room and she could see that he'd been into the booze, an open bottle of whisky and a glass holding a single melting ice cube.

'Excellent tactic: humiliate the man in front of a good portion of the country,' he began in a shrill tone. 'What did you think you were doing? Do you really want to collapse my campaign? Because I think that's where this is going. You don't want to see me succeed. You don't want to mess with the balance of power in this household.' His voice lifted with outrage and during the speech, Martina stepped out of her high heels and placed them neatly on the mat, then unbuttoned her jacket and hung it in the closet.

He made a show of clapping his hand against his forehead. 'That man is dangerous—you don't seem to understand this fact.'

She hunted for a black pottery vase, souvenir from the state of Oaxaca, filled it with water, and arranged the flowers. Then she stood back and looked at it, reached and made an adjustment until the arrangement suited her. She was aware of her husband's penetrating gaze. No hurry to calm his fears; if it hadn't been for his recklessness, she would have concluded the interview with Ms. Brisbois by now and money for refugees would be flowing in from all corners of the world.

Alejandro didn't understand that El León was not interested in another frightened citizen seeking approval, treating him with obsequious caution. Much more refreshing to be taken on as an equal. It was an instinct nurtured after years in show business that had led Martina to ask prickly questions after she'd seen boredom creep into her guest's face.

She poured herself a drink and pretended not to notice that her husband was staring fiercely, waiting for her to protest so that he might escalate the scene. Her mind darted back to the stage set, to the lithe man who sat with an arm flung over the back of his chair, legs crossed, the material of his suit perfectly creased.

She dropped onto the white couch and set her stockinged feet on the coffee table.

She yawned. Her toes played with the latest copy of *Hola* magazine. They were sent a free subscription. Friends could be found between its covers flouncing from one charity to another or participating in roundtable discussions where brilliant ideas were expressed and nothing was ever achieved.

Alejandro picked up one of the sofa cushions and threw it against the fireplace. He winced, his back acting up, as it did when he was under stress.

Formidable.

She quite liked the word. An image blew through her brain, so quickly that she barely had time to acknowledge it: she was in the back of the assassin's SUV, straddling his lap, her hand yanking the zipper of those expensive trousers. His head tilted back, eyes shut, arms at his side. Helpless.

'You seem to have no comprehension of what you have just done,' Alejandro told her and the room jolted back.

He'd stopped pacing and the candlesticks and decorative plates no longer trembled on the mantel. She lifted one hand and made a dismissive motion.

Now he sounded worried in a different way. 'You seem drugged.'

'I have not taken drugs, Alejandro. As for the Lion who makes you shiver in your boots, I don't think we need to fear him.'

'Because?' Chin jutting out.

'He and I have come to an understanding.'

'Really?' Scoffing—but interested. 'What is the nature of this understanding?'

'If you leave this matter in my hands—' She trailed off. That image again, her hand unleashing the stiff prick of the murderer.

'I don't understand,' Alejandro said. He was buttoning the front of his jacket, ready for battle.

His hair stuck straight up, electrified. She'd thought, years ago, that he would settle down, given the passage of time. This did not happen. She was half-pleased that he hadn't mellowed, for there was nothing middle-aged about Alejandro; he was the same charged-up guy she'd met when they were grad students at UNAM, he in political science, she enrolled in Literature of the Hispanic Countries. He ran the student paper and she already had her own program on the university's radio station, emitted at such a low frequency that her own family couldn't tune in. This was many years after the massacre at Tlatelolco and a new generation of student activists was beginning to appear out of the darkness.

She reached up and tugged the vent of his jacket. 'Luis Bartolo is not angry,' she said. 'Look.' She nodded at the flowers sitting on the antique telephone table.

'From him?' Alejandro was shaken.

'So it seems.'

Alejandro wasn't convinced. Flowers from an assassin could mean anything, could be a coded message meaning— prepare yourself for a funeral.

'A powerful man yearns to be challenged,' she said.

'How do you know this?'

She gave him an arch look. 'Sit down and put your head in my lap.'

This was their habitual posture at the end of the day when Alejandro fell onto her like a languid house cat. Soon he was purring in her lap, a damp furry creature, while her fingers raked through his tousled hair. The sun disappeared behind the neighbouring highrise and the room became cool as well as dark, the furniture retreating into shadow.

As always, sirens wailed below and drivers pressed their horns, the ever-present soundscape that always seemed louder after sundown.

Dinner was going well. Alejandro, after his nap, was as relaxed as he ever allowed himself to be. Perhaps he could sip wine without falling into some dreadful hole of need. He seemed to be proving this ability now in the restaurant, lifting his wine to his lips with no show of urgency. He'd shaved and changed his shirt and combed his hair and looked the part of a future state governor. Walking the few short blocks to the restaurant, they'd passed a rally of supporters who, upon spotting Alejandro, had charged towards him with their signs, pleading for autographs. Martina stood aside, watching as her husband pulled out his Sharpie and complied, then gave an off-the-cuff speech. Polls reported that his numbers were surging. His face was on the cover of *Proceso* magazine. Even the most jaded reporters sensed that change was in the air.

Guests in the restaurant noticed their entrance; Alejandro's image was plastered everywhere these days and she, of course, was used to recognition. A quartet of well-dressed men approached their table and each shook Alejandro's hand and wished him well, then turned to Martina and said, 'Honoured to meet you, *Señora*.'

It was hard not to feel like the golden couple. By the way Alejandro was glowing, she suspected he felt it was true, that they were somehow blessed, yet she understood that these admirers might not vote for her husband. They were simply covering all eventualities in the event that he might win.

The neighbourhood restaurant served food typical of the region; they were happily eating fish coated with a light batter and plenty of peppery sauce and a cactus salad laced with peanuts. The glass showcase tempted with half a dozen desserts, though Martina would stay clear of them; the camera was not kind to an extra pound or two. This evening she wore a jacket decorated with a bold yellow and black geometric pattern. Magenta lipstick. As a public figure, she wasn't about to step out in jeans and sneakers.

She tilted her head so that her chin sharpened.

Her husband was talking between mouthfuls of fish; she must pursue this curious relationship with—here he lowered his voice to a whisper—'Luis Bartolo. Put that together with our arrangement with Don Victor and—'

'Are you so sure about the painter?'

'He is remaining at the resort, which is an excellent sign.' Alejandro topped off their wine. 'He is finding that he rather likes the lap of luxury. Tomorrow I will head back there and we will finalize our agreement.' Alejandro ripped his tortilla in half and used it as a scoop for his rice. This was the sort of restaurant where it was expected that patrons would eat in the old way. 'You should come.'

He looked so eager and youthful with his smooth cheeks and clear bright eyes. Did he look at her and see someone who had suddenly aged? She checked his expression for ill-concealed surprise; so far he'd been careful—or else he truly didn't notice any change in her. Alejandro had the knack of seeing only himself mirrored in the faces of others.

They were surrounded by the muted clatter of diners. This restaurant appealed because the music was discreet and one could talk without shouting. The other guests were, for the most part, of their generation—except for two young men sitting near the entrance. They'd come in late, hence their position by the door. They'd nodded at Martina as they settled in and she'd nodded back. It pleased her that a new generation found her program to be of interest.

Alejandro slid a hand across the tablecloth and grasped hers. 'I am fully aware that I am the luckiest man on earth to have you as my lover and life partner,' he told her.

Uh huh.

'I am too impulsive; you see things that I don't see. You have feminine wisdom.'

Martina could have rolled her eyes, but she didn't. This was because she was looking past his shoulder at the young men who kept casting glances their way. When she caught them at it, they offered stiff smiles.

'Alejandro,' she said, leaning forward so that she could speak in a near-whisper. 'I would like us to leave now.'

'But we—'

'Just do as I say,' she said and placed her napkin next to the plate that was still full of food.

'Are you ill?'

'I'm going to act as if I am receiving an important call and you are to follow me without question.'

Now he looked alarmed. 'What's going on?'

'Possibly nothing.' She had already pulled out her phone and was peering at the screen, making a show of texting, though she was tapping random letters that the screen insisted on turning into words. She was thinking fast: leave via kitchen or front door? Front door was more natural. She shrugged her shoulders as if to say 'I have been summoned, what can I do?' and was on her feet, fingers raised for the bill.

She spoke in a clear voice to the waiter: 'I must race off to a meeting.'

She smiled courteously at the two young men as she strode past, opening the door to the chilly street that was crowded with pedestrians and kiosks selling snacks and newspapers. Half the population of the city appeared to be roaming the sidewalks this clear winter evening. Three policemen stood guard outside the bank, eyes staring straight ahead, semi-automatic rifles stashed under their arms. A pose of alert boredom. No one went to the cops for help; they were just as likely to be pitching for the other side. That was one of Alejandro's campaign pledges: clean up the force. Others had tried and all had failed.

Alejandro trotted to keep up. Martina felt her heart cartwheel; where was a taxi when you needed one? She angled into the traffic, hand raised, and after a moment a cab pulled a U-turn and swerved to curbside. Casting a final glance towards the restaurant, she let Alejandro open the door and they slid into the back seat.

'Where to?' Alejandro asked his wife.

'Home.'

He didn't speak until they reached their building, understanding that discretion was called for. During the brief trip he sat upright, face staring straight ahead. He had a slim aristocratic nose, so different from the wide flat noses of the Maya, though he was *mestizo*, as were most of their crowd—a mix of the conquerors and the indigenous tribes. Maybe that's why they were such a brittle nation: they couldn't figure out, even within themselves, if they were friend or foe.

Neither spoke until they'd stepped off the elevator and into their apartment.

'What was all that about?' Alejandro said, switching on the lights.

She set down her purse and hung up her jacket. 'I had an uneasy feeling about those two parked by the door. Why would two young guys want to hang out at such a stodgy place?'

'Perhaps you are on edge because of what happened last Wednesday.'

He meant the killings in their favourite Italian restaurant.

'Maybe.' She shivered, though the apartment was warmer than the street, then picked up the remote control and switched on the gas fireplace. This was a new feature of the apartment. Their friend, the eminent architect, would roll over in his grave if he could see how they'd desecrated the space with such a suburban fixture.

'I could phone Mauro and ask if the men are still there,' Alejandro said.

Maura was the owner of La Ruta Maya restaurant.

Martina moved to the window that faced west and would have an unfettered view towards the sea if it weren't for the neighbouring skyscraper. An eyesore so shabbily built that it was expected to collapse within the decade.

'I don't think it was Mauro and his restaurant that they were after.' She stepped away from the window. 'They were interested in you and me. Perhaps just one of us.'

'Because you are beautiful and famous.'

'Possibly.'

'We can't live like this,' he said. 'Running from our everyday lives. If we are to press on with this campaign—' Alejandro dropped a hand onto the fireplace mantel. Blue flames lit up his face, an eerie phenomenon. 'Tell me to stop, and I will. I can't bear it if you are frightened.' If he'd quit with this statement, she would have been impressed, but he kept going, sensing the nobility of his gesture. 'If you are afraid, then tell me now and I will immediately withdraw my name from the slate.' This was uttered in his sonorous public voice.

She perched on the armrest of the upholstered chair. 'Seeing those two men stare at us—' She let out a long breath. 'I felt ice.'

31

EQUIPPED WITH bottles of water and a tube of sunscreen, Bob, Lydia, and Iris jammed into the back of an ancient car driven by a kid called Dimitri. His father, he explained, was from the Greek island of Santorini.

Bob wedged between mother and daughter in the back seat. 'You won't regret this excursion,' he assured them, then spoke to Dimitri, who replied in Spanish. They were on the way to the ruins that Bob swore were hidden in the jungle, unknown to tourists. While a bus stuffed with hotel guests roared down the road towards the temples in the ancient walled city of Tulum, Bob told the two women about a recently discovered splinter tribe from the Maya, a separate culture that died out after only 150 years. It was the ruins of this brief civilization that they were soon to visit. Perhaps these people were killed by the real Maya who found their existence irksome, he speculated. There was reference to the offshoot tribe in the Maya codices; they were called Xenotahul, the 'X' pronounced with a 'sh' sound.

'Noted for imagining a universe that could be measured end to end,' Bob added.

'Richard, my first husband, would approve,' Iris said. 'Being a forensic tax attorney.'

Dimitri drove down the road that led through town and shot out the other end onto the highway. After twenty minutes, they swerved east onto a side road, surrounded by scrubby Yucatan landscape. Mid-morning humidity clung to their skin. Lydia gripped the back of the seat ahead as they clanged along the pebbly surface. Everyone swatted at no-see-ums that swept in through the open windows.

'What about Luis Bartolo?' Lydia said quietly. 'He will send his car and I will not be there.'

Bob clawed at his wispy beard. 'Best that none of us is present.'

She heard in his tone a new formality.

The gravel disappeared and they bumped along a dirt road that passed through a modest settlement, no more than a cluster of shacks with laundry hanging from branches, sad-sack dogs lolling in the sun, and a pungent smell of burning brush and garbage.

'Last end of nowhere,' Iris said cheerily.

Bob sat up straight but his eyes were half shut. He was so thin that his collarbone created troughs of sweat. They entered a rutted single-lane road through the jungle and Bob spoke to Dimitri in a low voice. The driver steered to an even rougher trail that was close to being a burro path, so narrow that they cranked up the windows, despite the oppressive heat, to keep the tangle of foliage from scratching their faces. The car became a sauna, with the jungle pressing in, flailing at doors and closed windows. Dimitri swung the wheel and lurched on, though perhaps not as slowly as he should. Lydia gritted her teeth with each bump and rattle.

A grey bird with frilled wings sailed overhead and disappeared into the greenery.

Bob slapped the top of the driver's seat; Dimitri hit the brakes and the sound of leaves sweeping over grass and metal suddenly stopped. Everyone flung open the doors, desperate to escape.

'I could use an ice-cold margarita,' Iris said and held out her hand as if a waiter were poised nearby.

Bob spoke to Dimitri; some arrangement was being made. Then he clapped his arms around the two women and prompted them to move along the trail that was only navigable walking in single file. Casting a glance backwards, Lydia watched Dimitri lean on the bumper of the car and pull out a cigarette.

'Not far,' Bob said, taking the lead.

There were several levels of foliage, the mossy carpet then knee-stinging grasses and spiky plants that flashed in a sunburst pattern. Higher up, stunted trees bristled with leaves that broke sunlight into diamonds. The hikers were accompanied by a constant insect thrum, though now and then they stepped into patches of quiet, where monkeys and insects and birds seemed to agree to quit their noise, though there was nothing to indicate why this was so. The air felt sodden and particulated with decaying vegetable matter.

'Don't touch a tree that looks like this,' Bob warned, pointing to a trunk with pale bark and inky sap oozing down its side. 'Black Poisonwood. The Maya call it the Chechem Tree.'

Lydia wanted to know the gory details: what would happen to a person who brushed its flank?

'Worse than poison ivy, doll,' Bob said. 'Blisters bubble all over the skin and they last for weeks.'

'You sound like someone who knows from experience.'

He swung around so that he was walking backwards, facing them. 'I thought I had smallpox.'

'I'm sure you both know,' Iris said, panting, 'that some claim Native Americans were deliberately infected with smallpox blankets, fiendishly offered by British and American soldiers.'

They stepped into a dark area where the trees were more densely packed and bird racket softened. The trail become spongy.

'The tale may be apocryphal,' Iris went on, 'but I've never felt comfortable with those striped Hudson's Bay blankets, so popular with tourists.'

Lydia knew this statement was not true. Growing up, all the beds in the family house sported such blankets.

'How much further, Bob?' Lydia asked. Not because she was tired, but because she feared Iris was, and would never admit it.

'Remember that the journey is the destination,' Bob intoned.

Iris's breathing had become laboured. A metallic blue butterfly fanned its wings as it balanced on a leaf. That cawing sound belonging to the Yucatan Jay; insects and creatures they'd never heard of buzzed and cheeped and howled, so many pixels per square inch. They paused in a thicket of variegated green tones, ranging from olive to chartreuse, all shimmering. It was as if they'd had cataracts peeled off and this was the cleaned-up world, almost too intense to bear. Bob stood, hands on hips. Sweat coated his brow and upper lip.

Lydia lifted the plastic water bottle, took a slug, and passed it to her mother, who drank and made a face: the water was tepid. Bob stared straight ahead and following his gaze to a clearing, Iris let out a muted gasp. 'Is that the edge of a building?'

'Correct,' said Bob.

Lydia's eyes adjusted to the uptick in brightness. 'One of those eco-tourism hotels,' she said, feeling hopeful. There would be a spring-fed pool and cold drinks and hammocks strung up by a grotto. Off the grid, but lacking no amenities.

The threesome pressed forward, careful to avoid a stand of Poisonwood trees that was surrounded by a halo of butter-flies. A sudden glottal squawking made them jump as they entered the clearing. Light fell unfiltered and it was like step-ping on stage, into floodlights.

The ruins.

A large open area had been hacked out of the jungle, machete marks still visible on bamboo stalks. A moss-covered hill loomed twenty metres high and the cracked stone that poked out from its side like an elbow was carved with a frieze softened by time and the elements. Lydia ran her fingers along its pebbly surface. She had the sensation of touching something ancient and vulnerable.

'Think back to 600 A.D.,' Bob said. 'The tribe grabbed their belongings and fled from the main Mayan settlement. Perhaps they were being harassed or even murdered for their strange beliefs. This site is what is left. We expect there is much more to be uncovered. Each hill may hide a building, a tomb, a pyramid.'

Iris stumbled on the uneven ground then righted herself. 'I know all about the Maya,' she said. 'They were great astronomers, mathematicians, and keepers of time.'

'They predicted the end of the world a few years back,' Lydia added.

'The Maya measured time,' Bob said, 'while the Xenotahul measured space and the visible world. For this treacherous skill, they became mortal enemies.'

'Perhaps measuring what is visible was too literal for the Maya,' Iris mused. 'Even when space doesn't appear to be empty, it's always framed by something. If it were up to me, we'd ditch time. I don't like the way it creeps up on one.'

'The site is known only to a select group,' Bob said, lowering his voice. 'Tourists and locals would pick it clean.'

Iris peered at the stone frieze, running her fingers along its indentations. 'I see fossilized insects and other embedded creatures. And there's a stick etched alongside.'

It was Lydia who got it: 'A ruler.'

'Correct.' Bob lifted his hat and created shade over the stone so that the markings stood out. 'They took it upon themselves to measure everything in their world. The temporal was not to their liking.'

'Time is the great unknown that scares us all, because it leads to death,' Iris said. 'Am I becoming overly philosophical?'

'Such a place encourages metaphysical speculation,' Bob said. 'It is thought that this marks a tomb for tribal elders.'

As he spoke, a monkey with a blond beard scampered over the hill and disappeared around the other side.

'Who else knows about this site?' Iris asked. Her breathing sounded asthmatic.

'Very few,' Bob said. 'Word gets out and the place will be swarmed.'

The resort seemed very far away, its breezes and implausible luxuries and manicured jungle a barely remembered dream.

Lifting the edge of his shirt to wipe his face, Bob danced away from them, so light on his feet he left no imprint on the scattered leaves. He was an elderly elf, Lydia decided. He called over his shoulder, 'We are approaching the village square.'

This open area was oblong-shaped, flanked on three sides by a series of steep hillocks, each the height of a three-storey building and levelled on top. The area was starting to make sense as a village commons.

The hilly structures, covered in moss and dense foliage, felt architectural, the nucleus of some ancient city, blanketed by centuries of jungle growth.

The visitors paused, sweat pooling on their skin. Clearing her throat, Iris recalled aloud the sites she'd explored decades earlier with Richard, then Jake. They'd climbed the hacked-out steps of vertiginously steep pyramids.

'No ropes to cling to in those days.'

Striding forward until she reached the centre of the square, Iris said decisively, 'The ball court.'

'No, no,' Bob shook his head. 'You are thinking conventionally. It is thought that citizens used the plaza for a scarily efficient system of justice, a form of outdoor courtroom.' He indicated the tallest hill. 'Those deemed guilty were executed up there. You have to understand that they took their measuring very seriously—and temporal calendars were illegal. Blasphemous.' He made a slashing motion across his neck.

Iris used her shawl to wipe her upper chest.

They should have been warned to wear proper walking shoes, not sandals. And what about ticks, Lydia wondered. Not to mention snakes and fire ants. Sun belted down. Dark glasses were a meek defence.

'Shall we clamber up one of these hills?' Iris said in a tone of forced enthusiasm.

'You don't have to, Mum,' Lydia said.

Her mother glared; that settled it, she would start to climb the steepest, highest mound, though perhaps, if Bob didn't mind, she'd hang on to his elbow. Did anyone bring a cell phone to snap the view from the top? Phones were, it turned out, locked back in the hotel room safes. No service out here.

They dragged themselves upwards. Lydia unsnapped her bandage and stuffed it in her pocket. Pale skin seemed to gasp in the daylight, grateful for release. She made a fist and let go.

Iris turned to beam at her daughter. 'We are treading over the executioner's arena,' she puffed. 'I'm seeing a machete as his tool, or possibly an indigenous form of the guillotine.'

'It was a type of guillotine,' Bob said. 'And the executioner was not hooded; it was considered an honour to pull the shaft that would allow the blade to fall.'

They were silent for a moment, hearing that blade hit bone.

Iris was not looking well. Lydia glanced at her surreptitiously, for her mother hated to be seen as frail. Violet circles had appeared under her eyes, a sign of dehydration.

'Give me some of that,' Iris said, pointing to Lydia's bottle; she'd polished off her own water while still in the car.

As they stood drinking the heated water, hundreds of possibly malaria-infected mosquitos swarmed. The high-pitched whining continued as another sound formed, a low mechanical rumble that seemed to erupt from one end of the sky and cross to the other, creating a basin of sound. A small plane dipped and circled then sloped towards what must have been a landing strip in the east.

Bob made a visor with his hand and stared at the aircraft. 'You know what that is.'

'Rich tourists?' Lydia guessed.

'Archaeologists arriving from the capital?' Iris added.

'You are both wrong.' Bob continued to track the plane's descent.

It took Lydia a moment. 'Drug smugglers.'

'Pickup from the coast,' Bob said. 'They haul coca from boats to a camo landing strip in the jungle.'

'Too low for radar?'

'Something like that.'

Suddenly, they felt very exposed.

'Could be a police plane,' Lydia said.

Bob snorted. 'The police are the smugglers. And the anti-smugglers. They are both. Where do you think the coin comes to build your golden pyramids and infinity swimming pools?' His tone was sharp, as if he was accusing them for their naïvité.

The jungle extended on all sides, a canopy of vegetation that bumped against the turquoise sea in the east. They could just make out the main road that ran parallel to the shoreline and the tops of resort buildings where they nested in the landscape. Just south was another clearing, surrounded by more hills.

Lydia felt the ground beneath her sway. Not exactly an attack of vertigo, but the humming of ancient lives and burial grounds underfoot. With a little imagination she could hear the grinding of mortar against pestle and children's voices squealing in play.

Bob began to jog down the hill, followed more cautiously by the two women. Lydia stayed near to her mother, ready to snatch her elbow should she lose her footing.

At the bottom, Iris paused to catch her breath then said, 'Shall we head back to dear Dimitri?'

'No!' Bob said. Catching her surprised expression, he said more evenly, 'There is more to see.'

Lydia began to insist on their return but it was Iris who shot her a warning look. This was not the same Bob they knew back at the resort. This Bob had an edge to him, intent on going through with this field trip, start to finish.

'Can you go any faster?' Bob called over his shoulder.

32

ALEJANDRO SMILED modestly as the host of the *mesa redonda* introduced him, underlining and embellishing his accomplishments. These roundtable discussions were an inevitable part of the campaign. Martina darted a look at her phone, shielding its screen in the dark auditorium. Usual batch of texts from work and one from their old pal, Mercedes, inviting them for dinner if they were free. They were rarely free these days.

Alejandro reached for the mike and cleared his throat. She cringed; she'd warned him about this—clear throat *before* leaning into the microphone. No one wants to hear your phlegm. His hair shone, blacker than it should be, the silvery hairs covered by an artificial gleam. It had been the party leader's request that he get the dye job and Alejandro had been offended, then compliant.

She shot a look sideways. The auditorium was two-thirds full, a respectable showing for a mid-week political event. A huge banner plastered on the curtain behind the speakers read: *LA SEGURIDAD. SÍ.*

Security. Yes.

She'd positioned herself on an aisle seat, ready to slip away before the break. These things tended to go on for hours. Discreet glances aimed her way indicated she'd been recognized.

Alejandro began to speak in the plummy tones of a practised politician, then as he grew passionate he began gesticulating and suddenly he was the scruffy youth she remembered from university, standing on a soapbox, organizing a protest. Peeking at other audience members, Martina saw that they were mesmerized by this man who promised to clean up the state, to bring security to their families and workplaces, because—'We have a choice, my friends.'

The practised manner she had sought to teach him whisked away and he was abruptly and fully himself, and Martina realized that it was this self, not the new improved Alejandro that she'd tutored him to be, that would win the race. The people loved his passion and sincerity, and when he paused there was a wave of applause—even hoots of approval from students in the front rows.

Alejandro spoke of his 'three-pronged approach' to the security issues that plagued the nation.

Old Benito sat at the far end of the table; he was Alejandro's chief rival for the post, a party hack who'd been around for decades. A man who could call in countless favours, when required. He leaned back in his chair, arms crossed over his chest.

Truth was, Martina could hardly stand to watch her husband perform in public, knowing as she did his commotion of nerves, the way he downed a shot of whisky before stepping on stage. Maybe no one else noticed the tremor in his hands, but she did.

* * *

Branches parted with the scent of a cupboard flung open after years of being sealed shut. The jungle again broke into open space, and in its centre a small pool shimmered.

This was not the word they used here, of course.

'*Cenote*,' Iris said, pleased that the word had come to her. She plucked the drenched fabric of her dress to let in a thread of air, air that was hotter than her body, damper than skin.

The pool was one of the ancient sinkholes that dotted the Peninsula. She stooped at the edge of the earth's mysterious liquid eye and stared into it. A layer of scum drifted across its surface, no hint of wave motion in this soupy climate. The pool opened to the deep regions of the planet and some-where, perhaps a hundred metres below, spring water bub-bled from subterranean caves. There were no lakes or rivers in the Yucatan, only these collapsed pockets of limestone. Iris and Richard had bathed in moonlight in just such a pool near Chichen Itza, nearly half a century ago.

Primitive stairs had been hacked into its side and she might cling to the rim of the crater while lowering herself. There would be a point where she would have to let go and fall backwards into the water. That letting-go moment was not a sensation Iris craved.

When had she started mapping out activities in this way?

Bob was already crouching by the pool's side, rolling up his pants and dangling his bare feet in the water. Lydia peeled down to her underwear, sports bra and underpants, and reached with her good arm to test the water. She let out a gasp of shock: it was deliciously, improbably, cold.

That's all Iris needed to know. She stepped out of her dress, reminding herself to stand tall. If one bent over at this stage of the game, flesh spilled into an unattractive accor-dion motif. Clad in her underwear, she stood next to the mossy edge of the pool. The other two were watching, ready to spring to the rescue.

Iris began to clamber down the rudimentary ladder— and after a brief pause, let go. A hundred knives bit flesh. She gasped as she shot downwards, a captive to propulsion. It took forever to spin up, lungs jamming, arms windmilling, bursting through her own reckless spray.

She let loose a shriek of triumph.

Lydia's frown of concern melted.

The tips of her fingers numbed and her ears felt as if they'd been pinched hard. Somewhere below, her legs continued to beat the water. The film of algae broke into fragments. It occurred to Iris that this icy plunge could lead to something unpleasant, like a heart attack. Fear could spring like a jaguar, if she let it.

Lydia, with her flat stomach and modest breasts, leaned over the rim of the pool, gathering nerve to take the plunge. She looked like a cautious child. The image startled Iris. She remembered the pool party, such as were popular with her crowd in the 1970s. She'd brought tiny Lydia, cute as the dickens in her polka-dot bathing suit. A dozen guests gathered poolside and Iris was deep in conversation with a filmmaker when she spotted, out of the corner of her eye, her toddler daughter reaching from the deck to snatch the turtle toy that was floating away.

'She sank like a stone.' That's how she described the event to Richard later. Even now, remembering, she shuddered.

Iris had leapt into the water, fully clothed, as the drunk partiers erupted into applause, impressed and moved by her quick reaction.

Something else happened that afternoon: Iris understood that she could lose this girl through accident or illness, or her own carelessness. The love that had been so easy and natural began to feel the tug of a leash. She must shield herself from the prospect of devastating loss. Never again would she innocently give herself over to any living soul.

She watched now as her adult daughter reached with a gym-toned arm to lower herself into the pool.

Iris closed her eyes against the modest explosion. Ripples crashed against the sides of the *cenote* and in an instant, Lydia shot to the surface, hair plastered to her scalp, laughing. They paddled lazily as the tropical sun beat down and the coldness of the plunge wore off. Dragonflies settled on whatever flesh rose above the water, translucent wings beating the languid air. They need never leave this place, Iris decided. The unknown depths kept them afloat, a pair of grateful corks bobbing in the water.

Bob, content to dangle his feet at the edge of the pool, related grisly uses of the *cenote* during its heyday. 'Locals tossed in sacrifices to the gods—livestock, treasures, even children.'

'And virgins,' Lydia supplied.

'You throw out what you value most,' Bob said.

A rumbling sound began again in the sky, starting as a low hum then growing louder as the same small airplane ascended from the coast.

'A hundred keys of Columbia's finest heads for the border,' Bob said.

And then he did a curious thing: he drew his legs up from the water and darted to the centre of the clearing where he began to wave his arms, using his bandana as a flag.

The aircraft pulled upwards, a nervous butterfly leaving the jungle. Pointing northwest, it flew in a straight line, receding from sight, then abruptly turned into a tight circle and began to angle back above the *cenote*. Losing altitude, it skirted the treetops, veering so close that they could see paint peeling off its flank and make out the pilot's blue shirt.

Where Bob had stood, wet footprints printed the mulch. The women stared at the blank space as they treaded water.

His red bandana dangled from a bush.

'He brought us here,' Lydia said as she shimmied into her skirt. 'He will return us.'

This statement would have had more effect if Bob were anywhere in sight.

'What, exactly, do we know about Bob, other than the fact that he deals drugs. Hardly a sterling recommendation.' Iris grabbed her clothes and worked herself into them over soaked underwear.

They stood listening: nothing but faint engine noise.

'Maybe he's taking a leak,' Lydia said and called out his name.

Nothing.

It was two p.m. and the sun was fierce. Lydia cursed herself for agreeing to this adventure. They could be lounging at the fake pyramid under clarifying sea breezes, margaritas in hand. She would be deciding whether to allow El León's chauffeur to drive them to dinner.

'Call again,' Iris said. She tried to do so herself, but her voice was an old woman's quavering.

'Bob!' Lydia barked. A bird wheeled overhead. Her voice was instantly dampened by the jungle. Panic dissolved in her mouth, a biscuit of dread.

'We'll have earned our steak dinner at the beachside hut tonight,' Iris wheezed. 'I've made reservations for the second sitting at 7:30 p.m.' Her lips tightened. 'Unless you have decided that we are to visit the cartel leader in his domain.'

Lydia said nothing. She pictured the hours to come, sun sliding over the palms as the great hand of darkness pressed in. Yellow eyes peering malevolently from the surrounding jungle.

Iris reached for her daughter's bottle and sucked at the trickle of warm water.

Lydia frowned. 'We should ration ourselves.'

Iris took another slug. 'We can't stand here waiting for rescue like a pair of helpless females. Your friend Bob is a rascal.' She sounded almost approving.

'He's worse than that,' Lydia said.

'Trouble with you is that you expect too much from the male of the species.'

The jungle presented itself as a wall of buzzing foliage, every centimetre quivering and pulsing with life. They left the clearing with its *cenote* to enter spotty shade where sun created a piano key effect on the ground.

'It isn't very far,' Lydia said and calculated quickly: the walk to the pyramid had been no more than half an hour, forty minutes, tops. She strode forward, with frequent pauses to allow Iris to catch up. It was obvious that her mother was at the limit of her capacity, shoulders hunched as she stared fixedly at the ground, wary of tripping on exposed roots. Insects swarmed their legs and took ferocious nips.

The minutes passed. Half an hour.

'I remember this,' Lydia said and felt relief open her chest. A marshy section loomed. 'We passed it coming in.'

Iris paused to consider.'When Jake and I camped illegally at the Palenque ruins, we swatted away avaricious insects.' She spat out tiny corpses. 'We thought we were Druids, hiding in the pyramids at night. Tell me, dear, have you got any of that breakfast muffin left?'

Lydia passed her a chunk of pastry stuck to plastic wrap and resumed pushing along the trail. They entered the marsh terrain, the ground churned up as if a vehicle, perhaps an ATV, had recently turned around. This was not where they'd left Dimitri. Her mother laboured to keep up, though whenever Lydia asked, 'How are you doing?' Iris would reply 'Brilliant!' and raise a thumb.

A monkey howled and its brethren howled in answer, an unearthly racket that made Lydia shiver, despite the heat.

'I prefer the synthesized sound of rainforest, as experienced in the spa,' Iris panted. She was so determined to be game that Lydia felt her heart melt—an almost literal sensation. She held back branches so they wouldn't smack her mother's face. Machete cuts were visible on a grove of bamboo ahead; this was where they'd come in. A few steps further would be Dimitri and his car, and possibly Bob. Lydia closed her eyes, as if to will the image into existence.

A chips bag lay on the ground next to half a dozen cigarette butts. Maybe she'd always known he—they—wouldn't hang around. No Bob, no Dimitri, no car. Lydia kicked the foil bag and watched it float, another exotic winged creature.

Iris caught up and rested her hands heavily on her daughter's shoulders. They were silent for several seconds then

Lydia cupped her mouth and called both men's names. Not so much as an echo returned in the saturated air.

Iris seemed to have shrunk in the heat. 'Where *is* Bob, goddamnit?'

'Question of the hour.'

'I need to duck behind this bush and go to the toilet al fresco,' Iris said. 'Remind me of the name of that barbed fish that travels up a stream of urine and enters the vaginal canal?'

'That would be the *candíru*, Mum, and I'm pretty sure it's found only in the Amazon basin. One needs a body of water.'

'Here's hoping they know that.'

The secret was to keep a slow but steady pace and to talk no more than necessary. At one point Iris began to sink to the ground, her lips chalky. 'I need something to drink,' she gasped. 'Antifreeze would tempt.'

The sun had begun its descent and Lydia knew that once started, its slide was abrupt. She allowed her mother a tiny sip of warm water and helped lower her onto a log. Iris let out a whimper of pain and Lydia was reminded that any creature who keels over in the jungle begins to be ravaged instantly. Human remains are skeletonized within a week. She wrapped an arm around her mother's back and felt the quilted flesh twitch.

What if Iris couldn't—or wouldn't—get to her feet?

Iris began to speak in a drained voice: 'Berkeley people don't get me. I'm not nearly intellectual enough for Steve's crowd. In retirement, women my age are learning Mandarin.' She started to laugh but it turned into a cough.

'Mum, you need to get up.'

'I know, dear.' But Iris did nothing.

She'd spread her legs out in front, like a small child.

'Mum,' Lydia pleaded. The fear socked her hard; her mother was fading fast, with her chin sunk onto her chest and Lydia could hear slow, laboured breathing.

It was all she could do to beat off waves of panic. This seventy-year-old woman whom she loved despite or perhaps because of decades of missed cues and difficulties, her dear adventurous mother with soft shoulders and fleshy body, was decaying before her eyes. Dehydration had hollowed out her cheeks and she looked her age and then some.

'This is it, old bean. End of the story.'

Had Iris really said this?

Lydia tugged her mother's arm and managed to drag what amounted to a dead weight to her feet. Both women staggered and Lydia began to laugh, hearing a note of hysteria in it, as Iris started to charge off in precisely the wrong direction.

There is beauty here, Lydia reminded herself as they continued the trek, holding hands whenever the path was wide enough. People travelled thousands of kilometres to visit the Yucatan Peninsula, to set foot in a jungle and allow the humidity to soak their dry, wintery pores.

Iris rasped, 'The men in your life seem to disappear without warning.'

Lydia dropped her mother's clammy hand.

Iris seemed to revive as she pursued the topic: 'What with Charlie taking off, and now Bob.'

'Bob is not a man in my life. He is an acquaintance.' Lydia felt it rise in her, the old need to defend herself.

'I make a point of always being the one to disappear,' Iris said, seeming to gain momentum as she tramped behind her daughter. 'It is so important for one's state of mind.'

Then they both heard it, a shrill machine buzz in the distance. A lower register than the constant buzz of insects. They stopped and Iris leaned over, pressing her hands to her knees. Her back rose and fell, the spine curled like a fern.

'A chainsaw,' Lydia decided after a moment. 'Someone clearing brush.'

Reassuring, this evidence of human activity.

Iris slowly rose, wincing with the effort. She stared at her daughter. 'I never thought you'd turn out like this,' she said.

'Like what?' Lydia asked, then immediately wished she hadn't.

That ruddy face continued to stare at her, small intense eyes, high forehead.

'One has an imaginary map for one's children,' Iris said. 'You must know that, being a mother yourself.'

Lydia felt a flare of pleasure at the idea that when she was a child, her mother had hopes for her, had paid attention to that degree.

'I don't have a map for Doug and Annie.'

'Oh please,' snorted Iris. 'You want them to evolve in a certain way and it can feel like a betrayal when—if—they don't.' She set a hand on her daughter's shoulder then reached down to ping the strap of her sandal. 'This blister is a doozie. I don't suppose you have a bandage.'

'I do,' Lydia said, taking pleasure in the fact that she'd come prepared to this degree, and reached into her pocket and pulled out two Band-Aids and tore them open.

Iris snatched one and gave her a squinty-eyed look before saying, 'I'm the mother of a woman who carries Band-Aids with her, just in case. I've never done anything just in case.'

Don't react, Lydia instructed herself.

They walked side by side as the trail widened. Sweat pooled in the creases behind their knees. Iris's breath was rapid, like a small animal's.

They stepped through a pungent smell of decay, salad left in the fridge too long, and squelched over the vegetable carpet. Sap trailed from bark like amber waterfalls.

First date, more than twenty years ago, Charlie at her side at the High Park zoo, the pair of them staring at mountain goats climbing over the rocks, beards shivering. She'd slipped sidelong looks at this man, his solid build, wavy hair, deep-set eyes. Not a big talker, she was discovering. Would it surprise her mother to know that she, Lydia, had made the first move? Skin so sensitive that the first time she touched him, he jumped; it was as if he'd just been born. Even now, Lydia felt the lick of excitement, followed immediately by a crushing sadness.

A pair of iridescent dragonflies floated past, stuck to each other.

'I'm afraid, dear,' Iris said, 'that I'm flagging again.'

'Not much further to the road,' Lydia said, hoping she was right.

'Then what?'

'We hail a passing car.'

Iris was more than flagging, she was visibly weakening, tottering sideways. Lydia thought quickly: could she carry her mother piggyback, or would it be safer to leave her here while she raced ahead to the road for help?

Leave her alone in the jungle? Iris would be terrified.

The shack appeared in a hacked-out clearing; they'd spotted the dwelling on the way in, without paying much attention. Now it shimmered like the Emerald City.

'Glory be,' Iris said and staggered against her daughter.

The shack, the size of one modest room, featured a pair of plastic lawn chairs parked outside. Lydia felt her spirits lift; they would fall into the hands of friendly locals. The owner might have a burro leashed in the back and they would heave Iris on it and make for the road.

It was a revived Iris who swept past her to tap on the door. '*Hola?*' she trilled.

Nothing.

She pushed open the door and the two women peered inside. Dark, except for a sliver of light filtering through a high window. Dirt floor. A pleasant charcoal smell.

'*Hola?*' Iris tried again, her pink face looking optimistic.

Just the incessant buzzing of a chainsaw in the distance.

'That's where they're at,' Lydia said. 'Cutting trees and scrub for pasture land. Demolishing the rainforest.'

Iris stepped into the little house. A moment later she emerged, clasping two bottles of cola beaded in water. 'From the cooler,' she said.

Lydia grabbed one of the bottles, feeling pocked glass that had been recycled dozens of times.

'There was something else,' Iris said.

'Oh?'

'Blood on the floor. Not a lot.'

Queasy feeling.

'Still sticky.'

Lydia edged away from the house. 'We'd be wise to get on our way.'

'Someone might need our help,' Iris said, holding back. 'What if a girl's had a miscarriage, or there's been a machete mishap?'

'Mum ...'

Reluctantly, Iris let herself be guided back to the pathway, leaving behind the stamp of human difficulty. They popped open the bottles and drank with their eyes shut, the sugary liquid exploding in their mouths and when Iris cried—'I feel diabetic,' they started to laugh in giddy relief.

Lydia heard it first, the sound of human voices and the rustle of bodies moving through the brush. The cola started to back up in her gut, a hideous bubble. Half a dozen men approached them, armed with machetes, wearing shorts and singlets. A solo women tramped in front, dressed in camo pants, t-shirt, and an Oakland Raiders ball cap.

Lydia felt her mind skid sideways; so this was how they were going to end. Doug and Annie would get a phone call from the Canadian Consulate. Dismembered bodies had been found.

'Lyd?' Iris's voice was faint.

Within seconds the group had surrounded the two women, holding their machetes in a casual way, blades caked with grass. One man set a chainsaw on the ground between his feet. They were all sweating, showing weary expressionless faces.

The woman spoke in accented English: 'Where's Bob?' She pulled out a red handkerchief from her pocket: The bandana he'd left hanging on a bush near the *cenote*.

Lydia's hands crept with pins and needles. 'I have no idea,' she said.

'He is with you,' the woman said.

'Was,' Lydia corrected.

Mexico was crawling with renegade police, she knew; special forces trained by the U.S. to battle *narcotraficantes*, trained so well they'd formed their own gangs and had taken over the drug trade.

'You are from the resort,' one of the man said, also in English, glancing at their bracelets.

Iris started to appeal to their better nature. 'I hope you will steer us in the right direction to return there now,' she said.

He just looked at her.

'Bob deserted us.' Iris tried to sound indignant.

The man turned to speak to the others in rapid Spanish. They nodded, faces solemn.

'What are you going to do?' Iris rasped.

Lydia touched her mother's back; Iris was hyperventilating.

'My mother needs to sit down,' she said in a clear voice. Lydia felt her own fear turn into anger. 'I'm going to take her inside, out of the sun.'

The woman lifted a hand and beckoned to a teenaged boy in baggy shorts, who seized Iris's forearm and began guiding her into the shack.

As Iris disappeared there was a moment when Lydia thought, 'I'll never see her again.'

'Let me go with her,' she demanded.

The woman swept an arm as if to say, 'Be my guest.'

As Lydia's eyes adjusted to the darkness inside the dwelling, she made out a kitchen area, pots and pans hanging from nails on the dirt wall. Half a dozen cots sat on the earthen floor along with several folding chairs. In the far corner, the boy stood next to her mother, who looked very small and hunched over, as if she were hoping to become invisible.

'I don't know what's happening,' Iris panted. Her hair stuck up all over. 'I don't know what these people are about and why they are here.'

Lydia heard the confusion in her voice.

Iris set herself on one of the cots and gave a little bounce. 'This mattress is filled with hay or straw or something similar. How are your allergies? I know you suffered as a child.'

Lydia just stared at her.

The rest of the group crowded inside and the kid passed around pop bottles from the cooler.

'These people drink far too much soda pop,' Iris said. 'Did you know that Mexican Coca Cola is made with real cane sugar? Whereas north of the border it's sweetened with high-fructose corn syrup.'

When no one responded, she added: 'Hell on a person's pancreas and glucose level.' Her face had a pleading look.

The woman crouched so that she was eye level to Iris. 'Tell me where he's gone.'

Iris stared back at her.

Lydia had to fight to keep her voice from shaking; it was important to make a show of expecting that this episode would turn out well. 'He ran off,' she said, 'after signalling to the airplane.'

The woman twisted her head and spoke quickly to the others. There was a flurry of back-and-forth conversation as the information was digested.

'Painted in camouflage.' Lydia was eager to show that she'd been observant. 'A pilot in a blue shirt. He circled us when we were at—' She hesitated. The ruins were a secret. Maybe that was what this ambush was all about; big money in antiquities.

'At?' the man who had spoken earlier prompted. He wiped sweat from his face with the edge of his singlet. He was balding with a wide mouth, barrel chest.

'The ruins.'

Then an odd thing happened; the man laughed while kicking off his sneakers. Then laughed again.

'Sit down,' the woman said, meaning Lydia. She pointed to a plastic lawn chair, the kind she and Charlie picked up from Canadian Tire every summer.

Then the woman asked, in the calm voice she'd been using all along, 'Tell me about your friend, Bob.'

Lydia owed nothing whatsoever to Bob. 'He deals pot at the resort.'

'Of course.'

'Maybe deals other stuff.'

A knowing nod.

'He brought us to the jungle, a sort of field trip.'

'I want you to tell me where Bob went after he left you at the *ruinas.*'

'I wish I knew!' Surely she could hear that she was telling the truth.

The woman looked up at the ceiling, as if gathering her thoughts, then said, 'Your mother is not a young woman.'

Lydia stiffened. 'Seventy,' and reminded herself that Mexicans were kind to the elderly. This woman looked to be around fifty, crinkles spreading from her eyes, hair held back in a ponytail.

'Show them,' the woman said and beckoned to the kid.

The boy tapped the screen of his smartphone, which quickly came to life.

A still image appeared and the three women leaned to peer at it. The boy tapped again and a video began playing. Audio of men talking in Spanish, birds squawking and humming of insects. The tiny screen showed Bob, bandana cinched around his forehead, pirate style. That was when Iris stepped into the camera's eye, followed by Lydia. The *cenote* appeared. The three of them looked excited, Lydia starting to peel off her blouse.

Here, mercifully, the video ended.

It sunk in, this group had been following them—perhaps since the beginning of their trek.

Iris asked, 'Who are you?'

'*Campesinos,*' the woman said.

Farmers. Peasants.

As if to demonstrate this, the men found cloths and began to clean their machetes: tools, not weapons. One heaved the chainsaw onto the table and went at it with a rag and machine oil.

The woman rose from her crouch, grabbed a flashlight from a shelf, and slid its beam over Iris. Her dress was hiked up, caught in the waist of her underpants. Lydia hastened to fix this.

'Take us to your friend,' the woman said. She didn't look annoyed, just tired, her bare limbs covered in nicks and scratches.

The entrance to the shack filled with a dark form.

'Tia Clara?'

Aunt Clara.

'*Si?*' The woman tilted the flashlight to the newcomer's face.

It took a second. 'Cleo!' Lydia cried. She sucked in a breath; it was as if the glory and safety of La Pirámide had poured into the miserable jungle shack. She began to dart forward but he put up a warning hand. Cleo seemed less excited to see her than she might have hoped.

He and the woman called Clara exchanged words. She nodded, interrupted, and nodded again.

'Will you take us back to the resort now?' Iris said.

The question was ignored.

Cleo must have a car; how else did he get here?

After another flurry of conversation, Clara went to the kitchen and lifted the lid off a pot resting on a propane stove. With the aid of tongs, she extracted two tamales wrapped in banana leaves, then two more, and dropped them on plates which she brought over to Lydia and her mother. Sitting on the cot, side by side, Iris and Lydia peeled back the leaves to reveal warmish corn meal stuffed with chili and what might have been chicken.

Iris plunged in with her fingers and said, *sotto voce,* 'Hope this doesn't give us the runs.'

33

'I'M GOING TO win this thing.' Alejandro stood in front of Martina, fresh from the shower, towel wrapped around his waist. Steam leaked from the bathroom and he smelled of shampoo.

Martina looked up from her work and said, 'It's what you want, yes?'

'Of course,' he said, but didn't sound sure. He retied the towel. 'There is so much expectation weighing on my shoulders.'

His dinner jacket hung from a nearby hanger; shirt and trousers were spread on the bed along with his tie. Tonight was a donors' dinner.

'You're not afraid, I hope?'

He did not answer the question directly. 'You have such faith in me, Martina.' He said this with a smile, but she knew he needed her to remind him it was true.

Martina tipped her head so that she was staring directly into his eyes. They looked almost black this time of night. 'I do have faith,' she said.

He'd promised no more booze, not a drop, and she examined the flesh under his eyes for telltale pouches. Alejandro could never keep secrets from her; it was both a blessing and a curse.

He dropped the towel so he was naked, skin gleaming in this half-light. He wanted her to look intently at him, to see every inch of who he was.

'Have you heard from him again?' he said.

No need to utter the man's name.

'No,' she lied.

A second bouquet of flowers had arrived at the studio and this time the note was written in the cartel leader's own hand. *I am thinking of you, beautiful woman.*

She wondered, in just what way was he thinking of her?

Alejandro pressed closer and she reached up so her fingers brushed his inner thigh. The skin was still wet. His eyes closed; he loved to sink into pure sensation without the clutter of seeing her.

* * *

'How did you know we were here?' Lydia asked.

Cleo's hand fluttered in the air, dismissing the question. Instead he said, 'El León's man came to La Pirámide, to fetch you.'

Lydia felt her gut lurch. 'And?'

'You were not there.'

Obviously.

'Was he angry?'

'The chauffeur felt nothing,' Cleo said. 'Why should he?'

Lydia's mind scrambled to fill out the scene. 'He phoned his employer?'

'What do you think?'

'Bob said I shouldn't be there; that the man is dangerous.'

Cleo shrugged. 'Now there is difficulty for you.'

'What kind of difficulty?'

He turned his back and continued the conversation with Clara in Spanish. It sounded like a plan was forming and

Bob's name came up. Clara nodded slowly, perhaps skeptical of what her nephew was proposing.

'What are they saying, Mum?' Lydia whispered but Iris just shook her head. It was too fast, too idiomatic, and she was tired.

'You will stay here tonight,' Cleo finally said.

Lydia and Iris cried out in dismay but he stopped them with a raised hand.

'It is dark and my car has no lights.'

The *campesinos* were his cousins and his aunt, Cleo told them. He'd been summoned because—'There was trouble.'

Lydia understood that the trouble was her and Iris. 'Bob abandoned us,' she said.

Cleo allowed a thin smile. 'Bob believes that he is an important man.'

Aunt Clara approached with bottles of water. Would the *señoras* like a drink?

'It is purified,' Cleo assured them.

And indeed, the sealed plastic bottles bore the insignia of La Pirámide resort. Only after they'd emptied them down to the last drop did Lydia whisper to her mother, 'Do you think this is the last of their potable water?'

The *campesinos* had put away their machetes and a pair of men sat on folding chairs watching a soccer game on a small old-fashioned television set. Battery-operated? No other sign of electricity. Another lay on a cot, hands tucked behind his head.

'Were the tamales we ate their supper?' Iris whispered back.

Cleo kicked shut the door of the house and the interior quickly heated up. He was nothing like the man Lydia knew from the resort; this Cleo wore cut-off shorts and a singlet as he paced the floor.

'Will we get you in trouble?' Lydia asked.

'I hope not.' He turned his back to them and went over to a small desk in the corner.

Time ground by. No sign of supper preparation until it was close to ten p.m. when Aunt Clara began to rustle around the kitchen. Rice kernels drizzled from her fist into a frying pan coated in hot oil. She peeled a tea towel back to reveal a stack of tortillas then started chopping nopal cactus into cubes. The smell of singed garlic soon filled the shack.

Iris rubbed her eyes. She seemed dazed, as if unsure where she was. 'I have to go to the bathroom,' she said.

She looked so frail, hands dropping to rest in her lap. Cleo beckoned her to follow him outside. This diminished Iris was frightening. She might capsize under the night sky, snap her hip; she was so fragile, Lydia saw, a mended china cup.

When the pair returned, Iris bustled over to the cot, using the backs of chairs as support. Her face was flushed with enthusiasm. 'A perfect outdoor privy,' she reported, 'complete with standard toilet seat. Highly recommended.'

Lydia helped her settle on the narrow bed, seizing her arm as Iris hovered then lowered herself with a gasp. 'When did I become this sort of person?' she wondered aloud.

When it was Lydia's turn to go to the bathroom, she stepped outside and across the yard, avoiding chickens and a preening rooster. She recalled the bathroom in the Blue House where she'd gone to fetch Bob: its brand-new toilet, shreds of packing material stuck to the rim, an appliance that sat on the floor with no plumbing attached.

A bird gave a long, mournful hoot.

The privy must be the add-on she spotted at the rear of the house. A jerry-built affair with aluminum roof, wood sides, and a door with a padlock hanging on a couple of U-forms. The lock was opened with a tug and the door swung inwards. She braced herself for the smell.

But there was no smell. Once she became accustomed to the dark, she saw that there was no toilet and no wooden plank with a circle neatly cut out. Instead, a pile of square packages wrapped in plastic were stacked floor to ceiling. Such silence, like entering church.

A hand clapped her shoulder. 'What are you doing?'

She spun around to see Cleo standing shirtless, his free hand holding a rolled-up tortilla, as if his meal had been interrupted. He pulled her away from the entrance and after pressing the door shut, he set the padlock and waited for her reply.

'Bathroom. *El baño.*' It sounded feeble, though it was true. Obviously there was no privy in this room. By the looks of his face, he wasn't buying her explanation. She hardly believed it herself. He kept staring at her, waiting for more, the real explanation. All she could do was shake her head: sorry, sorry. Her tired brain began to click: smugglers' plane, Bob's signalling and sudden disappearance. These packages. And now, Cleo's anger and suspicion.

'*El baño,*' she repeated.

He tossed the remains of his tortilla to the chickens, who went to work, pecking furiously.

'You are mistaken,' Cleo said.

'Yes.'

'This way.' He pointed to an area beyond a banana tree.

Stars clogged the night sky and Jupiter dazzled. Lydia stared at what must have been a falling star as it shot through the southern sky. As she watched, its lights snapped off and all that remained was a muted engine rumble. Another cargo plane. She glanced at Cleo but he was staring at the bright screen of his cell phone.

The privy loomed as a miniature version of the main house, complete with palm leaves laid across its roof. She stepped inside, yanked the door shut, and the world popped into aural focus, the creatures outside crying a call and response.

What would it be like to disappear in this jungle with Cleo and his family, the kind of people who didn't make a fuss over visitors, but accommodated them? It had always been Lydia's way to anticipate guests by cleaning the house top to bottom and bringing in a shipment of food, most of which never got eaten. Charlie would roll his eyes at what he termed her 'over preparation' and carve the roast.

The smell inside the privy was what one would expect, mixed with—her hand patted the shelf—an air freshener emitting a pomegranate fragrance.

Cleo escorted her back to the house. She got the idea he was making sure she didn't linger outside.

Aunt Clara was sorting out who'd sleep where.

'No, no,' Iris insisted when she saw that their hosts meant to triple up on the cots so that Lydia and Iris could each have her own. 'My daughter and I will share.'

One of the cousins helped himself to a plate of rice and tortillas and cactus salad. He returned to his spot in front of the television and began to eat.

Aunt Clara made a gesture and said something in Spanish. Lydia looked at her mother for translation.

Iris nodded, figuring it out. 'We are to wash our hands.'

Clara directed them to a plastic container, the sort that might have held gasoline in an earlier life, and now contained water. She handed them a bar of soap, washcloth, a towel, and the guests happily poured water over their hands and splashed their faces.

When they were done, it was Lydia who realized that perhaps they shouldn't have been so profligate with water use.

Aunt Clara passed them plates laden with the simple dinner and they began to eat, perched on the rim of their cot. Nine people were packed in the small space and the air was heavy with cooking smells and human sweat. As Lydia reached to clasp her mother's hand, she felt the boniness of it, the thrum of veins pumping blood.

Cleo sat at the desk, sorting official-looking papers. 'It is because of my son's accident,' he said. 'Perhaps we will receive a survivor's pension.'

'Your government pays pensions to families of accident victims?' Lydia didn't disguise her surprise.

He peered at her over his glasses. 'Not exactly.' He put his pen down and leaned back in his chair. From the corner, a pair of young men let out a whoop of celebration: Los Tigrillos had scored.

'Not the government,' Cleo said. 'Certain people help those of us who work for them.'

'I don't understand.'

'Lydia,' her mother came to life. 'I don't think you are meant to understand.'

The two women lay on the cot head to toe, though the others seemed to find this arrangement hilarious. First thing in the morning they would pile into Cleo's Volkswagen Beetle, the one without lights, and drive back to La Pirámide.

All through childhood, Lydia had wanted more of Iris, more time, more attention, a less distracted mother. And now she had her as close as she could imagine and the intimacy was alarming, almost overwhelming. Iris barely moved in her sleep and exhibited no sign of dreaming as soft flesh pressed against her daughter's hip.

Sometime during the night, Lydia had to go to the bathroom again. She sat up in bed carefully, not wanting to wake Iris. Lowering her feet over the side of the cot, she found her sandals and stepped across the dirt floor to the door. As she pushed it open the metal latch fell with a clang.

An abrupt rustling in one of the beds.

'I will come with you.'

Cleo. Naked except for his shorts. She was wearing her clothes—neither she nor Iris had gotten undressed; there didn't seem a way to do this with any degree of modesty.

The outside air was still moist but after the stuffy cabin, it felt fresh and clean. She took several restorative breaths. Sounds were different at night, differently pitched squawks and moans as if she'd stepped into another landscape.

Cleo guided her along the path, past the addition where the mysterious packages were stored, to the outhouse where he finally let go of her arm. She pushed open the door, aware that he was waiting for her outside. Did he really intend to drive them to La Pirámide in a few hours? The existence of the resort felt less real than this tiny settlement at the edge of the jungle.

When she stepped out of the privy and saw him waiting, rubbing his face like any sleepy man, she said, 'Let's not go inside yet.' She couldn't bear to re-enter the stuffy shack. Instead, she sat on a log that had been fashioned into a bench and listened as a noise like scything filled the air.

Los grillos, he said. Crickets.

She pulled the hem of her skirt over her knees. Cleo lit a cigarette and she felt the space between them shrink. He stood behind her, a creature so heated he seemed to vibrate. She inhaled the smell of his cigarette and the pungent fragrance of rotting wood and moss. An animal moved stealthily through nearby foliage, stop and start, stop and start. A bark rose from the opposite direction, answered with a low hoot. She could see no animal, yet she was surrounded by activity.

Cleo tossed his butt on the ground and headed towards the door of the shack, not waiting for her to catch up. Tap of panic as her rescuer disappeared, leaving her in the darkness. At the last minute, he aimed the light from his phone onto the pathway and she hastily followed.

Leave the sultry outdoors to enter the stuffy hut, singing crickets replaced with the snores of *campesinos*.

'There you are,' Iris whispered and patted her daughter's leg as Lydia slid back onto the cot.

Tomorrow night they would pass out in queen-sized beds with fresh sheets, a mountain of pillows, and Lydia would remember to set the alarm so she could wake up in time for Yoga on the Beach.

34

AUNT CLARA STOOD over their cot, speaking quickly. Iris got herself to a sitting position and translated: 'Cleo left already.'

Beside her, Lydia gasped in dismay.

'He had to drive to the resort early.' Iris frowned as she sought to understand Aunt Clara's urgent speech. 'Gabriel will take us.'

Gabriel was the teenager, presently demolishing a bowl of Fruit Loops.

This morning, Cleo's aunt wore her hair tucked into a kerchief and was dressed in shorts with a Ramones t-shirt.

'Gabo!' Clara called.

The teenager reluctantly got up from eating and disappeared from the shack. Moments later he was standing at the entrance, leading a swayback pony by the halter. Its ears twitched as flies circled its grey head.

This was to be their mode of transportation.

Gabo heaved Iris up onto the homemade wooden saddle and fitted her feet into wooden stirrups. She put on a brave face but winced. 'This already hurts.'

Lydia hoisted herself onto the saddle behind her mother. Soon they were clip-clopping down the trail as Gabriel, earphones snapped over his head, led them towards the main road.

Twenty painful minutes later, the women slid off the back of the scrawny creature and staggered onto the asphalt road, its surface gummy from morning heat. Without a word of instruction or farewell Gabriel hopped onto the pony and began to trot back to the shack.

The empty road gaped, a long featureless strip of tar.

'I'm not sure that he was meant to dump us here,' Iris said.

They stood, considering the situation. Zero traffic, not even a burro they might commandeer. The road was lined by acres of cultivated banana trees.

Iris said quietly, 'I was paralyzed with fatigue in the jungle. Shocking, to find oneself so depleted. I thought we were done for.'

'Frankly, so did I.'

A car approached from the east and Iris made her way to the middle of the road and started waving. An American compact of the last decade swerved to avoid the elderly *gringa* and pulled to a stop on the shoulder. The driver was a young Mexican woman in an embroidered blouse.

Iris stooped to speak through the open window then turned to her daughter: 'Meet our saviour, Elizabeth. Her uncle is in hospital in Cancun and they need her to sign some papers.'

Lydia tugged at the back door and fell onto the seat behind the driver. Elizabeth hit the gas and they were off.

Their rescuer dropped them off at the lower entrance to La Pirámide. Mother and daughter began to totter up the hill, past the parrot's cage where the flamboyant bird squawked a cheery insult. Bougainvillea petals spilled over the cobbled trail, a sight so cheering that Lydia nearly wept with relief. Ocean breezes swept the air and they could hear the lobby band playing. It was just about noon. They'd been gone for twenty-four hours.

35

GRAB WALLET, RACE downstairs with cell phone in hand, hail a cab. It was Alejandro's point man, Tomás, who'd phoned, jabbering so breathlessly that Martina had to order him to slow down, to repeat everything. So it was happening, as what one most dreads must.

The street was insanely busy, traffic clogged at the round-about, spewing noxious fumes that had her covering her mouth, as if it mattered now, to protect her spongey lungs. To the west in Mexico City they were suffering one of the thermal inversions that socked air in the valley for days, a ghastly yellow miasma. That's why she and Alejandro had chosen to move to the modest state capital, where sea breezes allowed the city to clean its pores.

She dropped her cell phone in her purse. A cab made a U-turn and braked hard against the curb. Martina jumped into the back seat before the vehicle had fully stopped. She gave the driver instructions to the resort, that he was to take the old road out of town, to where it crossed the new four-lane highway. The sun was intense and she dug into the pocket of her purse for dark glasses and set them over her eyes. The world turned mauve. She would face what was happening and she would make decisions. The ambulance would be hastening now from the beach town to the resort, but she wouldn't let Alejandro end up in some third-rate clinic. He must be transported to the hospital whose fundraising efforts they supported so vigorously.

The *sicarios* rarely left their victims undead. Tomás said the shooter was one of the waiters, Patricio. Whipped out a .22 and came in tight, weapon shielded by a linen napkin, as if he were serving a cocktail. Characteristic pop of a small-calibre revolver. The guests would think fireworks. Those crazy Mexicans and their fireworks, night and day. But Alejandro was not dead; Tomás had been careful to repeat this half a dozen times. Then he'd shouted frantically into the phone: 'It was not my fault!'

She'd snapped her phone shut. Tomás was too vain, loved his muscular body too much, posing in any reflective surface. They would have done better to hire a working-class boy who needed the job, but Alejandro insisted that he only trusted family. Each family was its own cartel, suspicious of outsiders.

She'd grabbed his health insurance card, which lay on the oak dresser next to a spare set of keys. He never thought anything would happen to him. They were a special couple, not vulnerable in the usual ways, and she'd half-believed him. Now the illusion was over and if there was to be a funeral, she would place their wedding photo on his crossed arms as he lay in the ornate coffin and she would weep as he was lowered into the ground, just like all the other widows of big-shot men. Friends would drop by bearing food, but she would be alone after the commotion was over, after the kids returned to their lives. Everyone would be wanting to know if she would continue with her television program. And would she remain in the apartment? This question would be asked discreetly, for the apartment was prized, in a building much sought after.

The cab roared onto the highway, the driver a gaunt man who kept peering into his rear-view mirror. He recognized her, if not from the television show, then from billboards that were plastered all over the downtown broadcasting building.

'This is it,' she said as the gold pyramid loomed into sight, shooting off rays of light.

The taxi turned sharply and drove up bumpy cobblestones towards the Arrivals area that was framed by a pair of Mayan figures that appeared to be supporting the pyramid on their broad shoulders.

She slipped out of the car and realized that she'd neglected to pay the driver. He sped off—he'd seen the police, the ambulance.

The first person Martina recognized was Don Victor, who hovered at one side of the lobby entrance, looking out of place in his baggy *campesino* cotton, part of a stage set that was no longer useful. Her journalist's eye picked up every detail: the cuff sloping over his left *huarache* was soaked in blood.

Please make it his, not Alejandro's.

Martina pushed through the huddle of guests decked out in souvenir t-shirts and bathing suits, her heels clicking on the tile floor. A mariachi band was playing at the far end of the lobby. No one had thought to send them packing, and the musicians raced through a well-known *corrido* celebrating the conquests of Pancho Villa. Glory to the great man, to violence, to the poor defeating the rich. *Narcos* commissioned these narratives to celebrate their feats of thuggery and Alejandro would crank up the radio and sing along— ironically, of course. She guessed that he'd love it if Los Tigres del Norte decided to compose a ballad in his honour, a bouquet tossed to the rebel politician.

She was a drone, zig-zagging unerringly through the labyrinth of police and media, including a cameraman and the anchor girl from her own station. Natalia, dressed as always in a silk blouse and skirt and vertiginously high heels, was

speaking into the microphone while Felipe held the video-
cam steady. Media had gotten here within minutes of the
shooting, quite possibly before police and EMS. They would
have been alerted to the event in advance. This happened. A
phone call, voice masked by a layer of cloth—toss a prayer to
the Black Madonna. Last week, a detox centre near the border had been raided, its hapless clients pushed against a wall
and executed, one by one. Photos showed brains splashed
against adobe.

What Alejandro sought to put an end to.

Her colleagues jostled for position, making sure the elaborate lobby chandelier got into their pictures. Martina spotted the man lying on the floor, one knee popping up and
down under the orange blanket. She tore past the fountain
with its mermaid spouting water. Inside the lobby it was
dark and cool, a cavernous space. Police in sharp uniforms
calculated to impress tourists stood waving their arms while
a quartet of paramedics crouched on the floor, working on
Alejandro. One held an IV drip overhead. Another twisted
dials on a black box. Another dipped into a kit full of medi-
cal gear, picking up one item, dropping another. The police
stood by looking nervous; if there were more shooters waiting in the wings, they were ready to hit the floor. You could
say that all staff were cartel employees since El León owned
the place. Hotel workers congregated around the registra-
tion counter, horrified, yet, truth be told, elated that such a
thing could happen in a luxurious tourist palace—not just
in their scruffy barrios.

No one was allowed to leave.

Racket of police radios, static, crisp voices, all male
except for Natalia. Martina heard everything, saw everything. She noted the upended tray of orange drinks, the
sort offered to new arrivals as they lined up to register for
their week in paradise. Noticing was a chronic disease of
the journalist's mind, and nothing must be forgotten about
this scene.

'You will leave.' A policeman placed his grimy hand on her shoulder.

Her head snapped around and she must have screamed for he tottered backwards. Others turned to see what was going on.

They made room.

They knew who she was. Martina was recognizable even to this subspecies of mankind, the corrupt local police force. It might have been one of them who'd taken on the role of waiter, awkwardly balancing his tray, weapon concealed under a freshly ironed napkin.

Alejandro was not dead. He was moaning in a strangled cadence, lifting one leg then the other. Blood everywhere. You could smell it.

She actually paused, trying to find words to evoke the smell: rusted iron?

She fell to her knees, cradled his face, and the rest of the world disappeared. 'Alejo, do you hear me? Don't go, please don't go.' And whispered into his ear, 'I love you, my darling, *mi amado*.'

His breath stuttered. Where could she touch him where he wouldn't disintegrate? His eyes kept rolling back into his head but his handsome, beloved face was intact. The IV made a queer clicking sound. She touched his hair and drew her own eyes in close and felt his soft lashes brush against hers. His skin felt cold and uninhabited and his damp hair clung to his scalp. Her hand tucked under his neck and she was whispering, no, pleading, as her husband jolted in a spasm. Those strange blanks for eyes.

'Listen to me!'

Where had he gone?

Alejandro, my precious, where have you gone?

36

IRIS WANTED TO be home.

Home was the redwood shingle dwelling in the hills of North Berkeley. Dark wainscoting and a narrow kitchen with a deep sink, a holdover home from Steve's former marriage and his wife who was attached to the Arts and Crafts style. Steve and Bonnie had raised their children there. The place exuded an air of melancholy that Iris couldn't quite pin down. Perhaps because the woman had died in this house, in their very bed, a sturdy structure made to withstand an earthquake but not tough enough to heal her cancer.

She stood at the entrance to the hotel lobby.

'Something has happened,' Lydia said.

They stepped into a scene of controlled chaos where people stood about in clusters, speaking in low voices. In the centre of the lobby, the cool dark space Iris had been craving to enter for twenty-four hours, some poor soul lay on the floor, all but his head covered by an orange blanket.

Iris approached the front desk.

Un accidente, the staff claimed, but they wouldn't meet her gaze. Someone in the crowd had heard pings like gun shots. Vacationers had a flair for the dramatic.

'Where is Cleo?'

Embarrassed smiles and shrugs.

Iris forced herself to look at the victim, and quickly recognized him: it was the politician, the man running for governor. His face was the colour of wet cement and a dark stain crept across the floor next to where he lay.

The last twenty-four hours tunnelled in—too long, too much. She felt a wave of nausea.

A paramedic beckoned for the gurney and a policeman helped heave the wounded man aboard while another medic held the IV drip. There was a moment of clumsiness as the victim rolled sideways and had to be rescued from tumbling over the other side. A sea of smartphones waved, snapping photos. Police had given up trying to keep the media and tourists back. The mariachi band launched into a slow ballad.

It wasn't the injured man that Iris stared at now—it was his wife. She kept thinking of Jackie O in her pink Chanel suit, stained with blood, as she held her dying husband in the open car more than half a century ago.

'One of the waiters came up with a drinks tray,' someone said. 'There was a pop. Maybe two.'

'Which waiter?' asked Iris.

Tourists crowded around the two women, excited to be able to tell the news.

'Young guy who ran the beach bar.'

Iris felt her chest tighten. 'Not Patricio.' That kind boy with the sunny smile, who told her of his family back in Michoacán.

'Is that his name?' someone wondered.

Iris spotted the slingback shoe tossed on the floor. Without thinking, she pushed through the crowd and reached to pick it up. Silk on the outside, slender toe, slightly scuffed. A leather insole held the imprint of the woman's heel. She cradled the shoe, feeling its delicacy and heat.

Martina was being helped inside the ambulance alongside her wounded husband. Iris, feeling as if she were crossing some stage, approached and held out the shoe.

Moment of hesitation, then the woman's hand reached, but it was her face that made Iris gasp; her features had clamped down, showing a look of such determination that Iris felt ambushed. The shoe passed from one hand to the other and Iris retreated to the edge of the chattering crowd. A siren wailed as the ambulance wheeled downhill.

Anyone's life could change in an instant.

Hotel staff returned to their stations. A scattering of police remained but there was no further attempt to block off the crime scene. Onlookers were approached as potential witnesses, but what with the language difficulties, the officers quickly gave up.

The lobby felt empty, almost serene. There would be so much to tell Steve. He assumed the gals were lounging about drinking piña coladas all day with periodic dips into the sea. He thought he was the one leading a full and interesting life. Two maids began to mop up the blood. Banish the scene from the minds of guests; this was more important than forensics.

Lydia was nowhere to be seen. She'd melted into the crowd, leaving her mother to stand on her own in the middle of the lobby. The walls were tilting, the floor a vast open surface and the fountain with its water-spouting mermaid wasn't near enough to lean on.

She spotted El Pintor waiting by the taxi stand, but all taxis had been commandeered. Iris began to make her way across the tile floor, step by cautious step. An orange cone had been placed in the centre of the lobby with the warning: *Mojado.* Wet. The open area was a skating rink, nothing to grasp onto, and the slick floor seemed to pitch sideways. Pause to breathe. Equilibrium slowly returned and Iris managed to reach a pillar near where the painter stood and she grabbed it with both hands.

He had been watching her undignified approach but did not reach out to help. He looked shrivelled, hat pulled low over his head. He'd lost his entourage and with it, his air of celebrity.

'We must get out of here,' Don Victor said. 'This is just the beginning.'

'Beginning of what?' Iris asked.

'The other side, he must reciprocate. Eye for an eye, only here they will also remove your teeth and nose and ears.'

She squinted at him, his nervous energy contagious.

'Who's going to take me home?' he asked.

'Where are the people who brought you?'

'They ran off. I'm a foolish artist who shouldn't have come down off his hill.' He pointed to the cuff of his pants, which was smeared with blood. 'He fell at my feet; it could have been me who was shot.'

Iris felt it coming, that old sensation where the man, whatever man who happened to be around, sucked her into his flame of need.

'You will fetch a driver,' he said. 'You will get my things in the hotel room. Here—' His free hand dove into his commodious pocket and seized his room key.

His voice like sandpaper, like plaster dust.

Reaching for Victor's duffel bag, Iris pitched his few articles of clothing into it. He insisted on holding onto the sketch pad, and already he'd regained a level of his old bounce.

Lydia was standing in the doorway.

'We should leave, Mum.'

Iris looked at her with surprise. 'But our flight isn't until tomorrow.'

'Air Transat has laid on an extra flight. Gloria and Joe are going.' Lydia looked flushed.

'But why?' Iris was perplexed. 'What happened has nothing to do with us. It's some local difficulty.'

Lydia stared as if her mother was insane.

Victor patted down his pockets, making sure he had his jackknife, his stubby pencils. 'You look like your *mamá*,' he said, watching Lydia. 'As she used to be.'

Lydia gave her mother a puzzled glance.

Iris realized that she had failed to mention that she'd met the artist decades earlier, a lifetime ago. It was the sort of coincidence that would make Lydia roll her eyes, meaning, 'You are everywhere, Mum.'

Pair of dirty socks—shove them in the side pocket. Did that hip flask belong to Victor? Indeed it did. Iris felt her mind work in slow motion, frame by frame. She'd managed to calm down and must not allow her daughter's nerves to infect her. Lydia was always a dramatic girl, aiming to make the most of any crisis. As in this business of Charlie leaving, a sad and difficult event, but not a tragedy of unparalleled proportion. Iris had survived a pair of upended marriages.

'Where is my jacket?' Don Victor started opening drawers and slamming them shut. Iris pointed to the hook on the back of the door where his jacket hung, rough unlined cotton. He grabbed it and plunged his arms into the sleeves while Iris offered a tranquil smile. She was an old hand at dealing with high-strung artists.

By the time the three of them made it back to the lobby, half the guests from their arrival day were lined up at checkout, winter coats cast over their arms. Was that Lulu and Neil? Iris offered a tentative wave. They waved back, luggage crowded at their feet, straw bags full of souvenirs.

'Rats leaving the ship,' Lydia said. 'As should we.'

Iris understood that the girl felt responsible for their safety. Lydia was more than capable of fending, while she, Iris, had become the sort of person one needed to look out for.

Victor strode ahead, pushing past the group standing at curb's edge next to their heap of suitcases. He stepped onto the cobblestone and lifted an arm. Instantly, a cab roared up and the driver reached to fling open the rear door.

'You will sit here,' Victor directed Iris, pointing to the seat. He slid next to the driver after tossing his bag in the trunk.

'I don't have my things,' Iris protested. Everything seemed to have speeded up again. She stood by the car, uncertain.

Victor leaned out the window and smiled at her, his face a mass of wrinkles. Those startling eyes were full of mischief. She pressed against the side of the taxi, filled with a sort of desperate indecision. Perhaps Lydia was right; they should escape on the next flight. A man had been murdered. Go home to what? She scrambled to assemble an image, rooms with dark panelling and etched glass, deer grazing in the front yard as evening fog rolled in, chilling her to the bone.

A gecko scrambled up the wall and disappeared into the magenta blossoms of bougainvillea. A trio of idling buses waited curbside. Iris recalled again the gunman bursting through the door of that derelict saloon in Chiapas, and how she and Richard and everyone else hit the floor. And how, ten minutes later, they celebrated their survival with shots of *mezcal* all around. Never once did they think of fleeing for home.

She slipped onto the battered upholstery of the taxi's rear seat and rolled down the window. The cabbie began to ease past the buses with their gaily painted flanks of palm trees and beach.

Was she really leaving her dear brave Lydia, who had lifted her from the jungle floor and offered the last of her drinking water? Lydia whose slim body had lain pressed against hers all night, not daring to move in case she might waken her mother?

Iris planted her hands on the neck-rest of the seat ahead. Don Victor's hair smelled of seawater and cigars. The taxi began to bump downhill towards the main road. Taking a final glance backward she saw her daughter standing next to the pond, heatedly engaged in conversation with someone. She made a visor with her hand and looked harder.

Bob.

37

YOU JUST DON'T get it,' Bob kept saying.

Lydia was furious. 'You left us out there. My mother can't ...' Words failed.

'I saved you from this.'

Lydia rocked back on her heels. Bob, in fresh clothes, kept sliding a hand into his pocket to check his phone.

'How exactly did you save us?'

His response was to look at her steadily, the first time he'd met her gaze since she'd spotted him standing across the lobby next to the flamingos. Birds that seemed unfazed by recent events.

'You two needed to be far from here,' he said.

'Because you knew a shooting was in the works?'

A drizzle of sweat appeared on his forehead. 'You have no idea.'

'I'm trying to find out.'

He nodded, as if deciding how much to tell her. 'How would it have looked if I'd gone solo to the jungle?'

'Looked to whom?'

'You were never in any danger.'

Lydia felt her exhaustion replaced by full-bore anger. 'How can you say that?'

A shrug.

'You were signalling the smugglers in the airplane.'

He laughed, a cheerless sound. 'That, doll, was a Mexican army plane.' He leaned towards her and confessed, 'I'm scared too, kiddo.'

A new batch of guests was arriving at the hotel, stepping off their bus with whoops of pleasure. Waitresses in *folklórico* dresses greeted them with the usual cocktails. Where was Iris? Lydia followed the trajectory of Bob's skittish gaze.

He pulled out his phone, punched in a number, and listened to a spray of angry Spanish. Responding with a single sentence, he pocketed the device.

'My mother is not a young woman,' she reminded him. 'We ran out of water. I thought I was going to lose her.'

A look of pain flashed across Bob's face.

'If it hadn't been for Cleo and his cousins and aunt—' She didn't finish the sentence.

'They are good people,' he agreed.

'I stumbled into a shed full of parcels behind their house.'

That got Bob's attention. 'What exactly did you see?'

She told him then added, 'I suppose this means Cleo and his family are in the drug trade.'

He seized her wrist, the good one. 'Cleo's cool. His family are *campesinos*, going back generations. Do you think they have any choice in this?' He let go, and she stared at the white ring printed on her skin.

'I'm frightened, Bob.'

'A reasonable response.'

'I want to go home.'

'No no,' he waved in an unconvincing way. 'No one wants to harm tourists; your cash keeps the racket going. The resort, as you may have guessed, is an excellent laundry service.' His chilly laugh was interrupted by the cell phone ringing the opening phrase of *'Round Midnight.*

'Bob here,' he said and crammed the phone to his ear, turning away so she couldn't hear.

Exhaustion punched her in the back of the knees. The mariachi band had been replaced with canned music. Police radios crackled, bus doors wheezed open and shut.

'Things are happening,' Bob said, pocketing his phone and turning back towards her. 'I don't know the next move. No one does.'

'They're saying Patricio shot the politician.'

'They always say something.'

The newly arrived tourists began to make their way to the beach, towels and sunscreen in hand. Instructions from the activity pool rang out: 'Lift your arms and clap!' The same Ricky Martin song they'd been hearing all week blared.

'I'm going to find my mother and leave,' Lydia said. The idea of organizing such an exit felt overwhelming.

Bob objected: 'El León will make sure there is no more violence. Look around you.'

Lydia saw nothing but pale-skinned tourists, the turquoise infinity pool, a lifeguard stand—and rows of recliners topped with striped pillows.

'Look harder.'

Now she spotted them, half a dozen men dressed in fatigues lined up on either side of the property, automatic weapons hanging from their shoulders.

'Jesus,' she whispered. Attack dog of adrenalin.

'It's a situation, not the apocalypse.'

A game of beach volleyball was in full swing.

'Why shoot a politician who isn't in power yet?' she asked.

'There was the danger that he might get elected and feel he had to do something.'

'None of this is real.'

Bob gave her a sharp look. 'Some is, some isn't. You need to sort it out.' Then, slyly: 'What did you make of the ruins? Did you feel you were stepping back in time, to antiquity?'

Her turn to stare.

Bob went on: 'My boys built the site from scratch, and the lost tribe is my own invention.' He looked pleased with himself. 'Tourists who shell out extra bread will be able to dig for pottery and pre-Columbian figurines. Interactive. That's what people want now.' His voice rose. 'If it catches on, we'll franchise the concept.'

Fake ruins. Lydia almost laughed.

'We intend to replicate the feeling archaeologists had when they hacked through the jungle and discovered the ancient world.' Bob made a broad gesture with his arm. 'Everything here is fake, except for the sea. The pyramid, the miniature jungle with the decorative bridge—even sand has been carted in after the last hurricane. But that doesn't affect your pleasure in the least.'

'A man was just shot, Bob. That wasn't fake.'

His body shrank again. 'I love this country,' he said, 'but you've got to know what's real and what's theatre.'

A pair of pelicans swooped across the pier, on the hunt for flying fish. Some clown on a jet ski circled too close to the roped-off area where people were swimming. One of the armed guards raced through sand in his heavy boots and stood waving his weapon until the tourist veered off.

At least Lydia supposed the skier was a tourist.

Iris was nowhere to be found. She'd checked the room and saw no sign that her mother had returned. Lydia didn't recognize any of the tourists crowding the beach bar. A new bartender, not Patricio, pressed his hand on the blender's lid as it roared, pink liquid frothing under glass. Was that Joe with his domed head sauntering towards the swimming pool?

She looked harder; it was not. This man was younger, sporting bulky calves with tattoos: a serious bicyclist.

38

THE RIDE IN the ambulance was interminable, yet took no time at all. Martina held her husband's bloodless hand while the paramedics did something to his chest then wired up his neck, his jugular, with a tube. Alejandro moaned and gurgled, a horrifying sound.

'Come on, come on,' she kept repeating. For the ambulance to hurry up, for the traffic to part, for the blood to stop its relentless seepage, for Alejandro to squeeze her fingers, to just try. For his eyes to flicker with recognition. She shivered, ice cold, as if she'd slipped into his body.

'Come on, *angelito.*'

She tried to edge in closer in the cramped quarters but was shooed away by the professionals. 'I am sorry, *Señora,*' they told her. 'Your husband has been critically injured.'

Another said in a studied voice, 'Blood pressure dropping, seventy over—' Eyes pinned to the monitor showing a thready pulse.

Martina's mind stuttered; he would have been crossing the lobby with Don Victor, evidence being a bloodstain on the artist's trouser cuff. They would have heard the pop of gunshot and thought, not here, not in this place.

The vehicle tore into the highway and made a right towards town, zig-zagging through the clatter of tourist buses, motor scooters, beat-up trucks carrying workers to landscaping jobs. The hand lay inert in hers but he moaned again; Alejo was alive. The sound a lullaby to her frantic ears.

* * *

Lydia jogged up the pathway towards the lobby, though she dreaded entering that high-ceilinged area again. She lined up impatiently at the front desk, watching Cleo deal with room changes, lost passports, changed dinner reservations. He would help; he would have seen that Iris was wilting, found her a place to recover.

Yet when everyone had gone, instead of looking at her, Cleo busied himself neatening a pile of index cards. He seemed nervous, as if he wished she'd go away. She recalled the peculiar serenity she'd felt in his family's modest house and how he'd waited for her outside, nearly naked under the stars, surrounded by the sounds of unseen creatures.

Now he was dressed in a crisp white *guayabera* shirt and avoided her gaze.

A car door slammed shut then a taxi took off, screeching down the hill too quickly. Iris entered the lobby from the driveway, setting each foot down with purpose, as if not sure of its location. Lydia felt a pulse of relief, and something else, a sweeping tenderness that made her eyes fill with tears. Her mother was walking like a hesitant old woman.

She hurried to help, though Iris brushed away the offered hand. 'He wanted me to go with him,' she said. ' He practically begged.'

'For Pete's sake, Mum. You didn't—'

'I chickened out,' Iris interrupted. 'I started wondering

266

what it would be like, would I make friends in his village, and what if I got sick, or my other hip started acting up.'

'It's called being sensible.'

Not the right thing to say.

'It's called "fear,"' Iris snapped. She was working to catch her breath. 'I didn't want to run off with the old coot; I just wanted to think that I could.'

39

THEY SWEPT HIM directly into the O.R. and Martina paced the tiny waiting room, her blouse smeared with blood. He isn't dead, she reminded herself. Or he wasn't when they took him in. The situation was 'grave': that's the measured word the medics used. Grave meant critical, but also meant that there was room for hope. She'd phoned her son in Texas and left a message on his voice mail. Then she texted him and he texted back. He was coming. Next flight. No, hang on, he'd let his passport lapse; they wouldn't allow him back in the U.S. What should he do? So many questions. The other son promised to fly in from Cuernavaca in the morning. She'd signed a waiver as they rushed Alejandro into the cold bright room. Questions about resuscitation and the perils of a general anesthetic.

'Just save his life,' she'd pleaded with the trauma surgeon, a Lebanese girl who looked no more than twenty-five.

There were three other people in the O.R. waiting room, a *campesino* couple with their teenaged son. The mother kept arranging a shawl over her shoulders; she wasn't used to air conditioning. All three were small and dark, and the man smelled of the field. The son wore mirrored sunglasses and acid-washed jeans. They were nearly silent, intimidated by the situation, yet Martina understood from their few words that it was their daughter, the boy's sister, being operated on. She'd had some sort of accident in the factory where she worked. This hospital, the IMSS, was publicly funded and catered to the poor of the state, but it also had the best doctors. There had been no time to drive back to the capital. This was what the EMS guys told her as she crouched next to Alejandro in the ambulance.

Time dragged on in the adroitly named waiting room and every few minutes they all fixed their eyes on the door leading to where loved ones were tilting between life and death. No use flipping through the worn copies of *Gente* magazine and *Hola*. She couldn't work up a flicker of interest in the goings-on of celebrities, though she noticed, with a cringe, a copy of *Hola* from last year sitting on top of the pile. She knew it contained photographs of her and Alejandro in attendance at the charity ball for Children of the Mist.

She kept checking her phone, waiting for the ping that signalled a message had arrived. The wafer-thin gadget was her connection to the world beyond the hospital and texts were pouring in from friends and colleagues and media.

The door from O.R. hadn't swung open in an hour. The journalist in her insisted that yes, this horror really was happening. The deeper self refused to believe it. Images of Alejandro took over her mind, snapshots of when they first met, his bushy hair pulled into a ponytail as he hunkered over a typewriter in the campus newspaper office. She was in her denim period, purposeful and perhaps a little dour.

She'd felt so protective towards the boy from the *rancho* and was shocked to discover he had such soft skin, especially his hands. His mother never let him do manual labour.

The family stared at her from across the room then looked away, the teenager slouching in his chair. His eyes were invisible behind the aviator-style shades. He wore a gold chain around his neck and she spotted the tattoo there, a tiny illustration of the Grim Reaper, *Santa Muerte*, an obvious link to *narcocultura*. This boy, Martina decided, was a wannabe. He'd view the narcos as heroes, outlaws who knew how to make money.

When you remember someone in detail, he cannot disappear. Alejandro had wide-set brown eyes and high arched brows. She would kiss the wrinkles that spread from the corners of his eyes, the blooms of crepey skin.

Finally, the door swung open. Ignoring Martina, a nurse strode up to the trio and spoke in a low tone. Good news, their daughter was faring well. She had come through the operation without excessive bleeding and would soon be conscious. In an hour they could go to her.

Martina stared at the face of the mother, taut and inexpressive, not daring to hope, not believing anything until she could see the girl for herself. The boy lifted his sunglasses just enough to wipe his eyes, and Martina saw that he was crying. The father, clutching his straw hat, looked dazed.

The nurse retreated into the depths of the hospital without so much as a glance towards Martina. Alejandro must be alive; she would have said if he wasn't. Martina clasped her phone to her chest.

The family of the injured girl began to chatter in subdued voices and Martina understood that they were being considerate because she had not yet received news. Would she have been so kind in their position? The mother dropped her chin and began to pray, fingering her rosary. Martina looked away, disconcerted by this unabashed religiosity. She'd never had an intimate discussion with God, despite the nuns' teachings. Was it too late to start? Surely it was a good omen that these people were spared tragedy; doctors could do so much these days with trauma patients like their daughter, like Alejandro. They'd had plenty of practice.

Where had his eyes gone? Rolled up inside his head. She'd reached to touch his hair and flickering eyelids, and now she lifted her palm to her nose and inhaled deeply. Blood stained her skin; she hadn't dared clean it off.

The mother spoke from across the room: 'I hope that your husband will recover.'

Thank you, I hope so too.

'The doctors will do their best.'

Of course.

Only a week ago she'd interviewed an eminent transplant surgeon. The doctor from Monterrey told her, on screen, that he favoured pop music as accompaniment while he worked: Beyoncé. Shakira. The beat kept everyone on their toes.

If the Lebanese surgeon would push through the door now, peel off her mask and smile. That's all Martina asked for—one smile.

The family conferred amongst themselves and left the room without saying a word of farewell; they'd forgotten she was there.

Time trickled on as Martina rose from her chair and paced the windowless cube, compulsively checking her phone. Everyone wanted to know the latest news—but there was no news. She could hear heels clattering on the corridor floor outside the room, and even laughter. A voice on the public address system: code blue.

Cardiac arrest. Don't think it, don't start.

Finally the O.R. door swung open and it was not the nurse who'd appeared earlier, nor was it the young Lebanese surgeon. This stocky middle-aged woman in scrubs lowered her mask and walked directly over to where Martina stood.

The woman was not smiling.

She motioned for Martina to sit and perched on the chair next to her and reached for her hand. Martina felt the powdery flesh seize hers and inhaled a whiff of latex.

She introduced herself: Doctor Sofía Colón. I'm sorry, she kept saying as she squeezed Martina's hand. Your husband lost too much blood. The bullets exploded inside him, so much organ damage. I've seen your show many times, *Señora*. You have brought civilization and intellectual life into our homes. This is my third gunshot wound in two days. What a country, yes?

Martina fell back in the chair, head propped against the wall. This was it, the worst had happened and there nothing left to anticipate or dread. She must have gone very pale, for the surgeon spoke from the ether, '*Señora*? Are you all right?'

Martina must have nodded, for the doctor then asked if she wanted to see Alejandro before he was taken to the morgue.

Take as long as you like.

And so it had come, the moment where everything changes. She thought of El León and his bouquets of flowers, the card that flattered her by declaring she was a 'formidable woman.' Not so formidable now. Was he responsible for this assassination? Surely he wouldn't want a murder in his resort.

His enemies were legion, and now they were hers.

She rose from the chair and said, 'I will go and see my husband now.'

She followed Doctor Colón down the narrow hallway, focusing on putting one step in front of the other. She did not notice the whiteboard crammed with names, some crossed out, others written in red. She didn't hear the sound of whispering coming from behind the door of B102. Nor did she mind the flickering light from a dying florescent bulb. The surgeon strode ahead, her shoes covered with paper slippers, turning left, down another hall, before pausing outside room B665. It seemed important to note these numbers, to remember them.

The doctor turned to Martina, as if waiting for permission to open the door.

Martina breathed deeply and nodded.

The heap on the bed was oddly small; they must have made a mistake. Tincture of hope. This grey-complexioned man was not her Alejandro, never had been. Such stillness here, such silence. Not even the whoosh of machines, now unplugged.

No one was present here, least of all her husband. She turned around and stared at the surgeon waiting in the doorway, hands folded across her chest. A woman who had seen many such scenes. The surgeon nodded. It was indeed Alejandro.

Martina kicked off her shoes and climbed onto the bed to lie next to what used to be her husband. He did not move to make room, nor did he reach out to touch her thigh. Her own breathing was an outrage, an embarrassment.

There was a click and the light went off. Dr. Colón had left the room.

40

'WE ARE NOT going home.' Iris sounded like an insistent child. 'We have one more day and we are going to enjoy it!' Her voice was fierce and just as Lydia began to insist that they must leave, as others had left, she stopped herself. Her mother's face grew heated with determination, and Lydia understood: Iris was scared. Scared as Lydia was, but was not going to let fear rule her life.

After a nap and a run at the buffet, they'd made their way to the pool deck. Newly arrived guests were toasting each other with syrupy margaritas, a drink they would weary of in a few days. They'd all heard of 'the incident,' but since there was no visible sign of difficulty, it was understood that any danger was past. Besides, they noted, pointing to armed guards lining the perimeter of the property, no one would dare ambush paradise now.

* * *

Iris pushed open the bathroom door, letting loose lilac fragrance from her shower. She was singing that Dean Martin song, 'Little Ole Wine Drinker Me', as she slipped into her nightgown and climbed into bed. She seemed far away in the dark as the paddles of the fan circled overhead. Lydia lay on her own bed, staring at the ceiling.

Iris said, 'That poor woman. Did you see her face when she was being helped into the ambulance?'

Lydia nodded but said nothing. Outside, the giddy whoops of guests started up.

'Are you awake, dear?' Iris said.

'Yes.'

'Might I get into bed with you?'

Lydia felt her muscles tighten then relax.

She lifted the sheet so her mother could join her. They lay head to head this time, Iris's shampooed hair drenching the pillow.

Last night they'd huddled on a cot in a shack in the middle of the jungle and then it was this world that seemed implausible.

The train tooted and a group of guests clambered on, delighted by such a charming mode of transport.

41

'I **HAVE AN** understanding with these people. Everything's copacetic,' Bob said.

'You're leaving.' Lydia stated the obvious.

Bob had slung a duffel bag over one shoulder and was headed for the lobby.

A shiny white SUV pulled up to the resort's entrance. Observing this arrival, Bob's expression changed, his mouth tightened.

'Maybe not just yet,' he said. With a studied calm, he slipped down the corridor that led to the washrooms and booths advertising day trips.

The doors of the SUV opened and a slim man in a beautifully tailored suit began to cross the tile floor. He was followed by a pair of bulky men in polo shirts and jeans. The guests stared at the formality of the man's dress; such a contrast to their own t-shirts, shorts, and sandals.

El León made his way to the front desk where he leaned over to ask a quick question. Cleo answered with a nod.

Lydia perched on the rim of the fountain, the mermaid squirting an arc of water behind her. Maybe the man wouldn't spot her here; there were at least a dozen tourists milling about, waiting for guides to take them diving.

El León turned away from the desk and stared straight at her. Had Cleo told him she was here? She felt herself rise from the fountain, mouth open, ready to apologize for her absence yesterday. She knew that she'd been rude in a way she couldn't fully understand.

His face betrayed no sign of recognition. She froze, mouth locked. He lifted one hand and gave a dismissive wave, as if she were a fly or an annoying child. The two barrel-chested men who'd arrived with him began to hasten down the corridor where Bob had disappeared. Lydia sank back onto the rim of the fountain; she'd seen the look on Bob's face as he'd made his exit. Gaze darting in all directions, a bird ready for flight.

El León remained by the desk where Cleo stood doing nothing, hands flat on the counter. A phone rang, then another, but he made no move to answer them.

A plume of charcoal smoke wafted into the lobby, issuing from the beach barbeque; today was grilled fish, Hawaiian style. El León stood absolutely still, though Lydia was sure she could detect the humming of his body under the material of his suit.

A clattering sound and Bob tumbled back into the lobby, flanked by the two men who gripped his arms. He looked terrified and his scant hair stood straight up. Was that a scrape on his temple? His eyes were wild as he lunged forward, spotting Lydia.

She rose to her feet, then backed up against the wall. It felt reassuringly cool and firm.

El León said something in a mild voice and one of the men flung an arm over Bob's shoulder, a mimicry of comradeship. Don't scare the tourists.

Bob's face was ashen, a word that struck her as being accurate. Her mind scrambled; what was she to do?

'Help me, Lydia!' Bob croaked, duffel bag swinging from one hand.

He never called her Lydia, always said 'gal' or 'doll' or 'dame,' words from the last century, from smoky cellar clubs and jazz and illicit reefer.

She bolted forward, then stopped. El León had raised a palm. A languid hand twinned with an amused gaze, eyelids at half-mast.

The two men hustled Bob towards the vehicle where they pushed him into the rear seat. She couldn't see anything through the tinted glass.

El León began to greet guests, shaking hands, beaming good will: *el patrón*.

Cleo busied himself with a stack of papers. The life of the lobby had folded neatly around the incident.

Bob would have yelled if he were in big trouble, Lydia insisted as she related the disturbing event to her mother.

'I'm sure,' Iris said, sprawled on the lounger, facing the sea. It was their final day and archery was in full swing nearby. Preschoolers filled the kiddie camp. The grilled Hawaiian-style fish was a big hit.

Lydia lowered her head onto the pillow. 'They're taking him in for questioning,' she said, nearly convincing herself.

Who were 'they,' Iris might have asked, but didn't.

The tide rolled in, sloshing around boulders that rose like a tropical Stonehenge. Did he really expect that she would jump to rescue him? Bob, who insisted that the people here needed him more than he needed them. Yet she couldn't shake his muted cry for help.

In a day she'd be home, climbing the steps to her house, lugging her carry-on suitcase. Would Doug have shovelled the walk in anticipation of her return?

Pushing open the door she'd call his name and hear a series of pings and explosions before he put his game on hold and dashed downstairs.

Her gangly son would scoop her up in his arms and twirl her around, a parody of welcome, yet also true.

Staff had begun to set up another wedding, styrofoam columns raised against the sun. Bouquets of flowers featuring stalks of Bird of Paradise poked out of urns. These urns were also made of styrofoam, splashed with an antique patina. A sound system was being tested—Madonna singing a song that Lydia dimly recognized from decades earlier.

'What ever happened to Wagner's Bridal Chorus?' Iris murmured from her lounger.

A boy arrived with their drinks and lowered them cautiously into their waiting hands. First day on the job, he confessed.

The two women pretended to clang their plastic cups, a salute to their final day.

'Charlie has a girlfriend,' Lydia said. She'd been on the phone to her son last night.

'Does that bother you?' Iris said then answered herself: 'Of course it does. One wants total freedom for oneself, and resents it in others.'

The sun sparkled so intensely off the sea that staring at it felt like chewing on foil. Staff positioned chairs into rows for the ceremony, directed by a woman holding a clipboard. The stools at the *palapa* bar were occupied by a group of recently arrived tourists. Bob's usual spot had been taken by a woman in a bikini, her shoulders already burned.

The wedding party made its stately way towards the red carpet. The bride, dressed in a pale green dress and holding a bouquet, was at least Lydia's age. Her hair was streaked with grey and she looked radiant—no other word would do. That must be her father grasping her elbow, hair slicked back. He used a cane, painted in tropical colours. A dozen guests had taken over the chairs and on the front row a pair of teenaged boys elbowed each other and looked anywhere but at their mother.

The groom, a thin man standing between the foam pillars, awaited the bride's approach. He looked kind, Lydia thought, and a little embarrassed at this public display.

Beyond the wedding party, at the perimeter of what would creep into some of the photographs, a commando perched on a rock, tricked out in full camo gear, his weapon tight against his chest.

The bride reached up and touched the groom's cheek, a moment captured by a fleet of camera phones.

Iris reached for a corner of towel to wipe her eyes. 'I think I'm going to cry,' she said.

42

THE SKY WAS tinted mauve and Don Victor stood on top of the hill—his hill—looking down at the sprawl of the village. Not so picturesque, some might think, people without proper eyes. Smoke rose from charcoal braziers, set out for dusk-cooking in the doorways. He'd soon tramp down for a *gordita*. Air filled with the usual howling of dogs.

Home again. He told himself this was good, that this was the only place on earth where he was happy, his studio a few metres away, the turmoil of sea-level activity left behind. The man who was to be governor had been taken down, and he, Victor, had managed to escape.

He buttoned his jacket against the evening chill. The humidity was glorious while it lasted, but this dry biting cold was better. A scorpion began to rattle towards him, slinking out of the woodpile. He aimed the heel of his shoe, then stopped; the cuff of his white pants was stained rust. Hastily he rolled the pant leg up, hopping on one foot.

That woman had watched him through the decades, saw him timeless.

He stomped hard on the *alacrán*, feeling the crunch of its exoskeleton as it broke apart. He'd been stung once, had curled up in a blanket and laid still for a day, not wanting to stir up the lather of venom in his blood.

* * *

Campaign headquarters had been plunged into chaos. Martina sat in a corner where they'd planted her, a bundle of papers on her lap that she was meant to sign. Alejandro would want this, his staff insisted. She was to run for office in his stead. The widow was well known across the country. Respected at all levels. Take your time, but sign here. There is so much to be done.

They tiptoed around the widow's grief.

Sign here.

Alejandro's bristled chin rubbed against her cheek, making her skin tingle. His fingers crept inside her blouse as he whispered into her ear. He slipped into bed in the dark, body slick and fragrant with lavender oil.

She shuddered; a sheet of paper floated to the floor. Someone picked it up and handed it back to her. Phones rang non-stop and voices were urgent yet muted, aware of her presence. Her gaze dropped so that she was staring at her shoes, one of them stained with his precious blood.

ACKNOWLEDGEMENTS

Toronto Arts Council for financial aid.

For invaluable editorial feedback and support over many drafts, I thank Tim Deverell and Jenny Munro.

ABOUT THE AUTHOR

ANN IRELAND is a prize-winning author of five novels. She teaches creative writing at The Chang School, Ryerson University in Toronto, writes feature articles about visual artists, and was a contributing editor for *Numero Cinq* online magazine. Her first novel was made into a feature film, *The Pianist*, directed by Claude Gagnon. She is a past president of PEN Canada.